Acclaim ...
an...

"Romantic, entertaining, and sexy enough to leave you wanting more!"
—Lori Foster, *New York Times* bestselling author of *Hard to Handle*

"Spicy sweet success." —*Romantic Times*

"Sizzling heat and a creative story line." —Romance Reviews Today

"Readers will be caught up in the story from page one." —Love Romances

"The plot is carefully crafted, characters fully developed, and the level of writing is superb." —A Romance Review

Improper Etiquette

"Erotic romance at its best . . . tasteful and steamy . . . utterly charming." —Romance Readers at Heart

"*Improper Etiquette* is sassy and delicious. . . . Maynard is a must-buy author." —A Romance Review

Play with Me

"Passion + Fun = *Play with Me*. Janice Maynard delivers. . . . By the end . . . three women's secret fantasies come true, and readers will be left wanting another provocative tale." —Erin McCarthy

Suite Fantasy

"All three novellas feature likable characters in sensuous scenarios. What sets Maynard's work apart from others in this genre is that she develops her characters and plotlines to the extent that the reader cares about what happens outside of the bedroom as well as within it." —*Romantic Times*

"Heated and passionate." —The Best Reviews

The Perfect Ten

Janice Maynard

A SIGNET ECLIPSE BOOK

SIGNET ECLIPSE
Published by New American Library, a division of
Penguin Group (USA) Inc., 375 Hudson Street,
New York, New York 10014, USA
Penguin Group (Canada), 90 Eglinton Avenue East, Suite 700, Toronto,
Ontario M4P 2Y3, Canada (a division of Pearson Penguin Canada Inc.)
Penguin Books Ltd., 80 Strand, London WC2R 0RL, England
Penguin Ireland, 25 St. Stephen's Green, Dublin 2,
Ireland (a division of Penguin Books Ltd.)
Penguin Group (Australia), 250 Camberwell Road, Camberwell, Victoria 3124,
Australia (a division of Pearson Australia Group Pty. Ltd.)
Penguin Books India Pvt. Ltd., 11 Community Centre, Panchsheel Park,
New Delhi - 110 017, India
Penguin Group (NZ), 67 Apollo Drive, Rosedale, North Shore 0632,
New Zealand (a division of Pearson New Zealand Ltd.)
Penguin Books (South Africa) (Pty.) Ltd., 24 Sturdee Avenue,
Rosebank, Johannesburg 2196, South Africa

Penguin Books Ltd., Registered Offices:
80 Strand, London WC2R 0RL, England

First published by Signet Eclipse, an imprint of New American Library,
a division of Penguin Group (USA) Inc.

First Printing, January 2008
10   9   8   7   6   5   4   3   2   1

SIGNET ECLIPSE and logo are trademarks of Penguin Group (USA) Inc.

LIBRARY OF CONGRESS CATALOGING-IN-PUBLICATION DATA:

Maynard, Janice.
    The perfect ten/Janice Maynard.
      p. cm.
    978-0-451-22290-9
    1. Aphrodisiacs—Fiction. I. Title.

PS3613.A958P47 2008
813'.6—dc22   2007021781

Set in Berkeley Oldstyle Book
Designed by Elke Sigal

Printed in the United States of America

For Anne Bohner

*I appreciate your professionalism
and the important part you play
in the creative process!*

The Perfect Ten

Prologue

*B*eyond the French doors that led to a flagstone patio, the late April moon hung full and heavy just above the inky-black treetops. Inside, the edges of Jeannie Killaney's übermodern kitchen were softened by the glow from a half dozen scented candles, though the task at hand did demand illumination from the utilitarian light beneath the stove hood.

Three female heads bent over a stainless-steel pot. The thick, fragrant contents, a pale milky green, bubbled slowly with burps and blubs. Nearby, a heavy glass beaker labeled NUMBER TEN sat waiting.

Jeannie straightened and looked at her cousins. "Well, what do you think?"

Diana, the youngest, nodded. "I believe it's ready. The eucalyptus smells fabulous. And it's not too girly, which is good since we want to market it to both sexes, though I still don't see quite how that works."

Jeannie inhaled the veil of steam. "It's all about the pheromones. Each person's skin gives off unique scents, so our products aren't the same in the end, at least not when they're out of the bottle and on the body. They're assimilated and influenced by chemical reactions. I've tried something new this time. For a little extra kick."

Diana's eyebrows rose. "Do you mean some kind of erotic love-potion effect?"

Jeannie chuckled. "Wouldn't that be great? Talk about making a fortune . . ."

Diana looked inside the pot once again. "Well, you're the chemistry geek. You make the call."

Jeannie glanced at the silent member of their group. "Elizabeth?"

Elizabeth gave the ceramic spoon one last experimental pass through the pot. "I vote yes." She paused and set the utensil aside. "It's hard to believe this is the tenth new formula we've created. And that it's been five years since we opened the store."

The other two hugged her. Diana smiled. "And it was all your idea, Elizabeth. You were the one who made it happen. Lotions and Potions wouldn't exist if you hadn't brought us all together."

Jeannie nodded. She slid the spoon back in the pot. "Put your hands on mine. Let's make a wish."

As the other two shifted positions and covered Jeannie's hand with one of their own, a shaft of moonlight sneaked through the window and fell like a benediction on the heavy pot. A loud *pop!* sent a shower of bluish sparks into the air, and all three women jumped back simultaneously.

Elizabeth and Diana hovered anxiously as Jeannie turned off the stove burner and examined the contents from a careful distance.

"Is it scorched?" Elizabeth's voice reflected her worry.

Diana winced. They had already been through a slew of variations. And the ingredients weren't cheap.

Jeannie sniffed the brew. Now that the heat was off, the rapidly cooling mixture seemed benign. She shrugged. "Must have just been an overheated bubble. I think it's fine. You want to try again for a wish?"

The other two shook their heads. Diana frowned. "Let's not press our luck. It looks like we've come up with another winner. I suggest we call it a night."

He Loves Me,
He Loves Me Not

One

Damian Bennetti loved sliding his hands over sleek, beautiful curves. Cars and women. He didn't play favorites. Of course, the cars weren't as moody and hard to handle. But then again, a car, no matter how exciting, didn't offer a man the gut-tightening possibility of sweet, hot, mind-blowing sex.

Unfortunately, Damian's relationships with fast cars were prospering, and his free time for the opposite sex was dwindling because of the backlog of new business. He'd come to Asheville, North Carolina, three years ago from a small, rural Kentucky town that offered few opportunities for a young, ambitious man. Armed with the money he'd managed to save from a series of dead-end jobs, a newly inked small business loan, and the fierce determination to succeed, he'd opened his automobile-repair shop.

His specialty was high-end European imports, and the skills he'd learned from his uncle back home included not only the basics of body work, but the mechanical know-how, as well. Damian might have missed out on a college education, but he was smart, he had a gift for understanding engines, and he was making a hell of a lot more money than he could ever have imagined.

He'd chosen Asheville carefully. It was a beautiful area for one thing, tucked into the Blue Ridge Mountains, and the climate was temperate. Those two realities were what drove his clientele. Well-heeled retirees flocked to the area, drawn by the small-town feel, the cultural opportunities, and the relatively low housing costs. And the wealthy, over-sixty-five crowd could afford to indulge their addictions. Including a lust for cars.

Maseratis, Alfa Romeos, Porsches, even the occasional Lamborghini—when they gave their owners problems, the sleek, expensive vehicles found their way into Damian's shop for some TLC. It was a win-win situation.

He'd even had clients come from as far away as Raleigh-Durham and Nashville and Roanoke, and he hoped, as his reputation grew, his business would only get better.

He picked up a chamois and gave one last wistful rub to a vintage Aston Martin. Damn, he loved his job. This baby belonged to an irascible geriatric fellow who only drove it twice a year . . . literally. The rest of the time, it sat in a climate-controlled, tile-floored garage.

But in the spring and in the fall, on one picture-perfect day each season, the lovely car headed out on the Blue Ridge Parkway for a triumphant spin. Damian thought it was a criminal waste, but it wasn't his place to criticize. As long as he could make his house payment, his sometimes-eccentric customers could do what they liked with their pretty status toys.

He glanced at the clock and gave a yell back to his high school–age apprentice. "Kevin. I'm taking an early lunch. Can I bring you anything?"

Kevin's response was a negative, so Damian tossed the rag aside and went to clean up. His sometimes-snooty clients might want a mechanical genius to work on their cars, but they didn't expect his hands to be grimy. Somehow, Damian thought they probably envisioned him coaxing their precious babies back to life while at the same time keeping his fingernails completely clean.

So he tried his best to preserve their illusions. But the subterfuge had a price. His knuckles split and cracked frequently, and the skin on his hands was rough and occasionally painful. The only thing he had found that really helped was a jar of stuff he bought from a little shop just up the street. The store was called Lotions and Potions, and it was run by three lovely cousins whose Irish heritage explained their fabulous red hair, in varying shades.

The tall bombshell with the amazing body had just a hint of strawberry in her shoulder-length blond locks. The buttoned-up woman who rarely smiled had fiery red streaks in her chin-length chestnut bob. And the baby of the group, Diana, had a headful of bright, springy ginger curls that made a man's fingers itch with the need to touch them.

Not that he'd ever had a chance to follow up on the urge. Diana didn't spend as much time out front mingling with customers as her two cousins did. For some reason, even though the blonde was an undeniable knockout, and the serious one intrigued him, it was Diana who appealed to him the most. He couldn't really explain it.

He'd flirted with her on and off for months, inventing any pretext to stop by the store. He had a closet full of "lotions and potions" he'd never used, simply because he'd wanted to spend time with Diana. Maybe it was her slight air of shyness that drew him. The times he'd chatted with her, she had been soft-spoken and almost hesitant. He'd done his level best to charm her, but if she'd been impressed by him, she hadn't let on.

When he was with her, he felt different. As though his past was not quite so disappointing. As though his future might hold some incredible surprise if only he could find the key to making it happen.

With anticipation urging him on, he walked up the street, wondering whether to eat first. But then he saw Diana enter the building ahead, and his appetite waned—at least his craving for food.

Lotions and Potions was located in the old Federal building, better known as the Grove Arcade. When old E. W. Grove built it back in the late 1920s, it was one of the last shopping arcades constructed in the U.S. During World War II, the government took over the premises, and all the thriving shops and businesses were evicted, literally overnight. Damian had heard the history from one of his clients, whose daddy had been a lawyer in those days.

The building was listed on the National Register of Historic Places back in the late seventies, and finally just after the new millennium, the creative structure was restored to its original purpose. The Killaney girls were among its first new tenants.

Damian followed Diana inside and tilted his head back to examine the skylight that ran the length of the wide corridor. You could look up and see three stories of commerce bustling on a busy Saturday afternoon. Normally he enjoyed studying the architecture and the various building features, but today he had a mission: catching Diana.

The shop was on the ground floor. The tiny bell on the door was still chiming as he followed her inside. Immediately he was enveloped with myriad scents and colors and sounds. Nothing was overpowering. The stimuli to the senses were subtle. It was like walking into a mythical fairy forest on a warm summer afternoon and holding your breath with the sure knowledge that something magical was about to happen.

Damian saw Diana greet her cousins and start to head for the back of the store. She had her pocketbook over her shoulder and a zippered bag from the local bank under her arm. He upped his speed and managed to intersect her path.

"Hello, Diana."

Her cheeks turned pink, and she gave him a fleeting smile. "Mr. Bennetti." She inclined her head in oddly formal acknowledgment.

He gave her his best I'm-on-my-good-behavior smile. "I was hoping you could show me some of that cream you gave me for my hands the last time I was in."

She hesitated, her wide eyes a clear, true blue. "Elizabeth or Jeannie can help you. I've just come back from an errand."

He took a chance and touched her arm lightly. "I'd really appreciate it if you could spare me a few minutes of your time."

The feel of her soft skin had an unexpected effect on his libido, and he forced himself to draw his hand back slowly, rather than jerk it away, as was his instinct.

She seemed equally dazed by the contact. She licked her lips. "Okay, then. Give me a minute to get rid of this stuff and I'll be right with you."

He concealed his impatience and browsed casually while he waited for her to return. Even though Diana's two cousins were each with other customers, he avoided their gazes. He sensed they were amused at his persistence, particularly Jeannie, and he wasn't eager to have them see him crash and burn if the outcome didn't go as he wished.

It seemed like an eternity before his reluctant saleslady reappeared. She came to him and stood by his side. When she didn't speak, he picked up a jar at random. "Is this any good?"

That made her smile. She took it away from him and placed it back on the shelf. "That's for nursing mothers to use on their breasts. It might do the trick for your hands, but I doubt you'd be able to overlook the connection."

He felt his face turn red, and groaned inwardly. God, he hoped she didn't think he was trying to be cute. And clearly she wasn't as meek as she seemed.

Diana picked up yet another jar. "This is the stuff you bought last time. It has a strong lanolin base, and if you use it right before you go to bed, you'll get the best results."

He decided to test the waters. "Don't you know you should never mention lotion and bed in the same sentence when speaking to a man? Unless, of course, you're interested in getting something started."

Her face went blank with shock for a half second, and then she grinned. "Think of me as a medical practitioner," she said drolly. She unscrewed the lid and held it up to his nose. "Does this smell like what you had before?"

He let his lips accidentally brush her fingers as he bent his head and put his nose to the jar. He straightened, trying his best to look innocent. "Yep, that's it."

Her eyes narrowed, saying she wasn't fooled a bit by his naughty maneuver. "Good. I'll ring you up." She turned her back on him and headed for the cash register.

He felt his window of opportunity closing, but Diana didn't seem any more receptive to him today than she had the other hundred times he'd tried. Although there was that moment when he'd touched her arm . . .

Jeannie was kneeling behind the counter, arranging a row of bottles in the display case. She stood up and smiled as they joined her. "Hello, Mr. Bennetti. How are you?"

Under normal circumstances, a man would be hard-pressed not to take note of Jeannie Killaney's impressive . . . attributes. But today his attention was focused firmly on her pretty cousin. "Call me Damian," he said absently, watching as Diana's quick, graceful hands made short work of wrapping his purchase. "I've been coming in here for over a year. It's about time we were all on a first-name basis, don't you think?"

Jeannie laughed and agreed. They both studied Diana while she concentrated fiercely on getting the tape exactly straight as she secured the white butcher paper around his jar of cream.

He leaned a hip against the counter. "Diana . . . are you okay with me calling you that?"

She looked up from her task, a tiny frown between her eyebrows. "Of course."

She took his credit card and ran it quickly, all the while managing to avoid his gaze.

Jeannie nudged her cousin with a hip. "That cream he's buying is great for dry hands, but why don't you give him a sample of the new stuff?"

Diana looked at her cousin and the two seemed to exchange some kind of silent message. "We don't have it ready to put out yet," she said.

Jeannie shrugged. She pulled a tiny plastic container from her pocket. "Take this one. And don't just hand it to him. Show him how to massage it into the skin."

Diana's mouth gaped open.

Damian smothered a grin. He was getting an unexpected assist from an unlikely quarter. He leaned forward. "I'm always up for something new," he drawled. He held out his hands and smiled benignly.

He was pretty sure Diana's fingers trembled as she fumbled with the small cap. He might have felt sorry for her if his own stomach hadn't been flip-flopping at the thought of her slender, soft hands touching his.

He took a deep ragged breath when she smoothed a dollop of lotion on his left hand and held the hand with both of hers. His other hand fluttered uselessly and then dropped to clench the edge of the counter. Sweet Jesus. This was way too much like foreplay for his peace of mind.

Jeannie might have left them alone after that, but a customer came up and demanded her attention. Damian scarcely noticed the conversation taking place close by. He gulped as Diana gently massaged the cream into his knuckles.

She glanced up at him, her habitual shyness reflected in her tentative smile. "You need to let it get warm and then keep rubbing. For it to be fully absorbed into your skin, you have to do more than slap it on. It's full of all kinds of minerals and antioxidants."

When her thumbs pressed into his palm, he was embarrassed to feel his dick getting hard. But he couldn't for the life of him imagine pulling away. Something odd was going on. His skin seemed to be heating from the inside out, and the feel of her strong but feminine hands grasping his was sending some kind of shock wave up his arm.

He chanced a look at her face and saw in her eyes that she felt something, as well, but she quickly looked away. Her pale skin flushed.

He tried to speak and had to clear his throat and try again. "When can I buy the real thing?"

She smoothed in one last spot of lotion on the back of his wrist and released him. "We should have our first shipment in another week or ten days. I'll save you a bottle if you want me to."

He nodded jerkily. "Sounds good."

He sensed this encounter coming to its inevitable conclusion, and his agitation convinced him to do something he hadn't planned at all. "Would you like to have lunch with me?" he blurted with a sad lack of finesse.

Both women went still. Even the customer broke off what she was saying.

But Jeannie relaxed immediately and smiled when she realized he was speaking to Diana. Jeannie waved a hand. "Go, sweetie. I've already eaten, and so has Elizabeth. Enjoy yourself."

For a half dozen seconds, Damian was sure Diana was going to refuse. But then she and Jeannie exchanged another obscure look and Jeannie grinned. "*Ten*-minute sandwich breaks at your desk aren't healthy, my girl." It sounded like she emphasized the first word, but he was probably imagining things.

Diana ignored him and shot back at her cousin, "I have at least *six* more things I need to get done this afternoon."

The other woman pushed her from behind the counter. "Go, my chick. You're in my way. Get lost."

Diana finally looked back at Damian. "Do I need a pocket-book?" she asked, her tone challenging and clearly frustrated.

Damian grinned widely, too pleased at his victory to comment on her less-than-enthusiastic capitulation. "Not with me around. I'll take care of everything."

Diana preceded her lunch date out the door of the shop and then onto the street, feeling awkward and excited at the same time. Her manipulative cousin had neatly boxed her into a corner, and though Jeannie might think the brash, cocky Damian Bennetti was a ten, Diana knew his type far too well to be taken in.

She'd had a serious crush on the man for a long time, and she wanted to give him the benefit of the doubt, but her father's penchant for flitting from relationship to relationship had marked her. She was wary of charming men who flirted as easily as they breathed.

Even so, Damian fascinated her. Beneath his outrageous behavior, she'd managed to glimpse from time to time a man whose feelings ran deep. He had a gentle sense of humor and he wasn't afraid to stand up for things he believed in. The time she'd asked him for a pledge to her favorite children's charity, he not only wrote her a five-figure check, but he also volunteered to do a stint in the dunking booth at the fund-raising carnival.

The image of Damian Bennetti soaking wet was one "brain picture" she'd never been able to erase. His body was clearly accustomed to physical labor. It was hard and sculpted and taut with restrained strength.

So there were many things about him she liked. But his reputation with the ladies reminded her too much of her dad's, and it was hard to get past that mental hurdle.

Diana couldn't sustain her momentary pique at Jeannie's interference. It was a perfect spring day, the sky a robin's egg blue dotted with fluffy clouds, and the sun-kissed breeze warm and gentle. She lifted her face upward and sighed.

Damian didn't comment. He merely led her down the hill to a popular small restaurant that boasted a handful of umbrella tables on the sidewalk. Once they were seated and the waitress had taken their order for vegetable soup and corn bread, Diana studied her companion.

He was tall and gorgeous. There was no denying that. His slightly shaggy black hair could use a cut, but the disheveled look suited him. His gray eyes held a keen intelligence, and he was well respected in the community as a decent and reliable businessman.

The heavy drawl in his sexy voice indicated he was originally from Tennessee or maybe Kentucky. She wished he would quit grinning at her. That flash of white teeth and the curve of those sensual lips didn't play fair. He had to know what the combination did to a woman's equilibrium.

"So why today?" she asked bluntly.

He blinked and his smile dimmed a fraction. "What are you talking about?"

She waved a hand. "This lunch date. As you pointed out, you've been coming in the shop for over a year. Why ask me out now?" It bothered her that his impulsive invitation seemed to come on the heels of her rubbing the lotion into his skin. Good Lord, surely the number ten formula wasn't really an aphrodisiac.

For a moment she thought her question had genuinely stumped him. The humor faded from his expression, and an odd look crossed his face. He shrugged. "I don't know. I've always thought you were cute. And I like you."

"You don't know me," she pointed out wryly.

He leaned back in his black wrought-iron chair and frowned. "I was hoping to remedy that," he said mildly.

She cocked her head. "Did you come up to the shop today with the intention of asking me out?"

The fingers of his right hand drummed restlessly on the table, though he seemed unaware of it. "No. I came to buy more of that cream or lotion or whatever the damn stuff is called. Seeing you was a bonus. You're almost never out in the shop. Why is that, by the way?"

It was her turn to shrug. "I do the accounting . . . the books . . . everything financial. It's what I was trained for. Elizabeth is the organizational and marketing expert, and Jeannie is the science nerd."

He choked out a laugh. "Not hardly."

Her eyes narrowed. "What is that supposed to mean?"

He spread his hands palm up. "Hey, don't shoot the messenger. That cousin of yours may have a fine brain, but it's not the first thing that grabs your attention."

"How rude."

"It's a compliment."

"Maybe from a man."

"I *am* a man, honey. Or perhaps you haven't noticed." He moved his chair closer to hers, and their angry gazes collided. "What's with the third degree, anyway? Are all your dates this complicated?"

She stared him down. "You're a player, Mr. Bennetti. And your reputation precedes you. Everyone in Asheville knows you spend your time with fast cars and fast women."

His eyebrows rose and he gave her an admiring gaze that was patently false. "That's clever," he murmured. "Should I have it printed on my business cards?"

"Don't be flip," she said, wishing she didn't feel the insane urge to drag him close and kiss him.

He scowled now. "I thought you were shy, but maybe you were just afraid to admit that you're attracted to me."

"Attracted?" Her overloud, incensed response was uncomfortably close to a screech. "How do you get that big head of yours through doorways?"

He leaned even nearer, his eyes glittering with devilment. "Shall we put my theory to the test? Pucker up, sweet thing."

She didn't have red hair for nothing. Her heart pounded, and her hands gripped the arms of her chair to keep from strangling him. "I am *not* attracted to you."

"Could have fooled me."

That was it. Even the knowledge that he was probably goading her was not enough motivation for her to keep a lid on her temper. She jumped to her feet, dumped her glass of ice water in his lap, and slammed it back down on the table. "Ask some other girl to lunch, Mr. Bennetti. This one's got your number, and if it's all the same to you, I'd rather starve."

Two

$\mathcal{E}$lizabeth stared at her in shock. "You did what?" Even Jeannie seemed nonplussed, and it took a lot to rattle her calm.

Diana shrugged uneasily and sat down in her desk chair. Her two cousins had followed her back to the office. The shop was empty for the moment, and they were curious about her abbreviated lunch.

She fiddled with a paper clip, knowing she had behaved badly. "He provoked me."

Elizabeth frowned. "He's a customer. That's not like you, Diana."

Jeannie's sharp gaze was speculative. "Did he make a pass or what? The guy's an out-and-out ten, baby girl. How on earth could you toss that one back? He'd curl any woman's toes."

Diana glared at her. The three of them had played this game of rating men for years. "He's not a ten. Just because he's passably handsome doesn't override the fact that he's arrogant and conceited and—"

Elizabeth whistled. "Wow. He really pushed your buttons, didn't he?"

Jeannie laughed softly. "I'll be curious to see if he comes back for more."

Diana dropped her head and banged it softly on her desk. "I'm going to have to apologize, aren't I?"

Jeannie patted her hair. "Best to get it over with quickly. Just like pulling off a Band-Aid. And the sooner the better."

Elizabeth's smile was sympathetic. "Blame it on your hair. All men like the idea of wild redheads."

"But I'm not like that," she wailed, feeling panicky at the thought of facing him again. And she really was even tempered . . . most of the time.

Her two cousins grinned in unison. Jeannie tugged Diana to her feet and hugged her. "Try telling that to the man with the wet crotch."

Damian left enough cash on the table to cover the uneaten meals and hustled back to the garage. He changed quickly into a pair of coveralls before Kevin could notice his boss's soggy condition and start asking questions.

As Damian picked up a wrench and climbed down into the pit, he couldn't suppress the smile on his face. All in all, the date hadn't gone too badly. It might have ended abruptly, but there had been enough electricity in the air to light up the city during a blackout.

Diana Killaney clearly had issues with him, but she wasn't indifferent. And he had a solid plan for round two waiting in the wings.

Which was a bit surprising. Because he'd been telling the truth when he said he hadn't gone to the shop earlier with the intention of asking her out.

Was it simply seeing her on the street that had prompted his impulsive behavior? Or was it the feel of her hands on his, rubbing so gently with the new lotion that had pushed him over the edge?

He lifted the back of his left hand to his nose and sniffed. The faintest trace of scent clung to his skin. And even in this short amount of time, his knuckles looked better. Maybe that new stuff had special properties. Healing and softening and making a man's libido go nuts.

He chuckled to himself and slipped on a pair of thin gloves. They were a hassle, but he hated the thought of mucking up Diana's mini-massage with axle grease.

For the next three hours, he worked steadily, concentrating on the task at hand with the analytical half of his brain, but not quite able to subdue the heated fantasies that were skating around in his more susceptible right brain. He could blame his creative imagination on an overlong period of celibacy, but in truth, it was all Diana.

Being close to her, seeing the sparkle of humor, and later anger, in her expressive eyes. She smelled good, no surprise there. But it was the softness of her skin and her gentle hands that really set him off.

He tried to loosen the same bolt for the third time and sighed disgustedly when it broke off in his hand. Maybe this was just one of those days.

He had finished for the afternoon and sent Kevin on his way, when he heard the unmistakable sound of female footsteps on the concrete floor. He froze, his coveralls stripped to his waist in preparation for changing back into his regular clothes, when Diana's head peeked around the corner.

She spoke before she saw him. "Mr. Bennetti? Damian? Are you in here?"

He stepped out from behind a half wall and lifted a hand. "Yeah. Getting ready to close up pretty soon, though." He didn't smile. It wouldn't hurt for a minute to let her think he was mad and see what happened.

She had changed from her skirt and blouse into jeans and a fleecy cinnamon-colored pullover. The skies had clouded over during the late afternoon, and it was noticeably cooler outside. He liked the way the casual clothes made her seem more approachable.

She had her hands shoved in her pockets, and she seemed uneasy. She looked around his work space for a minute or two, and he wondered if she was really curious or if she was simply stalling.

He picked up a tool and put it back on the rack where it belonged. He was almost obsessively neat when it came to the garage. Then he turned to face her. "Can I help you? I don't normally work on Sentras, but I could make an exception for you."

Her expression mirrored confusion, and then she shook her head. "My car is fine."

He rocked back on his heels, his own hands now shoved in the pockets of his coveralls. His bare chest seemed to be giving her a problem, because she averted her eyes when she spoke.

"I came to apologize."

"For what?"

That lit the flame in her eyes again. She gave him a tiny frown. "You know for what. Don't be obtuse."

He picked up a notepad and jotted down a word.

Her frown deepened. "What are you doing?"

He smiled faintly. "I thought I'd make a list of all the insulting adjectives you toss at me. For those times when I find myself being rude and bigheaded."

A tiny grin tilted the corner of her lips. "Has anyone ever told you you're outrageous?"

He started to write again and stopped. "Is that an insult or a compliment?"

She laughed softly. "I guess it would depend on the woman."

He felt a kick of desire in the pit of his stomach. This female seriously rang his chimes. It was almost scary. "No apology necessary," he said gruffly. "I stepped over the line. I always tease my two sisters like that. But I don't know you well enough yet, and I went too far."

She took two more steps in his direction, and the hair on his arms stood up . . . along with other things.

She met his gaze squarely, regret written on her face. "I still want to apologize," she said softly. "I overreacted, and I'm really sorry."

"You could make it up to me," he said, his voice equally low.

She went still. Something arced between them. Something hot and wonderful. Her eyes were on his face. "How?"

He reached out to brush her cheek with his fingertip. "You could give me that kiss I asked for earlier."

She cocked her head. "And then we'll be even? You'll be satisfied?"

He chuckled roughly, already reaching for her. "We might be even, but I sure as hell won't be satisfied." He pulled her nearer, his arms settling around her waist. She put her hands flat on his bare chest, as though warning him not to get too close. The prettiest little blush of pink warmed her cheeks.

They fit together well. *Whoa. Don't go there, Bennetti.* His libido shot instantly to the contemplation of another kind of fit that made his temperature rise.

He lowered his head slowly, still half expecting her to protest. Finally, when he couldn't wait a nanosecond longer, he covered her lips with his. They both gasped. If it had been the dead of winter, he'd have blamed the jolt on static electricity. But there was plenty of moisture in the air, even if his mouth had gone dry.

He dragged her closer and fought to keep the embrace within the traditional parameters of "first kiss." But it was damn difficult. Her fleece-covered breasts were pressed against his chest, and her mouth was as seductive as any fantasy he'd dreamed up that afternoon.

He slipped his tongue between her parted lips and probed gently. She tasted like sunshine and sin. When he put a hand to her breast, she sighed and murmured her approval. As kisses went, it was pretty chaste. But his heart was hammering in his chest, and it was a damn good thing there was nothing more comfortable than a concrete floor nearby, or he might have been hard-pressed to keep his intentions honorable.

Her hands moved suddenly, stroking, testing the contours of his chest. He gulped and broke off the kiss, burying his face in her neck. One of them needed to slow things down, and he was pretty sure it wasn't going to be him.

Diana had come to Damian Bennetti's place of work to make a quick, probably stilted apology, and then to get the heck out of Dodge. Nowhere had it figured into her plans to do a tactile exploration of his magnificent chest and to suck his tongue like a lollipop. But she appeared to be doing both. At least until he ended the kiss and started nuzzling her neck.

When her fingertips brushed his small, flat nipples, he jerked and muttered something under his breath. She had given up trying to deny the attraction. What was the point? Touching all that hot, smooth male skin set off internal explosions that were destroying any hope she had of convincing Damian that she wasn't interested. It was ludicrous to think she could even try.

His chest was lightly dusted with dark hair, and she loved the silky texture of it beneath her hands. She desperately wanted to feel her breasts skin to skin with his muscled contours, but she didn't have the courage, and besides, that was skipping way too many steps ahead.

Her thumbs slid down to span his waist, and he cursed softly, going rigid. She kissed the earlobe she could reach. "Damian?" she whispered, afraid to shatter the surprisingly intimate moment.

"Yes." His breath was hot on her neck, and still he didn't raise his head.

"Are you wearing anything beneath these coveralls?"

Long silence.

"Yes."

She debated the possibility of his answer being the truth. "Liar." Already she knew him well enough to see through that single, unconvincing syllable.

Suddenly, the possibility . . . no, the reality that he was nude beneath the heavy fabric barely caught at his hips made every bone in her body melt.

And she wasn't a bone-melting kind of gal. She was cautious in her relationships, for a lot of very good reasons. She didn't jump in bed with strangers. Not that Damian was a stranger. She'd had her eye on him for a long time. And Jeannie was one hundred percent correct. He was a ten. Way out of Diana's league.

A more aggressive woman might have cupped him through the cloth. She didn't dare. Instead, she moved her hands to safer territory and licked the curve of his ear. "Are we through kissing?"

She kept her voice light, even though she felt wildly out of control. This whole scene was improbable at best. Was the number ten lotion she was wearing to blame? It was the same substance she had massaged into his hands.

He finally lifted his head and looked at her. His cheekbones were red, and his eyes glittered with arousal. The intensity of that laser gaze should have scared her. Instead, it made her giddy with happiness.

He wanted her. Not that many men really had. And especially not after they met Jeannie. It was hard for a guy to focus on cute and small breasted when faced with the Victoria's Secret catalog.

But Damian clearly had a thing for skinny redheads. Hallelujah. She refused to believe that a hypothetical love potion had anything to do with it.

He sucked in a breath and rested his chin on top of her head.

"We probably should be," he said, sounding disappointed but resigned. "Would this be an appropriate time for me to invite you to dinner tonight?"

She winced. "I can't. I have a date."

He went so still, he might have been carved in wax. "A date?"

"Nothing important," she said hastily. "It's a blind date with a girlfriend of mine and her boyfriend. Set up weeks ago. I don't even know the guy they're bringing. But I can't bail at the last minute. It would be rude."

He released her with a disgruntled mutter. "And we know how you feel about rudeness."

She cupped his cheek with her hand. He was dark and his face was rough with late-day stubble. Would he shave in the evening if he had plans with a woman? Her knees wobbled and he grasped her upper arms. "Are we okay?" he asked, his gaze holding a hint of vulnerability that grabbed her heart and squeezed.

She licked her dry lips and tried not to think about what she had felt beneath his waist pressing insistently at her abdomen while they kissed—either a really big wrench or something that might keep a girl happy all night.

"Yes," she said primly. "I believe we are." Her stomach growled loudly at that precise moment.

He flashed the grin that did nothing to help her knees. "That will teach you to pass up lunch."

She wrinkled her nose. "I've been starved all afternoon."

He tugged her with him around the corner to his office, or what passed as such. "If you're going out with another guy, the least I can do is make sure you're in good shape." He unwrapped the foil cover from a small plate and handed her a large brownie laced with caramel. "Have one of these. Kevin's mom sent them."

"Kevin?"

"My part-time help. He begged to hang around just so he

could learn the business, but the kid's so damn talented, I had to start paying him. He graduates from high school in June, and I'll put him on the payroll officially then."

"He's not going to college?"

Damian's expression changed, and she sensed somehow that her innocent question had nicked him. "His parents can't swing it," he said quietly. "And his grades will never get him a scholarship. Even with financial aid, there are still a lot of families who can't afford all the other costs associated with college. Working with me he'll have a chance to build a good career."

She put a hand on his chest. "I didn't mean anything by that, Damian. It was a question—that's all. And how wonderful that he has someone like you to show him the ropes. He's lucky."

The light came back into his eyes and he wolfed down a brownie in one bite. "I'm the lucky one," he said, wiping his mouth with a paper towel. "He's a whiz with engines."

An awkward silence grew between them after that. She sighed. "Perhaps you should consider buttoning up those coveralls."

"Why?" he asked with a straight face. But she could see the twinkle in his eyes. "I'm just going to be taking them off in a minute."

It was staggering to realize how much she wanted to help him with that task. She straightened her pullover and ran a hand through her hair. Damian's fingers had rumpled it, and she could still feel his touch on her scalp.

She glanced at her watch. "Well, okay, then. I should be going."

He took her wrist in one big hand, his thumb finding her thundering pulse and stroking it. "Neither of us has to work tomorrow. Would you like to go for a drive with me and take a picnic?"

What a simply worded, prosaic request. No reason at all for her stomach to start doing Olympic-quality flips. She stared down at his hand. It was an extremely masculine hand. Hard, banged up, big and strong.

She cleared her throat. "Isn't it supposed to rain?"

He grinned. "Do we really care?"

She had a sudden vision of the two of them twined in each other's arms while the rain pelted down outside and they steamed up the car windows. She searched his eyes, trying desperately to see if he was half as off balance as she was. "No," she said softly. "I guess not."

He didn't ask for permission this time. And he moved so quickly that she was tucked up against his chest with her hands tangled in his hair before she knew what was happening. He made no pretense of being gentle.

The embrace and his mouth were hard, predatory, and hungry. And she met him kiss for kiss. His hand slid beneath her top for the first time and moved with disarming care to stroke her breast through the silky fabric of her bra. She whimpered and then gasped when he pinched her nipple.

"Damian . . ."

He must have heard it as a protest, because he released her with a groan and raked his hands through his hair. "Jesus, Diana, you'd better get out of here."

She managed to smile. "Is that a threat?"

His scowl was all frustrated male lust. "It's a promise, Red. As God is my witness, it's a promise."

Three hours later, she stifled a yawn behind her hand and wondered how soon she could politely excuse herself and head home. She had insisted on bringing her own car. She was no dummy.

She sighed silently when her date launched into yet another explanation of why his favorite MLB team was destined to have a stellar season. She listened with half an ear. While she enjoyed baseball, this guy was a bit too fervent for her tastes. She'd have to give him a five and a half if Elizabeth and Jeannie asked. He was harmless and polite, but a tad on the self-absorbed side.

And although she certainly didn't need a man to pull out her chair at the dinner table, it would have been nice if he had at least waited for her to be seated. Thank God, it was a double date. The other couple had helped diffuse the sports conversation with more general topics.

At nine o'clock, she made her excuses. Mr. Five and a Half didn't appear too disappointed, so perhaps she wasn't his type. Good news all around.

They had eaten at a new Thai restaurant out near the interstate, and it was only a ten-minute drive back to her apartment complex. Jeannie and Elizabeth had bought houses not long after they had first opened Lotions and Potions. But Diana had been out of college only a short time when they went into business together, so she hadn't had much opportunity to save. Plus, she didn't have the parental support the other two enjoyed.

She kept herself on a tight budget, and maybe in another twelve or eighteen months, she would have enough for a down payment. In the meantime, the place she lived was nice, and most of the tenants were young people like herself.

When she pulled into her usual parking place beneath a streetlight, she glanced up at the building and saw a man standing by her front door. Her heart leapt in her chest until she recognized him: Damian.

She got out of the car slowly and headed up the walk. Her neighbors on either side must be out on a Saturday night, because their windows were dark. She had forgotten to turn on her porch light, and the shadows were heavy, even with the nearby streetlight.

She paused three feet away from him. "Is it tomorrow already? My, how time flies."

Her sarcasm made him smile. He sat down on her top step and patted the spot beside him. "I saved you a seat."

She hung her purse on the doorknob and joined him. "Did you have a particular reason for dropping by, or were you just in the neighborhood?"

His deep sigh held a multitude of meanings. "I live on the other side of town."

She nibbled her bottom lip. "I see." Their hips were close, but not touching. He was leaning forward with his elbows propped on his knees. She sat, spine straight, and stared out into the night. "So why are you here?"

She felt him shrug. "I wanted to see how the big date went."

She grinned in the darkness. "Jealous, Bennetti?"

He huffed. "Of course not. I wanted to make sure he was a gentleman when he brought you home."

She snickered. "Well, if he *had* brought me home, wouldn't it have looked a bit odd for you to be lurking on my doorstep?"

"I would have disappeared discreetly."

"If I hadn't been alone."

"Exactly."

"How convenient for you that I was. Alone, that is."

"Indeed." He didn't bother to hide the masculine satisfaction in his voice.

She fired her first volley. "I'm not inviting you in."

He never flinched. "I know."

"And yet here you are."

"It's a nice evening."

"A bit on the chilly side."

"You should have worn more clothes."

She chuckled. "I never thought I'd hear you say that." She actually *was* kind of cold. She'd put on heels and hose, which might have been over the top for a casual dinner. But she'd been feeling guilty about kissing one guy senseless and then going on a date with guy number two. So she'd dressed up for the blind date.

Damian put a warm hand on her knee. "I like the dress. You look hot in black." His fingers lightly stroked the inside of her thigh.

Diana gulped. A sudden gust of wind sent her hair flying

around her face, and she shivered hard. He couldn't miss it. Without saying a word, he shrugged out of his leather jacket and wrapped it around her shoulders.

It was a simple, almost corny maneuver, reminiscent of a chick flick, but it made everything inside her melt. She wanted to put her head on his shoulder, but that would be taking things a bit too far. She gripped the lapels of the jacket with one hand and shoved her hair back with the other. When she sneaked a peek at her silent companion out of the corner of her eye, he was looking straight ahead, a contemplative expression on his face.

The jacket was warm from his body and smelled like the outdoors with barely a hint of some spicy aftershave. Beneath the leather, her nipples tightened and her stomach clenched with a shot of pure, unadulterated hunger. It scared her. She considered herself somewhat lacking in the romantic arts department. And she surely had never craved sex. Not until now.

She'd only been with two other guys, one a fairly long-term relationship in college, and one an ill-advised fling with a much older man here in town. Thankfully, he had moved away not long after they broke up, so she didn't have to bump into him. Neither time had convinced her that sex was as amazing and earthshaking as it appeared to be in the movies. She'd chalked the hype up to good special effects.

So how did that explain her response to a man she barely knew and had never actually dated?

The lotion. The answer came to her in a blinding flash of certainty. Something in that last batch of ingredients her cousins and she had cooked up. Eucalyptus wasn't a known aphrodisiac, but maybe in combination with something else . . .

Damian half turned to face her. "Are you a morning person?"

She choked on a nervous giggle. "That seems a bit personal at this stage." Even in the gloom, she could see the white flash of his teeth.

He took her face in his hands. "I was wondering how early I could pick you up tomorrow." His thumbs caressed her chin.

"Oh." All the breath had been mysteriously squeezed out of her lungs, and she felt dizzy. Without thinking through either her actions or her words, she tipped her face up for his kiss. "You can come whenever you want."

Three

Damian barely slept that night. After being knocked for a loop by Diana's unfortunate choice of words, he'd skedaddled from her porch like a scalded cat. It was either that or tumble her back into the bushes and screw her senseless. He'd been trembling all over, his cock hard as an iron pike, when he made his escape.

And in the hours that followed, as he tossed and turned in his lonely bed, he'd slipped in and out of sleep, tormented by raw, vivid fantasies of the two of them, nude, tangled in each other's arms.

He was up at seven, groggy and exhausted. He'd never been one for sleeping in, and today it was a relief to crawl out of bed. After three cups of high-test coffee and a blistering hot shower, he felt marginally human. He refused to examine the singing sense of anticipation that hummed through his veins.

He'd promised her a picnic, so he made a quick trip to the store and loaded up on sliced turkey from the deli, a container of fruit salad, some pickles, and a loaf of fresh sourdough bread. He tossed in a package of Oreos for good measure. Too bad he didn't have a classy picnic basket to put it all in . . . and some fancy silverware. But the plastic grocery bags would have to do.

Back at home, he dragged out a small cooler and loaded it with drinks. He should have asked her what she liked, but he hadn't been thinking that far ahead. So he put in a couple of cans each from the various soft drink packs he had bought and hoped one of the choices would meet with her approval.

He rang her doorbell at ten sharp. If a small part of him had been hoping to catch her sleepy eyed in a robe and pj's, he was out of luck. She was bright eyed and bushy tailed, as his mama used to say.

Her smile held a hint of the shyness he'd come to expect from her. "Would you like to come in?"

He nodded. "Sure."

She held the door wide and stepped back. "It's not raining. Can I credit you with that?"

He kissed her cheek. "If you like. I wouldn't mind being your hero for the moment. Consider the perfect spring day my gift to you."

While she finished doing whatever it was that women did in the last five minutes before an outing, he studied her apartment. It was cozy and cute . . . like its owner. The furniture looked comfortable, and although everything matched in shades of green and blue, it didn't look like a magazine photo. It looked like the kind of space where a man could feel at home.

And the sofa was nice and long and perfect for . . .

"Damian, you ready?"

He jerked his gaze away from the piece of furniture that had riveted his attention. "Sure," he muttered, turning away to adjust the fit of his jeans. "Let's go."

Diana came to a dead halt in the parking lot and stared at the small, sleek car Damian was unlocking. The paint color was cream, leaning toward buttercup yellow, and the design was totally unfamiliar. Not that she knew cars, but she had never come across one of these on the road.

Damian opened her door and she slid into the soft gray leather seat with a smile. "What is this? I've never seen a car like it."

He grinned, scooting in beside her and starting the engine that turned over with a quiet purr. "A 1999 Ascari Ecosse. A collector I know bought it at an auction after it was pretty badly wrecked and then he decided he didn't have the patience to restore it. I had the patience, but no money. So we made a deal. I got his other five cars in tip-top condition and he gave me this beauty as payment. It took me a long, long time to get it looking like new, but it was worth it."

"So how come I've never heard of it?"

He shifted down as he pulled out of the parking lot. "There are a lot of rare European sports cars that don't get much press over here. This company was named for Alberto Ascari, the first man ever to be a double world Formula One champ. And it's a small operation. They only produce twenty-five or thirty cars a year."

Diana raised her eyebrows, stroking the sleek dash with an appreciative murmur. "I'm impressed. I feel like a princess."

"Princess Diana?" he teased.

She wrinkled her nose. "My mom was pregnant when Charles and Di got married. She woke up at five a.m. or whenever it was and watched the wedding on TV. Daddy swears she got so wrapped up in the pageantry and romance of it all, that she insisted on naming me Diana."

"It's a very pretty name." His voice was soft and low.

The warmth in his words made her shivery. She licked her lips and tried to relax, which was tough given the level of sexual undertones between them. "Well, this is a very pretty car," she said lightly.

He laughed. "I'm glad you like it. But that's enough car talk. I've seen my sisters glaze over when I get wound up, so let's change the subject. Tell me about you and your cousins. How did you end up working together?"

She leaned back in her seat and watched as he eased smoothly around slower cars on the road. "Our dads are brothers, and our houses were on the same block growing up. The family business is bakeries—a string of them all over the Northeast. But by the time I had been out of college a year, Elizabeth hit her midthirties and she says she had an early midlife crisis and wanted to do something besides bake bread for the rest of her life."

"And Jeannie?"

"Jeannie was well on her way to getting a doctorate in chemistry, but she was feeling bored with the whole academic process, so everything just kind of came together. None of us has female siblings, and we were raised almost like sisters, so when Elizabeth laid out her proposal, it didn't take much to convince Jeannie and me that it was the thing to do."

"How did your families react?"

She chuckled in remembrance. "Their parents were horrified. I didn't have a problem. My mom died when I was ten, and my dad isn't really much of a parent, so I was free to make my own choices. It was fun and exciting to come here and plunge into something so challenging and different."

"And that was five years ago?"

"Yep. I'm twenty-seven now, Jeannie is thirty-two, and Elizabeth is thirty-nine."

"And none of you are married?"

She turned her head and grinned. "I am, but my hubby doesn't mind if I go out with cute guys on the weekends."

He took one hand off the wheel long enough to slap her knee. "Brat. You know I'm talking about the other two."

She put his hand back on the wheel pointedly and kicked off one of her tennis shoes so she could tuck one leg beneath her.

"I think men are intimidated by Liz and Jeannie. They're both so incredibly smart and talented, and of course, Jeannie is a knockout. I think guys are afraid they'll be shot down."

"And you?"

She smothered a grin and crossed her arms over her chest. "I don't intimidate anyone. I'm shy and reserved."

He snorted. "I'll give you shy . . . maybe. But it wears off pretty quickly."

"I don't fight with every guy I meet."

He turned his head for a split second, his gaze locking on hers with a look that made her stomach drop. "Fighting can be fun."

Fortunately, traffic demanded his attention, and Diana didn't have to answer. They wound their way out of town on highway 70, stopping at every light it seemed, and turned onto the Blue Ridge Parkway, heading north. After a cool start to the morning, the temperature was rising rapidly, and she soon shed the jacket she wore over her plain short-sleeved navy T-shirt.

Damian was clad equally casually, and he looked yummy. Good enough to eat. Even in her own head, that little thought seemed dangerous. She felt her cheeks heat, and she turned her face to the side window, studying the passing countryside with blind eyes.

Not long after, they rolled the windows down, and soon the warm breeze was tumbling her hair into an unruly mass of curls. She smiled to herself, caught up in the simple pleasure of the moment.

After an hour or so, they pulled off in a small parking area that overlooked a valley. As they unloaded the car and carried all the stuff to a nearby grassy area, Damian apologized. "I'm sorry I don't have a quilt or something nicer to sit on. I brought this tarp from the shop, but it's clean, I promise."

It was also wide and roomy. Plenty of space for two adults to recline side by side. Not that fooling around was really an option. The cars were few and far between at the moment, perhaps because yesterday's forecast had predicted rain. But once people realized that it had turned out to be a perfect day for a drive, the scenic road would get busier and busier.

Maybe that was a good thing. Diana and Damian needed a chance to get to know each other a bit before they gave into what was becoming an incendiary attraction. Impulsive behavior was not her style, but she had a feeling it wouldn't take much to make an exception in Damian's case.

She watched him bend to spread the tarp over the grass. His red henley shirt stretched across his broad shoulders, and it rode up a bit in back, exposing a strip of olive skin that looked smooth and warm. She'd never really considered the small of a man's back as a particularly sexy spot, but somehow Damian's body, wherever she looked, made her mouth water.

She helped him set the heavier items at the corners of the tarp to keep the wind from blowing it away. Finally, she sat cross-legged and watched him produce his bounty. There was something very sweet about having a man provide food for a woman, even if he hadn't made it himself. Perhaps it hearkened back to caveman times, when the male dragged in a woolly mammoth drumstick for his mate.

Damian held up a sandwich. "Hungry?"

She smothered a laugh and took it from him, unable to stifle her grin.

He paused, still on his knees, and cocked his head. "Am I missing something?"

She bit into the sandwich, chewed a bite, and swallowed. "Not at all," she said softly. "You seem to have thought of everything."

Damian lay back, his belly full and his heart light, and tucked his arms behind his head. Far above, a small black speck that might have been an eagle circled on the air currents. He closed his eyes and felt the sun warm his face. Except for the sound of the occasional car passing by, the stillness and quiet were absolute.

He was aware of Diana sitting near him . . . and even more aware when she scooted down beside him onto her stomach and pillowed her cheek on her arms. From the sound of her voice, he could sense that her head was turned toward him . . . her gaze studying him.

He kept his own eyes shut. That way he just might be able to behave like a gentleman.

She sighed. "I love living here. I don't think I would ever go back to Baltimore. How about you?"

His gut tightened for a moment and he shifted uneasily. "I like it here, too."

"Where did you move from?"

"Kentucky." He hoped she would drop the subject.

"That's a beautiful state, too."

"Not where I lived," he said bluntly, hearing the trace of bitterness in his voice and unable to do anything to erase it.

She was quiet for a split second, and then she laid her hand on his shoulder. Not in a caress. Just there. Not moving. He felt the warmth of it burn down into his flesh. She sighed. "Will you tell me about it?"

It was a simple enough request—a quiet understanding of his unspoken resentment. He felt ashamed and uncomfortably vulnerable. He didn't share much about his past with anyone. The successful Damian who lived in Asheville was the only guy who mattered.

He resisted the urge to shake off her touch. He took an arm and slung it over his eyes, blocking out the warmth of the sun. "Nothing much to tell," he muttered. "We lived in a narrow, dirty backwoods holler. As bad as any stereotype you've seen in the movies. My dad worked in the mines. He died of black lung when I was fourteen. My mother followed him three years later of what I'm pretty sure was a broken heart, though the doctor called it pneumonia."

"And your sisters?"

"They were eighteen and nineteen at the time. The three of us managed to hang on to the house, although God knows it was no prize. When I had saved up enough money working at the video store and any other odd jobs I could find, I left and haven't looked back. That was three years ago when I was twenty-eight."

She was silent for a moment. Then she probed again. "Who taught you about cars?"

"My uncle. He was pretty much the only male in my family who didn't work for the company. I used to hang out with him as much as I could and he taught me about cars . . . about engines. Some of it I learned from books."

"What about girls?"

Now it was his turn to be silent for a moment. "I tried to stay away from girls as much as I could. Or I was damned careful. If I had gotten anyone pregnant, I would have been stuck there forever. I couldn't bear the thought of that, so it was easier to keep my nose clean and work until I was too tired to do more than fall into bed."

"Eleven years is a long time."

"Yeah," he said quietly, "it is."

He jumped to his feet, suddenly unable to look at her. "I'm going to head into the woods for a bathroom break. I'll be back."

He left her behind, walking away at a normal pace when he wanted to give in to his urge to run. God, what a fool he was. He could have put her off with a half-assed story that would satisfy her curiosity, but instead, he'd ripped open his chest and exposed every one of his dark secrets. That was guaranteed to impress a woman.

He took care of business and then leaned his head against a tree, torn by the impulse to hide and the need to get back to Diana. The bark was rough on his forehead and he welcomed the discomfort.

He was leaping headfirst into something that was as new and scary as it was enticing. Diana and he had very little in common. Her family clearly had money. And education. And smarts. He still kept in contact with his sisters, but other than that, he had created who he was now from scratch. A new man. A new life.

Would it be enough? With any other woman, it might not matter so much. But he had an inkling that Diana was going to be more in his life than simply a passing fancy.

She was packing away their picnic lunch when he got back. He tugged her to her feet and brushed her chin with gentle fingers. "Oreo crumbs," he murmured.

Then he pulled her close and held her. Just held her. A car had pulled up at the opposite end of the parking lot, but the occupants were too busy taking pictures to pay any attention to Damian and Diana.

He stroked her hair. "Are you ready to head out?"

She broke the embrace and stepped back, tilting her head to study his face. "Your parents would be proud," she said softly. "You've turned into quite a man."

They drove for another two hours back in the direction they had come, passing the Asheville turnoff and heading south. The time for serious conversation seemed to have expired, and Damian was glad. He wanted to step back into the persona he had created for himself—the confident, macho guy who people responded to so well.

But it was difficult around Diana, and he didn't quite know why. She slipped through his defenses without even trying.

It was late afternoon when they finally headed for home. The gas gauge was getting low, and he hadn't brought enough food for dinner.

Diana had been unusually quiet since lunch. He wondered bleakly what she was thinking. She was a lady in every sense of the word, and he was simply a guy with rough, workingman's hands who had graduated from high school by the skin of his teeth. Not exactly a match made in heaven. But he couldn't discount the fact that she responded to him sexually. If he could coax her into bed even once, he was pretty sure he could live on the memories forever.

There was an awkward moment back at her apartment. He was trying to be a gentleman and escort her to the door, but he wanted to get out of there quickly, go home, and live to fight another day.

His stupid, overly detailed confessional had done a number on their romantic mood, and he felt not only responsible, but also helpless to get things back on a more even footing.

She unlocked the door and turned to look at him. "You're coming in . . . right? I may not be the world's greatest cook, but I can fix us something."

He lingered on the bottom step, his hands in his back pockets. "I'd better go. I've got some things I need to do before tomorrow."

"I thought the garage was closed on Monday like our shop."

Busted. He shifted from one foot to the other, not quite meeting her eyes. "Yeah . . . it is, but I've been really busy lately, and I need to catch up on paperwork."

"Oh." Her voice sounded small suddenly, her face blank and pale. "Well, thanks for today."

The words were stilted, and in a heartbeat, he saw past his own discomfort to hers. "It's not you," he said, the words tumbling out in a rush as he realized what impression he had given her.

Her gaze, tinged with the cynicism reflected in her smile, held hurt and stiff pride. "I thought you might be a bit more original than that. It's okay, Damian. I know guys don't like nosy women. I pushed too hard. I get it. Have a nice life."

And she shut the door in his face.

He froze for five or six seconds, gawking at the spot where the sexiest woman he'd ever met had stood just moments before, and then he dashed up the steps and pounded on the door. "Open up, Diana."

"Go to hell."

He heard her response clearly, even through the flimsy prefab door. She hid her natural hotheadedness well most of the time, but his pretty Red had a temper.

He leaned on the doorbell, listening to it ring repeatedly inside the house. "I'm not leaving." He had to raise his voice, and some of the neighbors who were outside on a pretty spring evening started to pay attention.

He kept his finger on the bell and pounded with his fist again. "I can do this all night."

The door jerked open so suddenly he nearly tumbled flat on his face. He grabbed the doorjamb to steady himself and heaved a ragged sigh. Part of him had been convinced things were torpedoed beyond repair.

"I was *not* rejecting you," he said quietly. He was very conscious of curious eyes on his back. Diana had opened the door, but she wasn't letting him in, not yet.

Her arms were folded around her waist in a defensive position. "What do you call it when a guy who was ready to screw my brains out last night tries to slink away without even a kiss?"

He raised his eyebrows. "Self-preservation?"

She frowned. "What is that supposed to mean?"

He shrugged uneasily. "I kind of dumped on you today . . . all that garbage about my childhood. I didn't think you'd be in the mood for—"

"Having hot, crazy sex?"

His mouth gaped open. He was shocked in spite of himself.

She glared at him. "Don't presume to tell me what I am or am not in the mood for, you big lug. I'm sorry you regret telling me stuff, but that's your problem. I don't judge a man by his past, and I don't think you're a sissy because you actually, God forbid, shared your feelings."

He cursed under his breath. This was not going well . . . from bad to worse in fact. "It was a little intense," he said carefully. "I thought maybe we needed time to reevaluate."

"Reevaluate what?" She looked mad enough to castrate him, given half a chance.

He must be some kind of sick son of a bitch, because the madder she became, the hornier he got.

He shifted uncomfortably, and her gaze dropped to his crotch. Her eyes widened, and her face flushed. "You do *not* have a hard-on," she hissed.

He crossed his arms over his chest and gave her his best cocky grin. "Apparently, I do."

He saw the muscles in her throat move as she swallowed. "Well, get rid of it."

He shrugged. "I can't. But you might be able to, sweet thing."

Blue sparks shot from her eyes. "Arrogant pig. Crude beast. Neanderthal . . ."

She seemed to run out of steam for a moment, and he smiled gently. "Shall I get you a glass of water?"

He'd never seen anyone actually turn that shade of pinkish red. He wouldn't have been surprised to see steam come from her ears.

"Get. Off. My. Porch."

"No." He didn't dress it up. She gaped in silence and he laughed. "You were apparently expecting a goodbye kiss and I disappointed you. I'm prepared to remedy that."

"Eat dirt." She'd found her voice, and it was a deadly hiss of rage. But interestingly, she made no immediate move to shut him out again.

He lounged in the doorframe. "I ate dirt as a kid. I wasn't impressed. Tell me, Diana . . . did you put clean sheets on your bed this morning?" He almost chuckled when the pink in her face darkened to red. God, this was fun. How far could he push her before she exploded?

She glanced wildly behind her, as though looking for reinforcements.

He nodded sagely. "I'll take that as a yes." He put one foot inside the door, risking life and limb. "I'm sorry, angel. I was a cad, a bounder, an insensitive son of a gun. I'm filled with abject regret, and I swear I'll never again leave without kissing you. Am I forgiven?"

Some of the fire left her expression, but she wasn't giving an inch. Her eyes narrowed. "You told me about the lack of female companionship back home, but interestingly enough, you never mentioned your sex life during the last three years. That seems an odd omission."

He gulped and pulled his foot back, just as a precaution. "I don't follow," he said, his words carefully spoken without inflection or heat.

She pointed a finger at him accusingly. "I told you before. Your reputation precedes you. You're a player, and now that I know the whole story, I'd say you must have been making up for lost time when you came to Asheville. Am I getting warm?"

He scratched behind his ear and looked over his shoulder. Right about now would be an ideal moment for a neighbor to interrupt. Sadly, they all appeared to have given up on the drama and had gone on to other pursuits.

He coughed, realizing ruefully that her newest tack had effectively taken care of his erection. "You know how people exaggerate things."

She crossed her arms again. "Not buying it, Mr. Bennetti. I want names."

He scowled. "I don't kiss and tell."

She smirked. "What a gentleman. I'll settle for a number. Ten?"

He flushed.

She gasped. "Twenty?"

He dropped his head, suddenly seeing his escapades through her eyes. God, maybe she was right. Maybe he was a scoundrel.

He sighed. "I didn't keep count, but that first year was not my finest hour."

She was pale now. "Thirty?"

He shrugged. "Do we have to do this?"

Suddenly, every bit of expression was wiped from her face, leaving her looking almost austere. "No," she said quietly, "we don't."

And for the second time that day, her door shut firmly in his face, this time with a gentle, silent motion that was far more intimidating than if she had slammed it with all her might.

Four

Diana scowled at her computer screen and wondered why in the heck the whole world had given up on pencils and paper. She had an error somewhere on her spread sheet, and for the life of her, she couldn't figure out what it was.

Of course, it didn't help that her head was splitting and that a raw sense of disappointment, not to mention sexual frustration, sat like a stone in her stomach. Had she blown her only chance to be with Damian? So he had been with a lot of women? So what? She had to get past her stupid phobias and insecurities. And it was pointless to deny the truth any longer, even to herself. She wanted to have sex with Damian Bennetti.

Jeannie poked her head in the office. "Someone's here to see you, Diana."

Diana sighed. "Can you ask them to make an appointment for this afternoon? I'd really like to get this damn report finished."

A tall, dark-headed man stepped around the corner. He

shook his head sadly. "Such language from a lady. I'm surprised at you, Diana."

She refused to allow him to bait her today. She'd spent a long, lonely Monday wishing he would show up on her doorstep, and then calling herself all kinds of a fool for caring when he did not. She tapped her pen on the desk. "What do you want, Damian? I'm really busy."

He turned to give Jeannie a quick, lethal smile. "Thanks, honey."

Jeannie, who had been fielding male admiration since she was fifteen, blinked and nodded slowly. Apparently even a sophisticated woman's ability to handle men wasn't immune to Damian's charm. When Jeannie returned to the sales floor, leaving them alone, Damian sauntered closer. "I have a proposition for you."

Diana's eyes widened in shock that he would be so blatant, and then narrowed in self-defense when she realized how very much she wanted to hear what he had to say. But she was darned if she was going to make things too easy for him. "You may have an entire folder of testimonials about your prowess in bed, Bennetti, but I'm not interested. Go seduce some other poor, unsuspecting woman."

He sat down in Elizabeth's desk chair and rolled it forward until his legs were practically kneecap to kneecap with Diana's. "I think you'll be interested when you hear what I have to say."

He leaned forward and kissed her smack on the lips. Her heart slammed into the ceiling and then settled with a lurch into her chest. She scooted back two inches. "I assure you, I will not."

He closed the tiny gap she had created, and now, trapped by her desk, she had nowhere to go. He put his big, warm hands on her knees. She had on a short denim skirt and sandals, so he was in contact with bare skin. The contact burned her thighs. She stood up and straightened a pile of papers on her desk.

He stood as well. "Look at me, Diana."

She was not a coward. She faced him, her expression cool. Or so she hoped. She raised an eyebrow.

He chuckled. "I'll keep my hands to myself for the moment so you know this is for real."

She frowned. "For real?"

"My proposition."

"You're talking in circles, Damian. And this is a place of business, in case you haven't noticed."

He held out his hands. "Okay, okay. Business is why I came. I want you to do my books, Diana. I've been handling the paperwork myself, but I'm pretty sure I've made a mess of it, and I live in fear of being audited. I'll pay you the going rate . . . whatever you think is fair. And you can do the work nights or weekends . . . whenever it fits into your schedule. What do you say?"

Of all the provocative things she might have imagined him suggesting, accounting had not made the list. And here she was, ready to be seduced, with no takers. She frowned. "Why me?"

"Are we back to that again?" he complained, humor lacing his voice. "You're smart. I know you. And I'd rather give the business to someone I trust."

She thought of the down payment she was trying to save for. She thought of being in contact with Damian on a regular basis. It was a measure of how far gone she was that the boost to her checkbook came in a dismal second to the idea of getting up close and personal with the guy who was making her crazy. Damian? No Damian. The devil and the deep blue sea.

She nibbled her lower lip and exhaled. "Can I think about it?"

"Nope," he said cheerfully, grinning as if he could care less whether she agreed. "This is strictly a onetime offer."

He named a price and she managed not to choke. She wasn't any more avaricious than the next woman who loved shoes and nice clothes, but hot damn.

She swallowed her misgivings and gave him a smile. "You just hired yourself an accountant."

Two days later Damian tried to focus on the axle he was replacing instead of staring at the ankles that sat primly in his line of vision.

Diana had taken a half day off from her real job to come in and start going over his filing system and his computer records. He thought it was cute that she mumbled and grumbled as she worked. He'd made excuses to stay in the office for the first half hour, but after that, she had chased him out, and he'd been forced to actually do his own work. The only reason he could see any of her at all was that she had left the door open, and from one end of the pit, he could keep tabs on just a narrow slice of the room on the far side of the garage.

Today, wearing a grease-stained T-shirt and old jeans, he felt the differences between them keenly. She was pretty and pristine in springy pink and white. She looked like a blossom just waiting to be picked and sniffed and . . .

He dropped the pliers and groaned when he bent to retrieve them. Maybe he should have insisted that she take the work home. He wasn't entirely clear about his own motives in hiring her. It was true that he needed accounting help. But buying some really good software or bringing in a temp probably would have done the trick.

One thing he noticed right off was her ability to concentrate in the midst of chaos. The phone rang constantly. Kevin made all kinds of racket when he came in from school. Customers tracked Damian down to ask questions in person. All in all, the garage was constantly in tumult.

But Diana was the calm in the storm.

At four thirty he ducked into the tiny shower stall in the rear of the premises, cleaned up, and put on a pair of khakis and a knit shirt. When he finally went back to the office, his hair damp and his jaw freshly shaven, she was still bent over his desk, hard at work.

He cleared his throat. She didn't flinch.

He tried again. No response. He wasn't sure he'd ever seen anyone stay that focused. When he dealt with numbers and invoices, he could barely tolerate it for more than an hour at a time. Diana had been here for almost five times that long. And the soft drink and peanuts she'd bought from his vending machine sat, only half consumed, on the desk.

He reached for the switch and flicked the lights on and off. "Earth to Diana."

She looked up and blinked, running a hand through the mass of soft curls, the image of which kept him up at nights. If she bent her head and he felt all that silky swath of firelight on his . . .

"Damian?"

He sighed and shook off his fantasy. Maybe there were a few things that could command his undivided attention. He tugged her to her feet. "I'm hungry. How about I take you to my place and I'll whip up some chicken parmigiana for dinner? It's my only specialty, but it's pretty good, if I do say so myself."

She smiled at him, a real, honest-to-God, uncomplicated smile. Uncomplicated, but possibly naughty. "Do we really want to waste time on cooking?"

His mouth opened and shut. Did she mean . . . ?

She reached up on her tiptoes, grabbed hold of his shirt collar, and kissed him. It was a good thing he wasn't standing in a puddle of water, because the electricity that crackled between their lips would have fried them both.

He might have been shocked by her about-face, but he was quick to catch up. He tangled his hands in her hair and tilted her head for a better angle. "No cooking," he muttered, nibbling her lower lip and sucking it gently. "What was I thinking?"

She unbuttoned the three buttons on his shirt, and he cursed himself for not putting one on that opened to the waist. He wanted to feel her, skin to skin.

Her hands were at his belt buckle. "Did you lock the door?"

His muddled brain tried to remember. "Yeah. Right after Kevin left."

"Good." Her response was muffled, possibly because she was busy putting a hickey in the crook of his neck.

He sucked in a sharp breath when her fingertips trespassed below his waistline. He grabbed her wrists, his chest heaving. "Not that I'm complaining, darlin', but I'm wondering what prompted this change of heart."

She muttered something indecipherable and licked his right nipple.

He jerked and tightened his hold. "Damn it, Diana. Answer me."

She went still and stepped back slowly, leaving him with the sick certainty that he'd blundered once again. Her face was hard to read, but she shook off his grasp and leaned against the desk. "Do we have to analyze this to death? I thought guys enjoyed living for the moment."

He ran a hand across the back of his neck. Hell, this woman was impossible to understand. "I thought you were still mad about Sunday evening." It might have been stupid to bring up past disagreements, but he felt as if he had missed out on a few important steps in the dance.

The slight but rapid rise and fall of her chest was the only sign that she was possibly a quarter as agitated as he was. She shrugged. "I was kind of witchy Sunday night. I'm over it."

"Why?" It seemed like a fair question.

She hitched a hip up on his desk and got comfortable, swinging her legs. "Would you believe I get turned on by a guy who keeps his books in the black?"

He managed a weak grin, though he didn't feel at all amused.

"Not really. I'd believe admiration maybe, but not horniness. Unless I'm way off the mark."

Her legs dangled, drawing attention to slender thighs and a narrow waist. "Maybe I'm just in the mood."

"At five o'clock on a Thursday afternoon? Ten minutes ago you didn't even know I was in the room."

She pouted. "Poor baby. Did I hurt the big man's soft, little feelings?"

He felt his temper kick. He'd learned to control it years ago, but Lord have mercy, this little tease knew which buttons to push. "Quit bullshitting me, Diana. What's this all about?"

Her eyes flashed, and the hair on the back of his neck stood up, like the tingling moment before lightning strikes. She smiled lazily. "Sex," she softly. "Plain, unadulterated sex. Hot, sweaty, fabulous sex."

Something about that explanation bothered him, but his penis wasn't interested in a debate over semantics despite what his brain might think. His erection surged and throbbed, drawing her attention.

She smiled slowly, sending every bit of testosterone in his body south to his dick. "What, no answer?"

He growled as he lunged at her. "You want sex? You've got it, sweet thing."

Diana gasped as he jerked her off the desk and into his arms. Her feet were hanging inches off the floor, and Damian was devouring her mouth as if he'd never survive without her kiss. Faster. Harder.

He released her long enough to undo the zipper on her jeans. She ripped her sweater over her head while he dragged her pants and panties to her ankles and then tossed them aside with her shoes.

He unfastened his own jeans and freed an impressively aroused cock from snug navy cotton briefs. Her hands cupped him reverently. "You're beautiful," she whispered, feeling sappy and emotional suddenly, and trying to remember this was only about sex.

He shuddered hard when she stroked him with both hands. The drop of liquid at the head of his penis beckoned her. She slipped to the floor and took him in her mouth, feeling his strong thighs tremble when she stroked his shaft with her tongue.

She winced when he pulled her hair. His voice was raw. "Jesus, Diana. Please . . ."

She nudged the warm weight of his balls between his legs and circled the head of his penis with a lazy pass of her tongue. He bit out a curse and dragged her to her feet. His hands closed over her sensitive breasts, and it was her turn to sigh and whimper.

His thumbs on her nipples made the ache between her legs sharpen to unbearable proportions. It took her a while to get there . . . usually. But not now . . . not today. "Condom?" She forced the word past dry lips, trying desperately to climb his body.

He looked down at her blindly and blinked. His pupils were dilated, and sweat beaded his forehead. "Condom?" He appeared not to know the word.

What the heck? She had come prepared, even if he hadn't. She evaded his embrace with no small amount of regret and rummaged in her purse on the desk, emerging triumphantly a moment later with a precious cache of six plastic-wrapped necessities.

He bowed his head and groaned. "Thank God."

She helped him roll one on, and he lifted her to her earlier perch on the desk with such ease that her stomach actually fluttered in feminine appreciation for his muscular strength.

She was naked except for her bra. He was fully clothed with his pants open. The contrast made her hot. So hot. He pushed her knees apart. She gasped.

She scooted her butt to the very edge of the broad wooden

desk and rested her heels against her ass. He froze, seemingly mesmerized by the sight of her feminine charms displayed so blatantly.

This was no time for ladylike deportment. She grabbed his hips and urged him closer. She'd expected him to go for the mother lode without delay. But Damian Bennetti was not a man to be rushed. He took his shaft in his hand and brushed the head of his cock in the wetness that signaled her complete and total readiness for this moment.

Her hands grasped his shoulders. Her head fell back. And still he teased her. Back and forth. Slower and faster. She arched her back. She was almost there. And then he stopped.

Her eyelids fluttered open and she gazed at him groggily. Was the man insane . . . or just a clever torturer?

She wet her lips, speaking as distinctly as she was able. "I would really appreciate it if you could get on with it, Mr. Bennetti."

His wolfish grin stopped her heart. With his free hand, he reached behind her and flipped open the catch on her bra. He ripped it free of her arms and bent his head to suck a nipple into his mouth. At the same time, he used his penis . . . again . . . to tease her weeping flesh.

Her orgasm slammed into her with such force that the fluorescent light overhead swung in dizzying circles. And she was pretty sure she yelled like a banshee.

When she hung limp and breathless in his arms, he bent his forehead to hers, his jaw clenched, his teeth gritted in a pained grin. "Save your ticket, baby. This next ride's on me."

Damian pushed into her incredibly tight, hot sheath and groaned aloud. Oh God. He could already feel the first distant tremors of his climax bearing down. Her legs wrapped around his waist in a viselike grip and she buried her hot face in his shoulder.

He pushed and withdrew and pushed again until he was

fully seated. The tight squeeze on his dick was so perfect, he almost believed he was riding bareback. But the damn condom was in place. He resented it suddenly, wanting desperately to feel her with no barriers. If they were married . . .

Whoa. Time out. Had he lost his freaking mind? Her arms tightened around his neck and he felt her breasts, smooth and cushiony, press against his chest. Somehow she had shoved his shirt up to his armpits, and now the two of them were about as close as two people could get.

He had his hands on her ass, lifting her into each thrust. But he had to stop for a moment. Had to try and stave off the inevitable.

He played with her butt, loving the feel of it, the amazing curves, the warm, plump flesh. He found her mouth with his, wildly out of control. "Can you come again?" He forced the four simple words from a throat that felt like sandpaper.

She squeezed him with internal muscles and chuckled roughly. "Oh yeah."

He moved faster, slamming into her and making the desk shake. He wanted to give her sweet words and romance, but the feelings tearing him apart were primal and urgent. He'd had sex aplenty. This was something far more overwhelming.

And then he abandoned rational thought in favor of sheer, blinding, shouted release.

When he recovered enough to wonder if she had made that last leap with him, his thighs were trembling, and Diana was slumped in his arms, panting and shivering. It occurred to him suddenly that the room was cool, and it must have gotten dark outside. The light that normally spilled into the hallway from the large windows out front had disappeared. He wanted to glance at his watch, but it seemed crass with the woman he had just screwed snuggled up against him.

He eased her back onto the desk and pulled up his pants. He

retrieved her shirt, bra, and panties and handed them to her. He would have helped, but the total lack of expression on her face made him uneasy.

While she dealt with the first three pieces of her wardrobe, he scooped up her jeans and shoes and stood quietly until she held out a hand for them. When she was more or less back to normal, he pulled her into his arms. They stood together in silence, beneath the harsh artificial lighting in his stark, unromantic garage.

He felt the sting of regret. She deserved better. Certainly for their first time at least. But she had instigated the tryst. Right? So why did he feel so damn guilty?

Perhaps because she wasn't saying anything.

He rubbed her back. "Are you okay?" It seemed like a dumb question in view of what had just happened, but he wasn't sure what else to say.

She nodded, still not speaking. He put his lips to her hair, inhaling her scent, learning the feel of her body in his arms. "Will you go home with me?"

Again, she nodded. And all at once, he felt the sunshine again.

Diana sat quiet and still in the passenger seat of her lover's utilitarian pickup truck and knew she was in deep trouble. She wasn't the kind of girl who could pull off casual sex. She had tried. Really. And for a brief moment during this evening's carnal proceedings, it seemed as if the hot, urgent encounter with Damian might be the cure for what ailed her.

But later, when he held her so tenderly and asked her to come home with him, her heart had tumbled that last dangerous distance between sexual attraction and honest-to-God love. She was such a sap.

Even knowing the eventual outcome, she was powerless to save herself. She wanted Damian in every way there was to want a man. He was sweet and sexy and so strong. But he was a man who had changed his world from what it had been to what he wanted it to be. And though she might figure into that picture in the short term, she was smart enough to know that men looked at life through different lenses.

Her dad had taught her that painful truth over and over from every possible angle during the seventeen years since her mother's death. Diana assumed he had loved her mother at one point. Before she died. But she was a child back then. She couldn't know for sure. All she saw was the endless succession of women who paraded through their house as she was growing up. All she remembered were the many nights spent sleeping over at her aunts' and uncles' houses, because her father needed privacy with his latest love interest.

It wasn't easy growing up with the black sheep of the extended family as your only parent. But in an odd sort of way, her unorthodox childhood and adolescence were directly responsible for the closeness she now shared with her cousins. They had literally lived under the same roofs . . . at least part of the time.

She glanced sideways at Damian. It was almost seven o'clock. He had promised to order pizza as soon as they got to his place. He had smiled and kissed her and acted as though everything was right with the world. Maybe it was. Maybe she needed to quit being such a worrywart. Maybe she needed to have a little faith. In herself. In the power of love. In men.

Damian's house was small but perfect. In addition to his skills as a mechanic, apparently he was a whiz at remodeling. When Diana saw the before and after pictures he had used to record his progress, her admiration grew.

She stood in the middle of his modern, airy kitchen and turned in a circle. "I love it," she said. "You're very lucky."

He looked puzzled.

She held out her hands. "What?"

He shrugged and rubbed his chin. "I'm surprised you don't have a house of your own."

Her grin was wry. "Do you think I have money, Damian?"

Her candor shocked him. She could tell. He was the picture of unease.

She sighed. "Jeannie has money. Elizabeth has money. Their parents have money. Me? I have a modest savings account and a deadbeat dad."

They stood facing each other in the silent kitchen as Damian absorbed what she had told him, and all the things she couldn't say. But he didn't speak a word.

Finally, he opened the fridge and pulled out a couple of soft drinks, handing her one with a slight smile. She cocked her head. "I had you pegged as a beer drinker."

A shadow crossed his face. "A lot of alcoholics back in the holler," he said simply. "So I never have."

She saw in his face the scars from those years, and in a flash, she realized that perhaps they had more in common than either one of them realized.

They squabbled over the pizza order. She liked hers loaded. He was a pepperoni guy. In the end they went half-and-half.

She ate three pieces. He devoured the other five. When she pointed that out in the interests of fairness, he took another swig of his drink and gave her the grin that was unfair on so many levels.

He swiped the last glob of cheese from her paper plate. "I need the calories," he said, brushing her boob with what looked like an intentional graze as he drew back his hand. "For later."

She licked her lips. "That sounds interesting."

He stood up and took her hand to pull her to her feet. With a gentle smile, he tucked a curl behind her ear. "Where do we go from here, sweet thing?"

She leaned into him, absorbing his strength, his warmth, the very solidness of him. "I have one question," she said softly as she played with a button on his shirt. "Did you change the sheets on your bed this morning?"

Five

Damian tried to look at his bedroom through her eyes. It was nothing special. A king-size bed with solid navy sheets and a matching comforter took up most of the space. The house had small rooms, and he should have picked out a double or a queen, but he liked to sleep sprawled out.

He looked at the window and winced. He'd hung a cheap set of miniblinds when he first moved in, but he'd never gotten around to picking out curtains. The chest of drawers was pine. On top of it sat a twelve-inch TV and an expensive Bose radio.

The decor was utilitarian, but at least it was clean. His mother had insisted he pull his weight around the house growing up, so he'd learned how to do basic chores early on, and the lessons had stuck with him.

He decided to distract Diana with sex. He flipped back the bedclothes and scooped her into his arms. She was smiling. That had to be a good sign. When he laid her gently on the mattress and started to ease down beside her, she shook her head and pushed at his chest with her hand.

"Not yet, Damian. I believe it's my turn to see a strip show."

He stopped, one knee down on the bed and one foot on the floor. If she was hoping to embarrass him, she was in for a disappointment. He'd grown up with two big sisters, and there wasn't much modesty to be had in a house with nine hundred square feet and five people.

He stood up and began unbuttoning his shirt. Diana propped her hands behind her head and watched him with a mischievous expression on her face. When he tossed the shirt aside and started unbuckling his belt, her cheeks flushed and he saw the movement in her throat as she swallowed.

He felt her reactions deep in his gut. He wanted her. It was as simple as that. He wouldn't examine any deeper emotions too closely as yet. Not when things were about to get really interesting.

When he was down to his skivvies, his cock was already prepared for action. Moments before, he had retrieved one of her condoms from his pants pocket and dropped it on the table. Despite how he felt about the damn things, he was eager to put it on. She stopped him then with an imperious wave. "Turn around."

He obeyed, and darned if he didn't feel the slightest bit bashful after all. He looked over his shoulder. "Can I finish now?"

He didn't wait for permission. He stepped out of his briefs, rolled on the latex, and went to the bed. Her eyes were glued to his dick. He liked that. A lot. And the aforementioned body part twitched and lengthened in eager agreement.

Diana was still fully clothed, a situation he planned on remedying without delay. He picked up his belt from the floor and used it to bind her hands over her head, anchored by a convenient spindly thing on the headboard.

Her breathing hitched and sped up. Another day, when intimacy between them wasn't so new, he might unwrap her slowly

like a long-anticipated package. But now, with his erection pain-
fully hard and his hunger not even dented by the snack in the
garage, he went after buttons and zippers with focused haste.

He figured he had her buck naked in less than thirty seconds. The unveiling was quick. But he had to stop and study the
amazing female beneath. Earlier, he had turned off the overhead
light, and now there was only the soft illumination from the adjacent bathroom. He wished he had candles. A woman like Diana
deserved candles.

He touched her collarbone . . . slid his hands from there on a
slow expedition south to her small, perfectly formed breasts, her
rib cage, the narrow waist, the flat stomach. When he touched the
light puff of hair between her thighs, she squirmed and panted.

He separated the plump pink folds of her sex and exposed
her clitoris. With a single finger, he stroked it softly. Her hips
came off the bed. "Damian, Damian . . ."

Was she protesting? He didn't think so. He scooted down in
the bed and replaced the finger with his tongue. She cried out
when he started licking her. Her taste was incredible. Sweet and
hot and so damn seductive.

She came with a long, low groan. He eased her through the
last tremors and then spread her thighs even wider. Her eyes
flew open, hazy and replete. "What are you doing?" Her voice
was hoarse.

He propped her legs on his shoulders. In her face he saw
the utter vulnerability she felt in this new position, especially
with her hands immobilized. He positioned his cock and pushed
slowly.

Diana gasped.

His own reaction was vocal and appreciative. He shoved
deeper, feeling her warm, moist flesh clasp him and pull him in. He
had one hand on either side of her, bracing himself on the bed.

He was so deep, he feared hurting her. Her blue irises had
darkened to indigo. Harsh breaths escaped from between her

moist, parted lips. She didn't close her eyes. And her challenging gaze spiked his hunger.

He bowed his head for a half second and sucked in some air. "Am I hurting you?"

She shook her head slowly. When he looked again, her eyelids had dropped to half-mast. He withdrew until only the head of his penis still filled her. She moved restlessly. He plunged back in, harder, faster.

Shit. He'd never felt anything like this. She was struggling now, trying desperately to free her hands. He would have helped her if he could, but his control had snapped, and he was drowning in a red haze that had only one possible conclusion.

With a mighty roar, he gripped her hips in a bruising grasp, pumped faster and faster, and came until he saw flashes of yellow light behind his eyelids. Moments later he collapsed in a heap on top of her soft, warm body.

Diana, her wrists finally freed, dozed lightly, wrapped in Damian's arms. When she woke up, it was difficult to gauge the passage of time. Physical satiation enveloped her in a warm fog of contentment, but her emotions were all over the map. Happiness. Fear. Hope. Dread.

He hadn't said any of those words women like to hear, but God, the tenderness in his lovemaking . . . she'd never felt so cherished in her life.

Even now, tucked close to his chest, spoon fashion, she felt completely protected in his arms. Already, the press of his cock against her ass told her he would soon be on deck for another round. She wouldn't object. How could she? But after that, she would ask to go home.

It was almost simplistic to say she had trust issues. It wasn't that she thought he was deceiving her in any way . . . but she was afraid to chance what the future might bring and afraid to end up getting hurt.

Perhaps it would be better to slip away now. It was still relatively early . . . buses would be running until eleven. In hindsight, she should have brought her car, but in the first flush of consummation, she'd never given a thought to *later*.

She sighed and played with the fingers of his limp left hand. He was dead to the world. She wondered what tonight had meant to him, if anything. Unfortunately, her father's hound-dog ways were not the only things causing her to proceed with caution.

In college, her roommate had dated someone a lot like Damian. Sexy, handsome, extremely charming. The unsuspecting girl had fallen hard, right up until the moment she found out her oh-so-cute boyfriend had been sleeping with two other women at the same time.

Diana's heart had bled for her friend. How did a woman ever know if a relationship had the depth and maturity to go the distance? The other thing keeping her awake at night seemed ridiculous, but she couldn't quite get past the fact that Damian had asked her out only after she'd put the new eucalyptus formula on his hands.

She vividly remembered the night in Jeannie's kitchen. The loud pop, the shower of sparks. Later, Jeannie's far from whimsical scientific brain had written it off as nothing, even though the night it had happened, she also seemed a bit intrigued.

Still . . . it was probably nothing. But Diana's other reservations continued to make her unsettled.

She tried to ease from Damian's arms, but he awoke instantly. His arms tightened around her. "Where are you going?" he mumbled, kissing the nape of her neck.

Not fair, she wailed inwardly, as her body responded to his practiced touch. She reached for her common sense. "I need to go. Tomorrow's a workday."

He froze, and she could almost hear the wheels turning in his brain in the sudden silence. His chest rose and fell against her back. Long moments later, his voice emerged, gruff and low. "I'll take you home. But first . . ."

He rolled her to her knees, stuffed pillows beneath her, sheathed himself, and entered her from behind with one smooth thrust.

It was very difficult for Diana to concentrate on work the next day. Images of Damian's large, nude body kept popping up on her computer screen. Time and again she had to blink and shake her head to remind herself that the vivid pictures were only in her imagination.

The sensitive flesh between her legs was still sore and tingling, and nothing could erase the memory of him taking her so dominantly in their third raw encounter. She muttered and shoved back her chair, reaching blindly for the bottle of water she kept on her desk. She was far too young for hot flashes.

Last night, after the amazingly carnal coupling that had eventually morphed into something sweet and slow, Damian had kept his promise and driven her home. As they got dressed and prepared to leave his house, neither of them spoke. Even the drive was silent.

On her doorstep, he gathered her close for an oddly gentle kiss. "Good night, Diana." He brushed back her hair and kissed her one last time on the temple.

She put her hand to his cheek, as afraid of saying goodbye in the short term as she was of the eventual outcome. "Good night."

He left without another word.

He hadn't called the shop today. But then again, the phone lines worked both ways. She hadn't made any contact either. She hated the uncertainty of the fledgling relationship. The sexual intimacy had progressed at lightning speed, but neither of them understood the other enough to predict what might happen next.

At lunchtime, she grabbed a quick cup of yogurt and a banana and then walked down the hill, ostensibly to pick up some more invoices. When she entered the garage, she could hear Damian's low, appealing laugh, and also the lighter tones of a woman's voice.

Almost afraid of what she might see, Diana stepped around the corner and stood silently so they would not notice her. The woman's identity was a bit of a shock. She was a well-known actress who had made her home in Asheville for years. It stood to reason that she would have the means to own a car that might require Damian's services.

For a long moment, Diana watched the two of them talking and laughing. Despite Damian's background, he didn't seem in any way intimidated by the woman's financial status or success. The two were interacting like old friends.

This little scenario was not an occasion for jealousy. Diana knew that. The woman had been happily married for years. And although she was no longer an A-list star, at forty-eight or forty-nine, she was still very attractive. And clearly, she was responding to Damian's sexy charm.

Diana made her presence known moments later, was introduced, and then wasted no time in collecting her paperwork and preparing to leave.

A flicker of concern crossed Damian's face, and he excused himself momentarily from his important client to pull Diana aside.

He lowered his voice and gave her an intimate smile. "I missed you today."

"Me, too." They were the only two words she could squeeze past her suddenly constricted throat.

He touched her cheek, a featherlight caress. "Can I come over this evening?"

A normal woman would have been flattered, right? But she was choking on her own uncertainties. Every cell in her body shouted *yes,* but she frowned and hesitated. And he saw it, felt it, and was hurt. His face shuttered and he stepped back with a hasty, almost clumsy move, which was behavior so unusual for him that she felt even worse.

She held out her hand. "Damian, I—"

He stopped her, his grim smile cynical. "No explanations necessary."

And he turned his back on her.

It hurt so badly, she pretty much ran out the door. She couldn't go back to the shop. Not under the watchful eyes of her cousins. So she went to her car, got in, and started driving. A half hour later, she was on the Blue Ridge Parkway, retracing the route she and Damian had covered a short time ago.

It was an even prettier day than last weekend and the traffic was markedly heavier. The dogwoods were blooming, pink and white splashes amid the spring green of the forest. It was a sight that usually brought her joy, but today her emotions were in turmoil.

She had to go back . . . eventually. She had flat out lied to her cousins. Invented a forgotten dental appointment. And then at long last at the end of a busy Friday, she went home to her empty apartment and buried her sorrows in a pint of mint-chocolate-chip ice cream.

All evening she hoped he would call. All evening she thought about calling him. But what could she say? *I'm scared that you're too much like my father.* Until she decided if she was willing to risk her heart, it wasn't fair to either of them to carry this any further.

The one time the phone did ring, it was Elizabeth. Her mom, Diana's aunt, was flying in on Saturday for a quick visit, and Elizabeth was having an impromptu dinner party. Diana accepted, of course. Aunt Tina was as much a mother to her as her own had been. Aunt Tina had been around for Diana's prepubescent years and adolescence, and for all the trauma and drama that came with them.

And it was Aunt Tina who had stood on the porch and cried when Diana drove off to college in a small used car crammed to the gills with blankets and pillows and books and CDs and a young woman's determination to strike out on her own.

Saturday afternoon, Diana showed up at her cousin's house early, offering to help with the food prep. But Jeannie and Elizabeth had it all under control. So Diana stole her aunt away for a walk around the neighborhood. They had always been close, but in Diana's mind, there was sometimes a bit of awkwardness in knowing that Tina was really Elizabeth's mother and not her own.

Tina was in her early sixties, but she was still a bright, attractive woman. She despaired of ever having grandchildren, as she complained to Elizabeth on a regular basis, but she had a full, busy life back in Baltimore.

The two of them talked about superficial topics for a while, and then Diana couldn't hold back any longer. She had to know. They were still strolling, so it was easy to look ahead and not meet her aunt's keen gaze.

Diana wrapped her arms around her waist. "I've been wanting to ask you something," she said, feeling tears sting the back of her throat.

"Anything, baby. You know that."

"Did my father ever love my mother . . . before she died, I mean?"

Tina stopped abruptly on the sidewalk, her face shocked. "Oh, Diana. Sweet girl . . ." There was a bench at the bus stop, and she made Diana sit. They faced each other, and the older woman gathered Diana's cold hands in hers. Her face had only the slightest of wrinkles, but her brown eyes held a wisdom Diana craved.

Tina sighed. "You father adored your mother. When she died, he nearly committed suicide."

Diana shivered in shock. "No."

Tina shrugged. "Yes. He was so distraught, we all had to take turns looking after him and at the same time caring for you. You were this precious, big-eyed, redheaded angel. So very fragile and in so much pain. We were terribly afraid he might hurt himself, and we couldn't bear the thought of you losing both of your parents."

"But obviously he didn't."

"No. Father Reynaldo spent hours with him, and your uncles of course . . . they talked to him. You see, your mother was the strong one in that relationship. She was your father's touchstone. His rock. Without her he was completely lost."

"But the women . . ."

Tina's gaze sharpened. "Did you never wonder why none of us criticized your father's behavior? It was appalling. But we knew the source, and we decided that if that was how he coped with the pain that was tearing him apart, who were we to step in and stop him?"

Diana was crying now. She felt the tears on her cheeks, but she made no move to stop them. Tina took a tissue from her purse and leaned forward to dry her niece's face. She held Diana close for a hug. "I'm sorry, sweetheart. I suppose we thought you would understand as you grew up. But we should have explained. He was staying alive the only way he knew how."

"I thought he never loved her at all," Diana whispered.

Tina's smile was wistful. "He loved her too much to go on. And for a while, we thought he wouldn't survive. But he loved you, too, so very much. And eventually, he regained a little bit of equilibrium."

"But not completely."

"No. Not completely. He saw a counselor for years. He drifted from job to job. That's no news to you, I know. But he tried, Diana. He really did."

"And did my mother love *him*?"

Tina smiled. "Oh, yes. Your mother was one of those lucky

people who always saw the good in others. And there was a lot of good in your father. Still is, I'm sure. But had the situations been reversed, she would have responded much differently. Your mother was an extremely strong woman. Even after her diagnosis, and during all the months that led up to her death, *she* was the one taking care of your father and not the other way around. You're very much like her."

"I never knew."

"How could you? We protected you as much as we could, but I suppose after years of keeping the family secret, it became habit. I think we did you a disservice."

Diana kissed her cheek. "You were wonderful to me. And I love you."

Now they were both crying.

"I love you, too, baby girl."

Diana wanted to tell Tina about Damian. For that matter, she wanted to tell both of her cousins. But the relationship was so new, and her feelings were so fragmented, in the end she kept silent.

Later that night she lay in bed, wondering what Damian was thinking. Had she merely hurt his pride or something much deeper? Despite his outgoing personality, she sensed a deep vein of vulnerability in him. The legacy of his difficult childhood had left its mark. To the outside world, it might seem as though the two of them had little in common, but she knew differently.

Both of them had become loners in a way. They had learned self-sufficiency at early ages, and perhaps they had learned to guard their hearts, as well.

It really boiled down to one thing. Was she brave enough to pursue with Damian a relationship that came with no guarantees? Could she enjoy him and love him and yet still be okay if it turned out to be only temporary?

Before today, she would have said no. The fear of hurt and

heartbreak was stronger than her desire to share her life for however long with Damian. But Tina had made her see the truth. Diana was not emotionally weak like her father. Diana was like her mother.

The words echoed in her head like a blessing. She was like her mother. Her mother, who had abandoned her through no fault of her own at a time when a girl needed her mom the most.

Diana rolled over in bed and plumped her pillows. She had some serious thinking to do and some decisions to make. Life was precious, and love was rare. Was it any less so if only *one* person loved? And was there any way to protect a heart in advance from breaking when the one-sided loving was not enough?

Six

*D*amian looked down at his bleeding knuckles and grimaced. His hands were a mess, and like some big-ass sissy, he couldn't bring himself to use the special lotion. It would hurt too much. Not the sting of the creamy ingredients against his cracked skin, but the memory of a woman's soft skin and firm touch on his hands.

It was Sunday night, and by his calculations, it had been almost exactly seventy-two hours since he had dropped Diana off on her doorstep. At the time he'd wondered if she might ask him to spend the night. Guys weren't attached to curling irons and hair products and junk like that, and he could have made a quick trip home the following morning to change clothes.

But no. She'd said good night, and he hadn't thought much about it. It was late. She was tired. They had already made love on three separate and memorable occasions. It made sense.

What didn't make any sense at all was her stilted, awkward visit to his garage the next day, or her not so subtle distaste for the idea of seeing him again that night. Even now the pain of it lodged beneath his breastbone, and the nagging sense of loss and disappointment had kept him up for two nights straight. Why did it hurt so much? Other women had given him the brush-off, and he had simply moved on to greener pastures.

But Diana's opinion of him mattered a lot. He didn't allow himself to ponder the reason. It was too damn scary to contemplate. Surely he wasn't . . . His thoughts skittered away from the L word. Hell, he really was in deep shit.

He tried to look on the bright side.

It was a good thing, really, that she had made her feelings clear right off the bat. Much better than him dating her for a month and then getting dumped like yesterday's trash. What was harder to dismiss was the notion that she had been slumming. That she'd been playing out some blue-collar fantasy and, having screwed him really damn well, realized that the wrong side of the tracks was not that appealing after all.

He knew he had a chip on his shoulder about his upbringing. He'd worked hard since coming to Asheville to put it behind him. To believe that people accepted him at face value. That he wasn't being judged by his past.

But he was such a dumb ass, he'd actually spilled all the not so pleasant details to Diana before they'd even had a chance to really understand each other.

So if she'd been turned off, it was his own damn fault. Although if he had deliberately evaded her questions, that would have left a sour taste in his mouth as well. He didn't want to be with a woman—not fuck her, but *be* with her—if he couldn't let her see the real Damian.

He was too old and too smart to live a lie just so some uppercrust, prissy woman would want him. He knew he was being unfair, but the anger helped him ignore the raw state of his emotions. And God knew, he wasn't about to wear his heart on his sleeve. He might have improved his image, but a coal miner's son from Kentucky would never miraculously transform into a "sensitive" metrosexual with a seventy-five-dollar haircut and a Starbucks cup in his hand.

He was a man. Real men didn't whine and moan when things didn't go their way. They sucked it up, swallowed the bitter pills, and kept on going.

Diana felt progressively worse with each day that passed. It was torture knowing that Damian was just down the street. And she couldn't blame him for not calling her. She was the one who had shot him down, and at a time when a guy's feelings were bound to be a bit fragile. Perhaps he thought she wasn't impressed with the sex.

Ha. Not bloody likely. There was no way Damian could think she hadn't enjoyed the sex. She'd been embarrassingly eager in his arms. And damn . . . he was good.

She refused to think about how much experience a man had acquired to reach that level of expertise with a woman's body. Speculation about his past relationships only compounded her feelings of uncertainty.

Over a week after her day with Damian, and her later heart-to-heart talk with Aunt Tina, Diana found herself on Sunday morning sitting at Jeannie's beautifully appointed table for brunch. Jeannie was a fabulous cook, and at least once a month, the three cousins gathered in her sun-kissed, cutting-edge kitchen, with its brushed-aluminum appliances and granite countertops, to eat a meal together.

The rules were no talk of calories and no business conversation. Anything else was fair game. For Diana, it was the perfect opportunity to broach the subject on which up until now she had been deliberately silent.

Over spinach-and-pancetta omelets, she eased into the subject. She swallowed an astonishingly sweet strawberry and pretended great interest in the arrangement of wildflowers at the center of the table. "Do you guys remember how Aunt Tina used to talk to us when we were little about her great-great-grandmother?"

Jeannie refilled a small glass pitcher with fresh-squeezed orange juice. "I loved those stories about Ireland and the little people."

Elizabeth nodded slowly. "I had the most beautiful pictures in my head of what it must be like. I can't believe I've still never been there."

Jeannie snitched the last of her own mouthwatering, bite-size pecan muffins. "Aunt Tina swore that we had a Celtic sorceress way back in the family tree. I thought that was pretty cool. Still do."

Diana choked on a bite of egg and swallowed a gulp of coffee as she recovered. "Do you think we have any power?" she blurted out uncensored.

Both her cousins turned in their chairs and stared at her.

Jeannie cocked her head, her blond hair sweeping her shoulder in a sexy tumble that Diana could never duplicate, even if she tried. "Power?" Her brow furrowed as though she were trying to figure out a confusing equation.

Elizabeth, always the efficient caretaker, stood up and began gathering dishes and silverware. She gave Diana a pat on the shoulder. "Single women as business owners are a growing demographic. Of course, we have power."

Diana and Jeannie smothered their laughter with a conspiratorial grin at each other. Elizabeth was a force to be reckoned with when she began lecturing on the subject of female independence.

Jeannie intervened. "I don't think she's talking about that kind of power." She studied Diana's face. "Are you asking if we have magical abilities?"

Diana felt her cheeks redden. "Well, when you say it that way, it sounds ridiculous."

Both of the other women shook their heads in bemusement. Jeannie scooted her chair closer to Diana's as though getting ready to dissect her somehow. "What are you talking about, Diana? And how much of that amaretto did you put in your orange juice?" She picked up Diana's cut-glass tumbler and sniffed it theatrically.

Diana grabbed it back, heedless of its value. "Very funny." She paused, feeling embarrassed, but unable to drop the subject. "I'm serious. Do you recall the night we finally got the new formula the way we wanted it?"

Elizabeth paused, transfixed. "Oh, I remember now. You're talking about the little explosion in the pot."

Jeannie raised her eyebrows. "Explosion? Let's not exaggerate. A bubble popped. That's all."

Diana nibbled the tines of her fork. "But there were sparks. And the moon was full."

Elizabeth nodded reluctantly. "She has a point. It *was* very odd."

Jeannie rolled her eyes. "Absolutely not." She said it flatly. "It was science, not a séance."

Diana wanted desperately to be convinced. "Are you sure? Isn't there a tiny chance that we might be . . . I don't know . . . maybe . . ."

Elizabeth stood by Diana's shoulder. "Magically gifted?" The two of them stared Jeannie down: the dreamers versus the scientist. Then all three of them burst into laughter.

Diana held up her hands in defeat. "All right, I know it sounds crazy."

Jeannie leaned back in her chair. "What's this all about, Diana?"

Elizabeth started the dishwasher and came back to the table. "Yeah, honey. What's got your panties all in a wad? You haven't been yourself all week."

Now the focus of two sets of eyes was on *her*. Diana squirmed. "It's men. Or one man. Or I don't know. I just can't figure him out."

"Who?" The other two chanted in unison.

Diana hung her head. "Damian. Damian Bennetti."

After that, she had no choice but to confess the truth, or at least as much of it as she could politely reveal. Some things a girl just had to keep to herself. Such as the memory of Damian touching her until she came apart in his arms. Or the way his beautiful smoke-colored eyes darkened when he was very serious. Or the feel of his work-roughened hands on her skin and how his touch made her shiver when he was so gentle with her.

When she came to the end of a severely edited rendering of her brief but powerful association with the man down the street, she fell silent. Her two almost-sisters wore slightly shell-shocked expressions. It was understandable. They were accustomed to their baby cousin living more or less like a nun.

Elizabeth found her tongue first. She narrowed her brows. "I think you're smart to be cautious. Damian does have quite a reputation."

Jeannie snorted. "No offense, Elizabeth, but you're hardly the one to be giving her advice. You're far too picky when it comes to men, and you know it."

Elizabeth opened her mouth to protest and then shrugged. "Perhaps."

Jeannie leaned forward and spoke earnestly. "You're twenty-seven years old, Diana. The perfect age to be out enjoying life. Enjoying men. So what if he has a past? If he's interested in you and the attraction is mutual, you should go for it. Not every relationship has to begin with a guarantee."

Elizabeth apparently couldn't resist jumping into the fray. "I hate to admit it, but Jeannie is probably right. And you won't be like your dad just because you go out with a few guys and have some fun."

Diana winced. "Aunt Tina told you?"

Elizabeth smiled gently. "We all love your dad, honey. But we know his limitations. He's not capable of loving any woman like he loved your mother. So he flits."

Diana sighed. "I don't want to flit. I want the one-man-one-woman, till-death-do-us-part thing. And I'm afraid Damian's not it."

Jeannie sat back in her chair and crossed one shapely leg over the other. "You'll never know if you cross him off the list now. Some guys have to warm up to the idea of marriage and forever."

Elizabeth was silent, her face pensive as though she had momentarily checked out of the conversation.

Diana sighed. "How can you know if a man will be faithful to you?"

"You don't," Jeannie said. "But remember, your dad was faithful to your mother because he adored her. It was only later that he started playing the field. Give Damian a chance. He seems like a straight-up kind of guy. I like him."

Diana dropped her head to the table and groaned. "*Liking* him is not the problem, believe me. The man is damn near irresistible."

Damian wondered how long it would take to get over Diana Killaney. They'd only been together one day and one night. Hell, you couldn't even call the brief amount of time they'd spent together a relationship. It was barely more than a one-night stand, and though he hated to admit it, even to himself, Diana hadn't cared for him at all.

There. He'd said it. He, Damian Bennetti, had been more than willing to tumble head over heels in love, but the woman in question wasn't all that impressed.

He stared at the computer screen and tried to make sense of the numbers. Three days ago he'd received in the mail a neat stack of invoices, already entered and processed, along with a polite note stating that Diana had underestimated the time it would take to do his accounting and suggesting that he probably needed to hire someone full-time.

She had signed the neatly typed letter in blue ink, and like a lovesick fool, he'd been carrying it around in his pocket.

Well, hell. It wasn't like him to take defeat without a protest. Where was his spine, for God sakes? He glanced around the garage in frustration and spotted the clock on the wall. Damn. Kevin had just arrived, and he couldn't bail on the kid. The garage was supposed to be open for two more hours.

Doggedly, he turned back to the car that demanded his attention. For the next one hundred twenty minutes, he made his mind a blank. At least when it came to infuriating redheads.

At a quarter till six, he showered. At six sharp, he said goodbye as Kevin headed out. Then he pulled the shades, turned off the lights, locked up, and bolted to his car.

An hour later, he cursed his own stupidity and headed for his house. Diana had not come home from work. She could be anywhere. His impulsive tendencies rarely served him well, which was why, over the course of the last decade, he'd tried to root them out. Case in point, the day he'd first asked Diana to go to lunch with him. He'd ended up with his dick covered in icy, wet denim.

Not one of his finer moments. And did he learn from that experience? Hell, no.

Feeling mentally and physically frustrated and hungry to boot, he turned onto his street and nearly rear-ended the vehicle in front of him when he got a glimpse of a familiar Sentra parked in his gravel driveway just a few hundred feet down the road.

He pulled in behind the other car and glided to a stop. His heart was pounding in rapid jerks, and his breathing quickened. This was a turn of events he hadn't anticipated.

Every window on the first floor was lit up in a welcoming glow. He unlocked his front door, stepped inside, and was met with the aromatic smell of food cooking. He followed his nose, hoping he wasn't dreaming.

Diana stood with her back to him, stirring something on the stove. She looked up when he entered the room.

Her smile was definitely nervous.

He could relate to that. He ran a hand through his hair. "This is a surprise." He kept his voice calm, though he felt anything but.

She wiped her hands on a dish towel and stuffed them in her pockets. "I owe you a meal."

He paused, taking in what she wasn't saying. "How did you get in?"

She shrugged. "Kevin. His mother is a regular customer at Lotions and Potions." She picked up something from the counter and held out her hand. "He gave me the extra house key from the shop. Here it is. I didn't want to forget to give it back to you."

When he took it, their fingers brushed. It looked like Diana's lips trembled, but she turned away to open the oven. When she bent over to remove an iron skillet of perfectly browned corn bread, eating dinner was the last thing on his mind. That vantage point of curved ass turned his brain to mush.

When she straightened up, she put the pan on top of the stove and glanced at him. "I hope it's not dried out. I expected you an hour ago."

"How wifely of you." He couldn't resist the dig.

She paled, and he felt like a heel. He was having a hard time deciding whether his anger or his relief had the upper hand at the moment. He couldn't quite erase the memory of her expression that day in his garage.

She waved a hand at the table. "It's nothing fancy—roast, potatoes, and carrots that I put in the slow cooker this morning before I went to work."

He watched her pull a bowl of salad from the fridge. "So you've been in and out all day?"

"No." She set his bottle of Italian dressing beside the bowl.

"Just long enough to prepare the corn bread. I carried the rest of the food from home."

They ate mostly in silence after a stilted conversation that never quite got off the ground.

He studied her as he chewed and swallowed. She was wearing a thin apricot top that hugged her small breasts. He could see her nipples clearly.

Beneath the table, his johnson rose to attention and stayed there. He barely tasted the food, only enough to recognize the fact that it was excellent. But other hungers took precedence.

At the end of the meal, when she began to clean up, he took her arm, holding her firmly just above the elbow. "Come with me, Diana." He led her to the den and installed her in a chair. He remained standing. Somehow, some way, he needed to keep the upper hand.

Her seated posture was prim, feet and knees together, hands folded in her lap.

He launched the first shot. "Why are you in my house?" He wasn't sure he wanted to hear her answer, but it couldn't be avoided any longer.

She licked her lips. "I'm sorry that things ended badly between us."

The knot in his gut grew bigger. So this wasn't a bid for reconciliation? His jaw tightened. "I've had worse." He mocked her deliberately, trying to get to the redhead's temper beneath her careful manners.

But she was not so easily baited today. Now she mutilated her bottom lip with her teeth. She bent her head. "Perhaps so. But I was unintentionally rude, and I'm sorry. It wasn't that I didn't want you to come over to my house that night. I just wasn't sure it was wise."

He folded his arms across his chest and leaned against the wall. "That makes me feel so much better."

Her spine seemed to melt, and she slouched back in the

chair, tucking her legs beneath her and kicking off her shoes. Her head rested on the back of the seat, and she looked at him steadily, her eyes dark with emotions he couldn't decipher. "I was afraid, Damian. Afraid of getting hurt."

His brows knit. "Why?"

She picked at the chair arm. "You have lots of experience in the love-'em-and-leave-'em routine. Me . . . not so much. I know you're a smorgasbord kind of guy, and I was afraid I couldn't keep that in perspective."

"And now?" He kept his expression impassive, feeling some kind of crazy-ass hope spring to life in his chest.

She pulled her knees to her body and wrapped her arms around them as though trying to protect herself. She smiled faintly. "I'm here to play. If you're still interested, that is."

"Play?" He spoke the word carefully, a sick feeling growing in the pit of his stomach.

She nodded. "I'm no starry-eyed kid. I'm a grown woman, and I'm entirely capable of having wild and crazy sex just for the hell of it."

The wild-and-crazy-sex part sounded promising, but that last bit was not what he wanted to hear. "And if I don't agree?"

She went white. It happened so quickly, he was shocked. She stood up. "Then I've wasted my time."

She was at his front door before he could process what was happening.

He grabbed her arm again. "Sit down, damn it. Don't be so quick off the mark. Can I say my piece now?"

Her face was sulky. "If you must."

He kept her there by the front door, but he put his back against it, just in case. "Tell me something, Diana. Do you enjoy screwing me because I fit some fantasy of a rough-edged mechanic to your white-bread-princess world?"

She smacked him. And it was a good one with all her weight behind it. His head snapped around, and he saw stars when his skull cracked against wood. She didn't look the least bit sorry.

He rubbed his face. "I'll take that as a no."

He looked deep into her pretty blue eyes and saw the apprehension and hurt lingering behind her belligerent stance. He couldn't have smiled if his life depended on it. He felt hung out to dry, and this vulnerable crap was hell on a man's ego.

He swallowed hard. "I'm not interested in having a fling with you. Sorry if that's what you wanted."

This time when she paled, her knees lost their starch, and she wobbled, big tears welling in her eyes.

He snatched her in his arms, finding her mouth desperately and raining kisses on it and her precious face. "Don't be such a clueless airhead, Diana. For God sakes . . . I'm falling in love with you."

He held her so tightly he could feel the rapid flutter of her heart against his chest. She was limp at first, and then slowly, as his words penetrated, her arms came up around his neck and she opened her lips.

She was trying to speak, but he sneaked in another kiss or two before she got the words out. Her voice was husky. "Really? You're not just saying that to get sex?"

He pulled back and stared at her, shaking his head. "You really have a low opinion of my gender, don't you?" He touched her cheek softly, trying to view this from her perspective. He chose his words carefully. "I may have had sex with a number of women, Diana. But I've never said *I love you* to any of them. Scout's honor."

Her nose burrowed into his chest. Her breath was warm through the fabric of his shirt. "Why now?"

He rolled his eyes, but she didn't see. He rubbed her back softly. "I never found one who excited me more than my cars."

She stepped back and stared at him. "More than your cars? Really?"

Diana was genuinely shocked. She'd witnessed him with those exotic vehicles, and she knew passion when she saw it. The man was nuts for a high-performance engine and a beautiful chassis.

He held up his hands, smiling that devilish grin that made her panties damp even when she was mad at him. "Swear to God. I'd drive a Ford Pinto if it meant having you in my bed every night."

Her hands went to his zipper, and he flinched. "What are you doing?" His voice was hoarse, but the length of firm male flesh beneath his jeans indicated guaranteed compliance.

She lifted him free of his underwear and stroked the smooth, velvety length. "I'm still looking for that wild-and-crazy sex you promised me."

A giant shudder racked his big frame. His hands tangled in her hair, pulling her closer. "I don't remember promising anything of the sort."

She dropped to her knees and licked her lips. "Let's see if this might help your amnesia."

He closed his eyes and a smile crossed his face. "Knock yourself out."

It was a tribute to her technique, or so she liked to think, that he didn't make it beyond a minute and a half. With an explosion imminent, he dragged her to her feet and over to the sofa. He went stock-still and gazed down at her, his chest heaving. "Condom?"

It delighted her to supply a half dozen from her pocket. With impatient, clumsy speed, he ripped off his jeans and hers, shoes as well, rolled on the necessary protection, and pulled her onto his lap. As she took every last wonderful inch of him into her body, he leaned back his head and groaned.

They were still dressed from the waist up. He shoved her shirt to her armpits and tried to get at her breasts. A very expensive bra ripped in the process. She didn't give a flip. Not when his tongue and teeth were teasing and nipping and tormenting . . . Oh geeez . . .

She arched up into an orgasm so white-hot, it made her shudder for endless seconds before she collapsed on top of him. At some level she was aware that he had climaxed, as well. His hands were slowly stroking her bare ass. His harsh breathing echoed in her ear.

He reached behind her and snagged the strip of five plastic squares. Seconds later, she heard him rip open another one.

And then he tumbled her to the floor. His words were jerky. "Sorry. That only took the edge off." Seconds later, with his fully erect penis standing proud and tall for its second time at bat, he knelt between her legs, positioned himself, and thrust deep and hard between her legs.

In theory, this round should have been soft and slow. Neither of their libidos got the memo. He was wild and rough. She was crazy and limber. They went at it like animals in heat, tumbling and rolling over and around and up against furniture, until both of their asses were bruised and carpet-burned.

He finally picked her up and went back to the sofa. His cock was buried inside her, and her legs had a death grip around his waist. When he sank down onto the cushions, sitting upright, his rigid length did magical things to the insides of her body.

She gasped and tightened her vaginal muscles with an involuntarily whimper. "Damian . . ." She was dizzy with love and lust. The smell of sex mingled with her light perfume and his spicy aftershave.

He moved lazily now, making his upward thrusts deliberate and slow. Her orgasm was just out of reach, and she was desperate for it.

She bent her head and nipped his bottom lip with her teeth. "Do it."

He put his hands on her waist and lifted her until they almost disconnected. "Not until you say those three little words."

The muscles in his arms quivered with the strain of supporting her weight at this angle.

She panted. "Do it hard."

His penis flexed. "Guess again."

"Do it fast." She wanted him inside her now.

"Nope." He was sweating.

"Do it, please."

He scowled. "The first one is *I*."

"I need it. I want it. Take your pick."

"Cruel, Diana. Cold and cruel." He jerked her downward so hard that the head of his cock thumped against her womb. She shrieked and shot over the edge, sobbing and laughing and writhing in his arms.

Still he didn't end it. He wasn't done. And his control was admirable. He licked a drop of sweat from her temple. "Please."

That one did her in. Her heart turned over. Hard. She felt something so strong and so incredibly beautiful that tears filled her eyes. How had she been so lucky as to find this remarkable man?

She took his beloved face in her hands, feeling the very life force of him filling her to the brim. "I love you," she whispered. "Forever."

He cursed and flipped her to her back, lengthwise on the sofa. His eyes were dark, his cheeks flushed. He started to move slowly, in and out. "Was that so hard?" he asked in a raspy mutter.

She held him tightly as he shouted and shuddered in her arms. In the emotionally laden silence that followed, she brushed her lips over his damp cheek. "Loving you isn't hard at all, Damian," she whispered. "Not hard at all."

Movie Magic

One

*E*lizabeth leaned over the sink to get closer to the mirror. Was that a wrinkle? She turned her head and sighed with relief when the shadow-induced line disappeared. She'd never been one to obsess over her looks or her body, but with her fortieth birthday looming on the horizon in just a few months, she was getting jumpy.

And it didn't help that her baby cousin was engaged. Although Diana and Damian had known each other for a long time, they'd been together as a couple barely three weeks, and already they were talking marriage. Elizabeth disapproved of the speed at which things were moving with the two of them, but she kept her mouth shut. She couldn't help wondering, though, if the number ten "potion" really did have some kind of power to make potential victims of Cupid's whimsy dive headfirst into lust and love.

She wasn't jealous. . . . Really she wasn't. She was thrilled to see Diana so happy. But Elizabeth was a dozen years older than Diana, and had nary a romantic prospect in sight. It was depressing, to say the least, even if it was her own fault. She'd allowed a traumatic episode in her past to practically eradicate her sexuality.

In the historical English romance novels she loved to read, the younger female members of the family were never allowed to wed before their older siblings. Which seemed only fair . . . at least from the standpoint of someone in kissing distance of forty. And forty wasn't all that far from fifty and a membership in AARP. And from fifty it was quickly on to retirement and pretty soon a grass-covered plot at the local perpetual-care cemetery.

She frowned at her reflection in the mirror. It was perfectly acceptable to be maudlin and overdramatic in the privacy of one's own home. Because in public, she was *never* a drama queen. Elizabeth Killaney was known for her levelheaded, responsible, and down-to-earth personality. All adjectives she had appreciated in the past . . . even aspired to, if the truth were told.

But now, because she was a daily witness to Diana's fresh-faced, dewy beauty and her contagious, bubbly excitement and joy . . . now, with the bridal magazines and the napkin samples and the gown fittings . . . Elizabeth was feeling a bit like the Scrooge of the wedding world.

She fluffed her chin-length hair and wondered what she would look like as a blonde. Brown was so boring. The natural red highlights she'd inherited from the Irish gene pool helped, but those only really showed up in sunlight. Other than that, her hair was just . . . brown.

She turned and faced the full-length mirror on the back of the bathroom door. She hadn't put it there. The previous owner had left it. Elizabeth tried to avoid its unforgiving accuracy whenever she stepped out of the shower. Only a woman as gorgeous as Jeannie might be able to gaze into it with impunity.

Slowly, Elizabeth untied the belt on her robe and held open the sides. Then, with a metaphorical spit in the wind for courage, she dropped the soft navy blue terry cloth to the floor with a soft plop. The nude woman staring back at her didn't flinch.

She studied her image clinically. If she didn't use the Hollywood standard as a measure, it wasn't too bad. Long legs . . . narrow waist . . . average boobs that still pointed in the correct direction. Even her weight wasn't really a problem.

Oh sure, she might like to lose five or ten pounds, but that was vanity talking. In truth, she was healthy and average for her height and age.

Average. God, she was learning to hate that word. She picked up her robe and slipped her arms back into the sleeves, tying the belt so tightly, she felt the squeeze. Just once, she would like to be out of the ordinary. Just once she would like to have a man's eyes light up in simple male lust, even though she was no longer a nubile twenty-something. Was that so much to ask?

But heck, what would she do if it really happened? She was so accustomed to freezing men out of her life, she probably wouldn't recognize genuine male interest if it smacked her in the face.

As she wandered into her bedroom and started getting dressed, she thought about the magazine article she'd read recently that dissected the nuances of sexual attraction. The author claimed that although it was true that men responded initially to visual stimuli like big boobs and a pretty face, in the long run, the thing men found most attractive about a woman was her air of confidence.

Over her usual breakfast of oatmeal and orange juice, she continued to think about the confidence thing. Lord knew, Elizabeth projected confidence, even when things were falling apart around her. It had taken confidence to persuade Jeannie and Diana to go into business with her.

And in the early days, when the probability of their success had been touch and go at best, Elizabeth never wavered in her belief that the three of them would make it. When her dad was diagnosed with cancer, Elizabeth was still in high school. She had sided with her mom in an unerring determination that he would pull through. And he did.

She knew how to do confidence. But no one understood the true price she had paid to learn.

After graduating from college summa cum laude, she had gone on to earn a master's degree in business administration with a concentration in marketing. She snagged a job with a high-profile firm in New York City and spent a dizzyingly wonderful five years with a creative and productive team. She'd dated a lot in those days.

Fun was a concept that wasn't as alien as it seemed now. But then everything came tumbling down around her ears, and even confident, talented Elizabeth had been unable to escape the calamity.

She'd fallen in love with her boss, a new vice president brought in from outside. The sexual attraction had been instantaneous. He was handsome, funny, and as smart as she was. They were in bed within three months. And the sex was hot and satisfying.

But Mr. Handsome, Funny, and Smart was also something else that was not so wonderful. Something he had concealed from her and everyone in the office. He was married. His wife had stayed behind in Phoenix to sell the house and to let their six-year-old finish his first-grade year.

Even now, almost twelve years later, Elizabeth still tasted the bitter memory of shame and heartbreak.

But no one in the family ever knew. Not even her mother. And Tina Killaney was an extremely perceptive woman.

The debacle in New York hadn't been pretty. Elizabeth had been blindsided when Mr. Handsome's family showed up at the office one day. It was the single-most-awful moment of her life. And though the rest of the staff had been as surprised as she was, at least they hadn't been sleeping with a married man.

Their covert looks of sympathy should have comforted her, but the fact that her humiliation was completely public made her feel raw and exposed. She never even allowed herself the satisfaction of telling him what a jerk he was. She couldn't risk hurting two innocent people.

So she simply quit her job and moved back home on the pretext that she needed a change. That much was true. She had also needed time to regroup and figure out what to do with her life. It was in that painful period that the idea for Lotions and Potions was born, though it didn't come to fruition until much later.

So in some ways, you could say that *jerkface* had done her a favor. His perfidy was the catalyst for Elizabeth to start an extremely rewarding career.

But her confidence was hard won, and the scars from that period in her life ran deep.

After peeking her head in at the shop to make sure their new saleslady was handling things well, Elizabeth decided to stop by the bank. She had some ideas for expansion, and she wanted to explore her options for a loan.

She was walking along the street, head down, texting a message to a friend, when something slammed into her shin just above the ankle and took the legs right out from under her. She cried out in pain and shock, and felt herself heading rapidly for a jarring collision with the sidewalk.

Before she could do more than flail her limbs in a futile attempt to save herself, strong arms came around her from behind, and her back *whumped* into a hard, broad chest.

Even so, her right knee made contact with the rough concrete, scraping off a layer of skin and ripping her expensive hose.

In the aftermath of the accident, the pain in her knee and shin was momentarily overshadowed by the reality of being sprawled gracelessly in a strange man's lap. He was warm and big, and he smelled delicious.

He helped her to her feet and their eyes met for the first time. *Wow*. She felt dizzy, and it wasn't from the fall.

The man eyeing her with quizzical concern was rugged, but a bit flashy by North Carolina standards. He stood at least six feet four inches tall, and his broad shoulders were clad in a tropical-print Hawaiian shirt in blues and greens. His dark wavy hair was a couple of inches longer than hers, and a small diamond stud winked in his not-gay earlobe. She'd picked up that bit of bling distinction from an issue of *Cosmo*.

He still held both of her hands, and he was caressing them lightly. His voice was deep and rumbly. "Are you okay? I would have given that maniac skateboarder a piece of my mind, but he was gone in a flash, and I was worried about you."

She glanced around and saw her belongings scattered across the sidewalk. For once, the practical side of Elizabeth Killaney was silent. She wet her lips. "I'm fine, thanks to your quick re-flexes. I'm lucky I didn't break something."

His eyes did a very deliberate and yet not at all insulting inspection of her body from head to toe. "I'm the lucky one," he murmured. He lifted her hands to his lips and pressed a warm kiss on her knuckles.

Then he released her with undisguised reluctance. He cocked his head and stared at her mouth. "Enrique Cantilano at your service, my lady."

All sorts of things in her body went liquid and gooey. Sweet heaven. If any other man of her acquaintance had uttered that line sporting longish hair and an earring, she would have laughed in his face.

Looking into Enrique's hazel eyes, she didn't feel at all like laughing. She tucked her hair behind her ears with a nervous gesture. "Elizabeth Killaney."

He helped her gather the contents of her purse, and man-aged to hand her a tampon without looking the least bit em-barrassed. Elizabeth, on the other hand, turned bright red and grabbed it furtively . . . then wanted to smack herself. What was she . . . twelve?

When she stood up again, she was shocked to see him still kneeling at her feet. He put his big, warm palms on either side of her injured kneecap and studied her raw, bleeding flesh. She could barely feel the pain. She was too distracted by the hot zings of pleasure radiating up her thigh. If he slid his hands eight inches higher . . .

She sucked in a startled breath when he looked up at her and frowned. "We need to clean this before it gets infected." He rose to his feet, making her feel suddenly small and dainty. Her nose was about even with his collarbone, and she realized she was in danger of actually sniffing the man to see where the delicious masculine scent was the strongest.

Maybe she'd seen too many Johnny Depp movies, but she could swear she smelled the salty tang of the ocean and the piquant aroma of a citrus grove.

He took her arm, steering her down the street. "There's a little mom-and-pop pharmacy around the corner. I saw it this morning. We'll get hydrogen peroxide and ointment and a small bandage."

He seated her courteously on a wooden bench outside the store while he went in to purchase first-aid supplies. The sun on her head was warm, and she wondered if she was having a heatstroke. Nothing else explained her docile behavior. Elizabeth Killaney was usually the one *doing* the caretaking and not vice versa.

He was in and out in record time, and he approached her with a triumphant smile on his face. "Nice place. They had everything we needed." He knelt in front of her again and tapped her thigh though her skirt. "Can you shimmy out of those panty hose?"

He asked it calmly, as though it was no big deal for a woman to shed an undergarment in his presence. Then he waited patiently for her to comply.

She would be mortified if he realized that his prosaic request had made her panties damp. For two cents, she would strip naked in the street.

She gnawed her lower lip. "They're stockings, not panty hose," she muttered.

A shot of something fierce and dark flashed in his eyes before he lowered his head. She actually felt the heat of his gaze on her trembling fingers as she slid her skirt up a couple of inches and unfastened the top band of the hose from the lacy pink garter belt.

She adored impractical feminine fripperies and dressed to please herself, though it was her private naughty addiction. Not at all in keeping with practical, conservative Elizabeth. Nevertheless, she'd never been more glad to be caught wearing such a tantalizing item.

He brushed her hands away after that and rolled the sheer fabric down her leg, carefully loosening it where the injured skin clung to the silky fibers.

She bit her lip. It wasn't all that comfortable, but watching him stroke her calf was a highly effective anesthetic. He lifted her foot from her practical black pump and dispensed with the destroyed piece of nylon.

For a long two or three seconds, the arch of her foot rested in his firm grasp. Her useless fount of mental trivia reminded her of another pertinent piece of information. Somewhere she had read that the part of the brain that responds to stimulation of the foot is immediately adjacent to the part of the brain that is excited by touch to the sex organs.

This was her first chance to test the hypothesis, but her clitoris was making itself known in the neighborhood. She wanted to purr like a satisfied kitten. But she wasn't ... . satisfied, that is. Or for that matter, a kitten.

Good Lord, this man was scrambling her synapses without even trying. Her leg looked pale against his brawny hands. He was tan all over . . . well, at least the parts she could see. He was probably too big to be a decent surfer, but the image of a sun-kissed outdoor lover remained.

It was early in the season, and his naturally bronzed glow made her feel unhealthy by comparison. She rarely had the time or the inclination to sunbathe, and this time of year, after a long winter, she was pasty white.

He replaced her shoe and tugged her to her feet as he stood up. With a completely natural gesture, he brushed the hair from her cheek. "I'd like to buy you lunch."

It wasn't phrased in the form of a question. Alex Trebek would take points off for that. But in a guy-meets-girl context, she realized it was very effective. He didn't give her the option of saying no. And how rude it would be to reject his offer when he had been so solicitous of her well-being.

She smiled up at him, momentarily blinded by the sunshine and the masculine beauty of his chiseled features. "That sounds nice."

Enrique leaned back in his chair and studied the woman across the table from him. He'd asked about her business, and she was describing how her personal-care store had come into existence. Her story was interesting, but not nearly as riveting as the constantly changing moods on her expressive face.

She talked with her hands, and her beautiful eyes, a deep amber-streaked green, flashed a range of emotions. Humor. Sly sarcasm. Biting wit. Smug satisfaction. He was charmed.

In repose, her features were pleasing, but when she spoke, all the fire inside her bubbled to the surface. He saw passion and drive and a deep vein of determination. She was fascinating.

He met many women in his line of work. Most of them were extremely aware of their beauty, their market value. They were defined by their ability to seduce the camera, to win over jaded studio execs. They were ego-centered in the nicest possible way. Self-absorbed, but fun to be with. And pros at gilding the lily.

Elizabeth Killaney was a lovely woman. Though she wore little makeup, perhaps a dash of mascara and some pink lip gloss, she had a natural, girl-next-door beauty. Her skin was smooth and creamy, and the cute way her nose tilted just the tiniest bit upward brought a hint of mischief to her otherwise calm, pretty face.

She was a restful woman. That was the word that came to mind. A sea of serenity in which a man could submerge himself and be refreshed. He blinked and had to ask her to repeat the question. He had zoned out for a moment.

She frowned slightly. "I asked if you were vacationing here."

He shook his head. "No. I'm a location scout for the movie industry."

Her eyes lit up. "How exciting. I've always thought that must be such a fun job. Do you work for a particular studio?"

"I freelance. It was a bit rocky in the beginning when I was trying to get established, but now I have steady work. I was lucky to have a relative in the business who put in a good word for me. It's all about who you know."

She cocked her head. "But you must be very good at it, or they wouldn't keep calling."

He grinned. "Let's hope so."

She leaned forward, her elbows on the table. "Can you tell me about the movie you're working on now?"

The hint of cleavage where her V-necked blouse gaped almost derailed his thought processes. Did her bra match that pretty piece of lingerie he'd been privileged to see earlier? He cleared his throat. "It's a period English piece with some time travel–alternate universe stuff thrown in. Sort of Jane Austen meets the Harry Potter gang. A lot of it will be filmed in England, of course, but I'm pretty sure they'll want to use the Vanderbilt house for the castle portion."

She nodded. "I've only lived here five years, but I know the estate and grounds are photographed quite a bit."

"You'd be surprised if I showed you the entire list of movies. And not just Asheville, all of western North Carolina. *Richie Rich* and *Patch Adams* were filmed at the Biltmore property. And of course, *Dirty Dancing, The Fugitive,* and *The Last of the Mohicans* were staged not very far from here."

"I can see why. I fell in love with the mountains. That's partly why we decided to locate our business in Asheville."

"You said you've only been here five years, so you didn't grow up here?"

"Nope. Baltimore born and bred. But a college friend of mine lives nearby, and I visited her from time to time, so I knew the area fairly well. How about you?"

He took a sip of his wine and shrugged. "I'm from Malibu. A native, actually."

She sat back and grinned. "I knew it. You've got California beach bum written all over you."

He raised his eyebrows. "Have I just been insulted?" He said it mildly, but something in her self-satisfied assessment stung.

She had the grace to appear mortified. "I'm sorry. I didn't mean to sound disparaging. But you do have that athletic sun-god thing going for you."

"Much better," he laughed, mollified. For some reason, he didn't want Elizabeth Killaney to see him as a dilettante. He worked damn hard. And he had a sneaking suspicion that his pretty Elizabeth might be a workaholic.

He decided to test his theory. "So, Ms. Killaney—or Elizabeth, if I may be so bold—what do you like to do for fun?"

She stared at him blankly. "Fun?"

He smothered a smile. "Is it a foreign concept?"

And just like that, her face shuttered. She gave him a noncommittal answer and glanced at her watch. He wondered what it was about his innocuous question that so clearly bothered her.

She stood up abruptly, gathering her purse and her invisible armor in tandem. "I'm sorry to run," she said formally. "But I have a meeting at the bank. Thank you for everything."

He grabbed her wrist, holding it gently but firmly. "I want to see you again."

He noted the instant repudiation in her expression and managed not to flinch. He wasn't accustomed to seeing that look on a woman's face. Her body language was one big negative.

He tightened his grasp. "Please."

Beneath his fingertips he felt her pulse racing madly. He wasn't exactly sure why he was pushing. Except for the fact that she had affected him deeply. And in a very short amount of time. He smiled at her, doing his best to seem nonthreatening. Not a hint of male hunger showed in his gaze. Not a suggestion of his determination to win her over.

He stroked her wrist with his thumb. "A phone number, Elizabeth. That's all I'm asking." He realized with some chagrin that she had never actually told him the name of her store, making it impossible to look her up that way.

Still she remained silent. She wasn't tugging on her arm, but the very absence of expression on her face was telling.

He sighed. "How about your business card?" Perhaps she was uncomfortable giving out her personal information.

Her lips were pressed together in a thin line. She looked him straight in the eye. "You're only temporary. I don't see the point."

At last . . . something he could argue. "I'll be here for two weeks or more. I would enjoy your company." He made his statement deliberately casual. Perhaps she was not the kind of woman to indulge in a brief liaison. Why that idea pleased him, he couldn't say, because it sure as hell didn't bode well for his libido.

She sighed, looking down at his hand holding hers, or near enough. "I'm a very busy woman. With a lot of responsibilities. I can't simply pick up and play hooky whenever I want."

"So you want to see me, but you're overbooked?" He teased her gently, hoping to see a rebirth of the vivid personality she'd exhibited before he had said something wrong. And he still couldn't figure that one out.

Her pretty white teeth worried her bottom lip. "I think you're a very attractive man. So of course I would like to see you again. But I am telling you the truth. My life is full."

He pushed to his feet. They had eaten a very early lunch, and the place was still mostly empty. He cupped the side of her face with one hand. "Too full for new experiences?" He made it a challenge, hoping he hadn't misread her innate competitive nature.

Her eyes locked on his, and he felt an odd jerk in his chest. Their faces were so close he could have kissed her with very little effort. But he forced himself to remember their public location.

When she didn't respond, he tried to seal the deal. "Make room," he urged, his thumb tracing the line of her jaw. He'd never felt skin so soft.

She stepped back and rattled off a phone number. She blurted it out so rapidly, he was sure she thought he wouldn't be able to re-create it on paper. But she was destined to be disappointed. Where Elizabeth Killaney was involved, he remembered everything.

Since he couldn't kiss her, he shoved his hands in his pockets. "Thank you."

She nodded jerkily. And then she left him standing there to watch her walk away.

Two

*E*lizabeth refused to admit that she was disappointed when he didn't call that evening. It had been a chance meeting. He was passing through. Nothing would have come of it, anyway. Best not to drag things out.

Still . . . it was hard to forget the way his dark chestnut hair shone in the morning sun . . . practically begging a woman to run her hands through it.

And the feel of his warm hands on her skin. *Phew,* it was enough to make a girl's bones melt. And those eyes, a dazzling mix of gold and brown with a hint of green. They were almost mesmerizing.

She did a load of laundry, painted her toenails now that warm weather was here and she could finally wear sandals, and washed her hair. During all of it, she thought ruefully about Enrique's off-the-cuff question.

Fun? Fun was having the luxury of sitting down to read the newspaper before it was three days old. Fun was finding a free minute to clean off her desk at home. Fun was opening a bank statement whose balance reassured her that the business wasn't going belly up anytime soon.

She didn't lie. Her life was full. She went to Pilates class three nights a week. She helped with a Girl Scout troop that met in her neighborhood. She often dropped by the store late in the evening to sneak in a couple of hours of work while things were quiet.

As she went over the list in her head, an unpleasant notion took hold. Maybe she *was* a workaholic. Jeannie and Diana were always urging her to take a day off. In the beginning the three cousins were the sole employees of Lotions and Potions. They did everything from putting out stock to cleaning the toilet in the bathroom.

Gradually, as their finances eased, they hired some part-time staff: a custodian, a shipping clerk, a Web designer. And eventually, two salesgirls from Western Carolina University and a stay-at-home mom who worked a set shift while her kids were in school. Jeannie loved helping customers, and so did Elizabeth, for that matter. But it was nice to be able to get away without feeling like you were dumping on the other two. Not that Elizabeth took advantage very often.

If she wasn't out front on the floor, she was in the back logging on to the computer and studying the Web site to see how they could increase traffic and sales.

She loved what she did. But maybe she *had* let it take over her life more than was healthy. In her late twenties and early thirties, when the hurtful episode with jerkface was still fresh and raw, work had been a panacea. She'd had no desire whatsoever for a social life.

It was possible that her frantic schedule had become habit. But Enrique's insistence on seeing her again made her pause and take stock. Did she want to go out with him? Was it wise? Did she even remember how to have fun with a man? All valid questions for which she had no answer.

Just thinking about him made her heart give a funny little hop and skip. The two of them together was an image that didn't come into focus. Even without an ounce of pseudohumility, she knew he was off the charts of suitable men for her to date. His striking looks and the unconscious charisma he exuded were powerful aphrodisiacs. In the jungle he would be the jaguar stalking a mate . . . or two or three. He wasn't merely a ten. He was a ten to the nth power.

She wondered about his Hispanic name. But he didn't have a trace of an accent (thank God, or she would really be in trouble). So his Spanish or Latin heritage probably came from a couple of generations back. His strong nose, which was a bit large for his face, was the only thing that saved him from being too pretty.

Despite the fact that he had rescued her and fed her, she found it hard to believe that he was really interested in her, even in the short term. He lived in California. He worked in the movie industry. Stunningly beautiful women sashayed through his life on a daily basis.

And then it hit her. Holy cow. Maybe Diana was right. Maybe the unexplainable spark between Elizabeth and her rescuer could have been the result of the newest eucalyptus mixture, their lotion number ten. Elizabeth had rubbed it all over her body that morning while she was still damp from her shower.

And Enrique had definitely been close enough to inhale it. And he'd had his hands all over her leg, so the stuff might have even worked its way into his skin. That would explain a lot of unlikely behavior, including his insistence on getting her phone number.

And the fact that he hadn't called tonight—well, that was simple. He was no longer under the influence of love potion number ten.

She laughed out loud at the idea that she and Jeannie and Diana were purveyors of natural sexual stimulants. Although, come to think of it, it wasn't a bad idea for next Valentine's Day.

Sex sells, and it couldn't hurt to pique the public's interest with a provocative and sexy sales campaign.

They could do a modest television ad and then . . .

She stopped dead in the center of her kitchen just as she was reaching for a pad to make some notes. Oh dear God, she *was* a workaholic. Shocking, but true. She couldn't even think about sex without turning it into a business proposition.

She put her hands to her hot cheeks, even though no one was there to witness her embarrassment. Self-realization was a bitch. No wonder her hunky lunch date hadn't called her back. She must have seemed like the most boring woman on the planet.

After eating a quick dinner of tasteless leftovers, she curled up on her comfy couch and grabbed her laptop. She opened a new file and typed in a heading: *Elizabeth's Complete Makeover.*

She was smart. She knew how to attack a project and spin it for the best result. All she had to do was admit her problem and change her behavior.

She typed in #1—*Relax more.*

Well, that was a good start . . . right? She could watch a sit-com or take a walk or meditate.

She tried to imagine herself meditating in the lotus position and snorted. Or maybe not. Moving on . . . #2—*Ramp up social life. Quit avoiding contact with men.*

Hmmm. What exactly did that mean? She was always getting invited to singles mixers over at the Catholic church, but she happened to know that at least half of the eligible men were seventy-plus widowers. But that wasn't the only option. She had friends. Perhaps she could throw a dinner party. She knew how to cook . . . maybe not as well as Jeannie, but enough to pass muster.

That was an appealing idea. Perhaps if Enrique was still in town, she could invite him to come over. Her fingers froze on the keys. Earth to Elizabeth. The man was momentarily dazzled by her damsel-in-distress routine. But that was then. This was now. The fairy-tale interlude was over.

She tried to think of a #3, but the cursor blinked unsympathetically. Before she could make herself feel guilty, she saved the embarrassingly brief list and pulled up a file of marketing statistics she'd downloaded from an online seminar. Ten minutes later she was deep into the figures, her mind racing with the implications for increasing the profit margin at Lotions and Potions.

The following morning she went by the shop, as she had yesterday, but this time both Jeannie and Diana were in the mood to talk. Jeannie nodded her head in approval. "You look very nice today, Elizabeth. What's the occasion?"

Elizabeth was wearing a hand-me-down outfit of Jeannie's: a khaki skirt and a turquoise silk wrap blouse. She'd added a simple gold chain and a bangle bracelet. She shrugged, hoping she wasn't blushing. She felt as if she had a neon sign on her forehead that said: *Elizabeth is horny for the new guy she met yesterday.*

She shrugged. "The sun is shining. It's spring. And I'm going out to the Inn, so I didn't want to look grungy." The Inn on the grounds of the Biltmore property was a lovely upscale hotel. The manager of the gift shop there had promised to carry a line of products from Lotions and Potions, and Elizabeth was meeting with her today to discuss some ideas for exclusive packaging. With a fancier presentation, they would be able to try a higher price point.

Diana studied her. "It's not just the clothes. You're almost glowing."

Jeannie's eyes narrowed. "Oh God, you're not pregnant, are you?"

Elizabeth rolled her eyes. "Now *that* would be an immaculate conception." She shook her head, savoring the delicious secret of yesterday's encounter. Nothing would come of it, but it was fun to hang on to the moment. "I'm in a good mood, that's all. Don't let your imagination run away with you."

She picked up a tube of exfoliating cream and fiddled with the cap before replacing it on the display. She was tempted to spill the beans, but to what end? Yesterday's brief interruption in an otherwise humdrum day meant nothing. She sighed and headed for the back. "I need the folder of those mock-ups we did, and then I'm out of here."

The meeting with the savvy gift shop manager went extremely well. Elizabeth left the beautifully decorated premises with a little bounce in her step. This new venture would be a win-win situation. She just knew it. She glanced down at the notepad in her hand and smirked at the figure on the bottom line. Hot damn. Martha Stewart, hold on to your apron. Elizabeth Killaney was on the way.

She rounded a corner into the hallway leading to the main lobby and ran smack into a solid male body. For the second time in as many days, her personal belongings went flying. Fortunately, this time she didn't hit the ground. Although if she had, the expensive Oriental runner would have cushioned her fall. "Excuse me," she said, breathless and mortified. "I wasn't looking where I was going. I'm so sorry. I—" She broke off her rushed apology, her mouth hanging open in shock. "Enrique?"

Warm hands, still clasping her shoulders, tightened momentarily before he released her. He grinned. "We have to stop meeting like this."

Her eyes narrowed. Time hadn't dulled the effect of his masculine beauty. His shirt was a bit more conservative today, but the devilish gleam in his eyes and the impact of his knee-weakening smile were the same. "What are you doing here?"

His lips quirked. He leaned against the wall, the picture of a relaxed, confident male animal. "I could ask you the same thing."

She glanced away, trying to protect herself from rampant sexual hunger. "I had a meeting." She squatted and gathered up the rumpled notepad and the personal items that had escaped her tote. She'd left her purse in the car. But if she was going to make a habit of klutziness, she would have to buy something that zipped across the top.

She reached for a renegade roll of mints, just as Enrique bent to help her. Their foreheads collided with an audible crack. His muttered oath echoed in her brain. God, this was embarrassing.

He helped her to her feet. They each rubbed their heads, avoiding the other's gaze. Finally, she chanced a peek. The look on his face was priceless. He appeared to be rattled, and she sensed it was an unusual occurrence for him.

She cleared her throat. "So tell me, Enrique. Are you stalking me, or did the CIA put out a hit on me and hire you to do the job?"

He managed a chuckle. "I'm beginning to think it would be more than a one-man job. You're cute but lethal. And I'm not a stalker, though your creative brain delights me. I'm a guest here."

Enrique watched as her face lit up. "Oh, how exciting. I've always wanted to see what one of those rooms upstairs looks like."

It took her about three seconds to hear what she had said. Her face went beet red, and her eyes rounded. "Oh, hell. I didn't mean that the way it sounded."

He laughed out loud this time. God, she was a piece of work. He took her arm and steered her toward the bank of elevators nearby. "I learned early on never to disappoint a lady. Feel free to come up and examine my etchings. And while we're at it, we'll put some ice on that knot."

As they passed a large mirror, he glanced at his own head. Other than a little red spot, he was fine. Obviously his was the harder noggin, because Elizabeth was sporting a small goose egg. And it was turning a nasty purplish shade, to boot.

He could tell she was nervous when they got upstairs, but she tried to hide it. While he went into the bathroom for a washrag, she roamed the large, well-appointed room. He hoped the king-size bed gave her a few ideas.

He handed her the washcloth he'd filled with three or four ice cubes. "Put this on your head. And let's sit outside for a few minutes." The room's narrow balcony wasn't spacious, but the view made up for it.

They sat in the decorative metal chairs and gazed out at the mountains. His earlier impression was reinforced. Elizabeth was a restful woman. She didn't always feel the need to talk, even though she could keep up with the best of them in a conversational give-and-take.

Her right elbow rested on the arm of the chair, and she was leaning her head on her hand with the rag pressed to the spot where his head banged into hers. Her eyes were closed, and he was suddenly concerned. "How's it feeling? Do you want some aspirin?"

Her smile was wan. "It couldn't hurt."

He brought her a couple of tablets with a glass of water and watched as she swallowed the pills. "Why don't you stretch out on the bed for a few minutes?" he said, doing his best to maintain a matter-of-fact tone. "I have to pick up some information down in the office. I'll give you a bit of privacy to rest."

She opened her mouth to protest, but he silenced her by scooping her up and carrying her inside. The warmth of her body in his arms and the trusting way she nestled her head against his chest did something funny to his equilibrium. So much so that he was reluctant to let go of her.

He didn't think pulling back the covers would go over well in her eyes, so he laid her on top of the heavy damask duvet and reached for a soft mohair throw in matching shades of ivory and gold. He took off her shoes and covered her from the waist down.

She held out the rag. "This is melting. And my head is like an ice cube."

He took it back to the bathroom and returned to find her with her eyes closed. He stood beside the bed. "Will you be okay?"

She opened her eyes and smiled faintly, her irises hazy with the discomfort she was feeling. "I'm fine. I probably should just go home."

He bent and pressed a kiss to her temple. "Don't even think about it. Get rid of that headache, and then we'll talk."

Elizabeth watched him leave and closed her eyes as she heard the quiet click of the door locking. God, who knew her skull could throb so badly from a mere bump? She lay there in the silent, luxurious room and pondered the vagaries of fate. Here she was, in Enrique's bedroom . . . in his *bed* for Pete's sake, and she barely knew the man.

Not that time had much to do with the way she felt about him. Call it pheromones or instant lust or even the fact that she had lived like a nun for the last decade, but he'd knocked her off her feet both literally *and* figuratively. First impressions weren't always valid, but she had a sneaking suspicion that Enrique would only improve on closer inspection.

She already knew he had a sense of humor . . . which she considered to be a nonnegotiable trait on her list of desirable male characteristics. He was confident and perhaps a bit arrogant, but it was a natural, integral assertiveness that denoted strength and not the need to ride roughshod over people.

And he wasn't too macho to be gentle. Yesterday had proven that. Even moments ago when he carried her to his bed, he had been tender and solicitous. Maybe he'd learned that smooth routine from the movies, but it was still darn effective.

She put her fingers to the bump on her head and winced. The headache was already easing a bit . . . and the bed was soft and comfy . . . so soft. . . .

Enrique eased into the room quietly. Despite his caution, Elizabeth opened her eyes immediately and sat up as he put a bag on the table and approached the bed. She eyed him warily.

He sat on the bottom corner of the mattress and put his hands on his knees. "Feeling better?"

She nodded solemnly. "The aspirin worked." She tossed back the throw and swung her legs over the side of the bed. "I should go."

"Wait, Elizabeth." His voice came out louder than he'd intended. More harsh. But he felt an alien sense of desperation. He didn't want her to leave. He tempered his words with a cajoling note. "Don't go. I have a proposition for you."

She lifted one perfectly arched eyebrow. "How very intriguing, Mr. Cantilano. Does that smarmy line work with all your women?"

He chuckled. "Are you offering to be one of my women, pretty Elizabeth?"

She lifted her nose in the air. "I am not."

He stood and raked his hands through his hair. "No sinister motives, I promise. I need to walk the grounds this afternoon. It's a beautiful day. I thought you might like to come with me."

She eyed him steadily, her hands clasped in her lap. "I'm not really dressed for tramping in the woods."

He nodded toward the bag. "I bought you a few things in the gift shop."

Though she tried to hide it, he could see she was shocked.

He exhaled. "Oh, hell, it's not what you think. You can pay for the damn clothes if it makes you feel better."

Her throat moved as she swallowed. "Do you really want company, or are you being polite?" Her words were almost a whisper, and a pained uncertainty shadowed her delicate features.

He scrubbed his face with his hands. It wasn't like him to be awkward around a woman, but Elizabeth evoked an entire repertoire of reactions that were both uncomfortable and unfamiliar. He huffed out a breath. "You're a very attractive woman, and I like you. Is that a sufficient answer, or do you need more? Maybe a photo ID and a major credit card?"

His sarcasm didn't appear to faze her. She stood up and faced him. "Are you married?"

He hoped his startled pause didn't make him look guilty. "God, no."

She looked over at the bag with the distinctive Biltmore logo. "In that case, then yes . . . I'd love to go walking with you."

Elizabeth understood why Enrique was good at his job. He was a problem solver. He wanted her to walk with him, so he simply bought her the appropriate outfit . . . and thought nothing about it.

The sleeveless coral top and matching drawstring shorts in crinkled cotton were extremely casual. The matching pair of Keds tied with coral laces was simple but comfortable. She looked at herself in the mirror. A very handsome man was wooing her, and some time between now and when he invited her to do more than doze in his big bed, she had a decision to make.

Enrique was passing through. He wasn't permanent. And his interest in her might possibly be the result of the lotion she was wearing. Under those conditions was she willing to have a brief fling with a charismatic, sexy semistranger?

She had certainly never done so in the years since jerkface did a number on her self-esteem. But then again, when she *had* flung herself into a hot-and-heavy affair years before, the man had been lying. Even though she thought she knew all there was to know about him. So there were no guarantees.

She called out before she opened the bathroom door, "Are you decent?"

His deep masculine laugh made the hair on her arms stand up. "Not often. Come on out and model for me."

She held her head high as she entered the bedroom. No need for him to know she was scared spitless of making another monumental mistake.

He whistled as his interested gaze swept her body from head to toe. "Best seventy-five bucks I ever spent. You look hot."

She glanced down at her pale arms and legs. "Oh yeah, I'm just one crooked tooth and an audition away from a Jennifer Aniston role."

He grabbed a digital camera and slung the strap over his shoulder. "Why do women never understand that it's their imperfections that make them interesting?"

She hooted with laughter as she followed him out the door. "Well, you're in luck, because if you're going by that standard, I'm about as interesting a gal as you're going to find."

Three

It took them a few minutes downstairs to get organized. Enrique had phoned in a room service order while she was in the bathroom. The concierge met them in the lobby with two boxed lunches and a small backpack, as well as a map of the Biltmore trails. While all that was going on, Elizabeth checked her cell phone for messages and texted a note to the shop to say she wouldn't be coming in that afternoon.

Calling wasn't a good option. Diana and Jeannie would have quizzed her mercilessly, and she wasn't up for the inquisition at the moment.

Outside in the parking lot, Enrique pulled an old faded quilt from the trunk of his car. The colorful soft fabric was too battered and worn to have much value, but it looked clean. He tied it into the lower straps of the pack, and they set off.

She walked beside him, settling into an easy pace. "Don't tell me you flew all the way from California with a quilt handy in case a spontaneous picnic opportunity cropped up."

He pulled a pair of sunglasses from his pocket and settled them on his craggy nose. "Not hardly. I flew into Knoxville and stayed with a friend for a few nights. I wanted to drive through the mountains to get here. Otherwise, I could have flown into the Asheville airport. The quilt is borrowed."

Elizabeth frowned, knowing he wouldn't notice. A friend? Already she was worrying about the competition. Which was ludicrous. When she had sex with Enrique—*if* she had sex with Enrique—it would be light and easy with no strings attached. She was not laying her heart on the line. Not this time.

She studied her companion surreptitiously. He looked like a rugged cover model for one of those men's outdoor adventure magazines. His long, muscular legs were tanned beneath a light covering of golden brown hair.

He wore a moss green camp shirt and lightweight khaki shorts made of some high-tech fabric. His shoes were low-cut hiking boots that looked more like sturdy walking shoes. And he had a navy bandanna stuffed in his back pocket.

She might have wondered if this was a "costume" designed to impress the ladies, but the boots were well-worn, and the shirt and shorts were clearly not new. He appeared to be completely comfortable and ready for an afternoon of exploring.

With an inward sigh, she abandoned her suspicious nature and decided to enjoy the day.

As they wandered, Enrique paused now and then to check for glimpses of the great house. He took pictures from several vantage points and even jotted notes from time to time.

She stood patiently, enjoying the feeling of being completely free. How long had it been since she had taken a day to goof off . . . to enjoy the nature that was in such abundance around Asheville? She exercised regularly, but seldom outdoors. She had forgotten how wonderful it was to feel the sun on her back, to hear the quiet buzz of bees, to smell the pungent fragrance of freshly mowed grass.

The estate covered eight thousand acres, and despite the many tourists who flocked to tour the house, it was still possible to find tranquillity and solitude on the grounds. Especially since she and Enrique were there on a week day. The weekend might be more crowded.

They walked for several miles before Enrique checked the map and doubled back toward the creek. Soon he was leading her across an arched wooden bridge over a picturesque, sun-dappled creek.

He handed her a pebble he had picked up on the path. "Make a wish."

She took it, shivering inwardly when his warm fingers brushed hers. "I thought that was for wishing wells and fountains."

He gave her a mock frown. "Those are *artificial* water sources. This is the real thing."

She closed her eyes and hurled her small rock as far down stream as she could. Her wish was a garbled mishmash of hopes and dreams.

Enrique ruffled her hair with careless affection. "You throw like a girl . . . no offense."

She grinned lazily. "None taken."

They stood there a long time, side by side, hips almost touching. They propped their forearms on the bridge railing and leaned in contented silence, gazing down at the always-changing water.

A thought occurred to her. "Do you miss the ocean when you're away from home?"

His profile was strong and masculine and yet strikingly beautiful. "Sometimes. I love to get up and run on the beach in the early morning when the mist rises off the water. Watching the sunrise never gets old."

"I've only ever been to the beach once. We fair-skinned Irish people don't have much tolerance for sun-worshipping. And my mother loathed the sand. So after that, Daddy took us to Hershey,

Pennsylvania, or to the Catskills, or to Niagara Falls—places like that."

"You'd love the Pacific Coast," he said quietly. "It has such a raw, wild beauty. You can't help but be awed by its phenomenal power. Especially during a storm."

She wanted to say that she would love to see it . . . but it seemed like an awkward statement. Their lives wouldn't cross again, and an empty, polite invitation from him wasn't what she wanted.

After a long while, they headed on. This time he dragged her up a steep hillside until they came into a clearing and were able to look down on the mighty Vanderbilt house. It never failed to awe her. Not just the architecture or the beauty of it, but the almost impossible-to-understand massive fortune it took to accomplish such a project, even in the nineteenth century.

They spread the quilt on a grassy spot, sat down, and dug into the food. It was nothing fancy: club sandwiches, apples, homemade cookies, and bottles of water. She was surprisingly hungry, and she practically inhaled her meal. Enrique matched her bite for bite.

When their tummies were full, they leaned back on their elbows and studied the view. Elizabeth wrinkled her nose. "I know this is magnificent, and I see how you could use the house for a castle, but why not simply film all of it in England?"

He lay back and closed his eyes. "The castle is not the hard part," he murmured. "Think about it. I might locate a suitably atmospheric, photogenic English fortress, but chances are, it would be in the wilds of the countryside with only a small village nearby. Then you have the logistics of feeding and housing a crew of hundreds. Not to mention things like Internet service and cell phone signals."

"Ah. Makes sense. I never thought of it like that. So you make it *look* English."

"That's why they call it movie magic." His voice was drowsy, and seconds later she saw the steady rise and fall of his chest.

Quietly, she got up and walked a few hundred yards away for a discreet pit stop. Afterward, she wandered back and joined him on the quilt, stretching out on her side, and studying his face while he slept. His lips were chiseled, and honest to God, until she met him, she always thought that was kind of a dumb description.

But now she was a believer. She couldn't wait to taste his kiss and feel his mouth on hers. Her breathing quickened as she imagined waking him by climbing on top of his prone body and straddling his hips. Her clothes were easy to get out of, and his zipper shouldn't present a problem.

The legs of his shorts were loose-fitting, and she could slide her hands up to his . . .

He made a grumbling noise in his sleep and settled back into a doze. Perhaps jet lag had made it hard for him to get to sleep last night. She pictured the two of them curled up together in his big, soft bed, and a pulse throbbed low and insistent between her legs.

She wished she had the confidence to wake him by stroking his cock and bringing him to life. But she couldn't bear to think that he might laugh at her or, even worse, be angry with her.

In the aftermath of that unfortunate affair with her boss, she had faced both. Jerkface had been furious with her for ending things so abruptly. And she had felt the curious eyes of her co-workers in the painful days before she had quit and fled home. She was sure they were laughing at her for being such a naive, credulous patsy.

With an impatient shake of her head, she willed away the old memories. Instead, she concentrated on the vista in front of her. If she were making the movie, she would cast herself as a heroine dressed in a pretty muslin frock holding a frilly parasol. Enrique would play the role of Mr. Darcy, and he would gaze into her eyes with the dark, brooding look that said he wanted her in every possible way.

Then they would lean toward each other across the quilt, and their lips would meet. She could hear the musical score in her head. Sadly, her version of the film ended abruptly, which was unfortunate, because she really, really wanted to see what Enrique and/or Mr. Darcy looked like beneath his clothes.

There was something so incredibly hot about all that repressed Victorian sexuality. She could feel his hands at the bodice of her dress, watch his fingers trespass beneath the lacy edge and brush ever so slightly against the tops of her breasts.

The parasol would be abandoned. He'd slowly remove the pins from her hair, and gradually, her artful curls would tumble to her shoulders. Then he would press her, ever so gently, back onto the quilt. He would loom over her, his dark shape blocking out the sun.

Her heart would race in her chest, her spine arching in silent pleasure as he toyed with her breasts. She could hear his soft murmurs, sense his growing hunger. Her legs would move restlessly, her thighs parting of their own accord to let his heavy body press between.

The throbbing hunger in her sex would make her wet and ready for him. He would unbutton his tight breeches and free his thick, erect penis. Perhaps she would gasp. Perhaps he'd give her a reassuring kiss.

She felt the raging battle between maidenly modesty and feminine hunger. His head lowered, his breath warm on her cheeks. And then their lips met. She murmured softly, begging him to make love to her. He resisted, a gentleman to the end.

But her need was too great to be dissuaded. "Kiss me," she murmured, ever so slightly.

Enrique sat up and Elizabeth yelped. Good Lord, had she actually said that aloud? The way he was looking at her suggested that maybe she had. But on the other hand, he seemed like a man who could read women. So maybe he was picking up on something in her expression.

She flicked a crumb from the quilt, not meeting his eyes. "You must be fighting jet lag."

The drowsiness had disappeared from his eyes, and now he looked wide-awake. He leaned forward, resting one hand on the quilt and using the other to gently slide into her hair and anchor her head. "What I'm fighting, pretty Elizabeth, is the urge to kiss you," he muttered.

She blinked and turned her cheek into his caress. "I wouldn't fight it if I were you," she said, trying to sound sophisticated and flirtatious. But instead, she probably came across as horny and naive.

Enrique groaned. The sound settled inside her abdomen and made her want to reach for him in every way possible. His head lowered. Their lips met in a tentative caress. He tasted like oatmeal cookies and aroused male.

He licked gently at the seam of her lips, and her mouth opened. She gasped when he played with her tongue, stroking it with his and then sucking gently.

Their bodies were not touching, except for the languid kiss and his hand in her hair. She tried to catch her breath, but the irregular rhythm of her heartbeat made it impossible. Her hand found his chest and explored the hard muscles through his shirt.

He settled back, tugging her with him. Now she lay half on top of him, and his steellike arm snaked around her waist to pull her tightly against his hot male body. He was still kissing her with drugging sensuality. Her hand slid from his chest to his waist. She felt every inch of his body tense when her fingers touched his belt.

She stopped, aghast at her uncharacteristic lack of modesty. She barely knew the man. Was she really ready to fondle his cock?

Oh, yes. Her fingers closed around his erection through two thin layers of fabric, and they each hissed in unison. Beneath her grasp, he was thick and oh so hard. She squeezed gently and then ran her fingernails up and down his shaft. He pulsed and throbbed in her grasp.

Now both of his hands tangled in her hair, and he dragged her face to his, kissing her wildly. She whimpered, trying to get closer. One of his hands found its way beneath her shirt, and in seconds her bra was unclasped.

When he rolled her to her back and she felt his fingers tug at her nipple and cup her swollen flesh, her world turned upside down. Had she ever felt this level of raw urgency? She wanted Enrique so badly, she was actually shaking.

He bent and sucked a nipple into his mouth. Her hips moved restlessly on the quilt. To hell with foreplay. She was primed and ready to explode with only the slightest provocation.

She spread her thighs, moaning with satisfaction when he took the hint and settled between them. She pulled at his hair, desperate for the main event. Her voice shook. "Do you have a condom?"

"Shit."

His disgusted expletive told her all she needed to know. She inhaled deeply and tried to ignore the tremors of need shaking her body. It was probably for the best. What was she thinking?

He dropped his head to her belly, his warm weight almost pleasurable enough to convince her this was enough for now. She ruffled his hair. "I'm sorry."

He nudged her shirt out of the way and licked her belly button. "No need for both of us to suffer," he muttered as he gripped her hips and pulled her shorts and panties to her ankles and ripped them free. The sun on her naked skin was shocking. But not as much as the moment his head moved south and he found her sex with his talented tongue.

She should have been worried about being discovered by other nature lovers. She should have been worried about having a man see her nude body for the first time in aeons. She should have been worried about her moral decay and total lack of self-control.

But all that worry was obliterated by the fiery shards of pleasure arcing from her clit up through her abdomen and radiating outward in a burst of sunlight and joy.

She came three times before he stopped. Even then, she might have come again if the sound of nearby voices hadn't intruded. She gasped and tried to evade his grasp. "Enrique, someone's coming."

He chuckled against the soft skin of her tummy. "I noticed. I think it's you."

She shivered as his teeth raked a sensitive spot. "I'm not kidding," she cried. "Let me up."

He released her with clear disappointment. His cheeks were flushed and his lips were wet with the evidence of her recent wild orgasms. She reached frantically for her clothes. The voices were drawing closer.

Enrique's erection tented the front of his shorts. He rolled to his stomach with a pained groan and buried his face in his arms. She picked up his camera and pretended to be taking pictures just as a mom and dad with four kids came around a corner and spotted them.

The noisy group waved and called out a greeting as they passed by. Elizabeth hoped they attributed her red face to sunburn. When the intruders disappeared, she touched Enrique on the shoulder. "Are you okay?"

He flopped to his back, his state of excitement not noticeably diminished. "Just peachy." The surly note in his voice was nothing more than sheer male frustration.

She stroked his thigh below his shorts. "I'm sorry. I didn't mean to let things go so far. I barely know you, and I can assure you that as a general rule, I don't frolic around in the great outdoors." In the past she had preferred locked doors and guaranteed privacy, although there *was* the time when she and the boy next door, her sixth-grade classmate, had taken turns educating each other behind the bushes with a strictly hands-off show of body parts. His less than impressive equipment hadn't excited any undue interest in her prepubescent imagination. But he sure as heck had enjoyed his first sight of a girl's breasts.

She wondered what to do now. Was there proper etiquette for this awkward situation? Enrique still had his eyes closed, and his poor, severely denied body part was deflating.

She glanced at her watch. "Shouldn't we be getting back? You probably have work to do . . . calls to make . . . whatever. And I need to check in at the shop."

He sat up and gazed at her with incredulity. Abruptly, she realized how callous her question had sounded. He had given her the most amazing pleasure, and now that she had gotten hers, so to speak, she was bailing.

She bit her lip, feeling her face heat. "Sorry. That came out wrong. I don't mean to be rude. But what we were doing probably wasn't wise. This is a public place. I'd hate to get busted for indecent exposure."

His eyes narrowed. "And if I asked you to come back to my room and pick up where we left off?"

She winced. "At the risk of sounding completely selfish, I don't believe that's a good idea. Don't you think we're moving rather quickly?"

His eyes darkened, and although sexual deprivation could account for some of it, she had the strangest feeling she had hurt him. He dropped his head, rubbing the back of his neck. When he looked at her again, she sensed he was choosing his words carefully.

He looked out toward the horizon and then back at her, his expression cajoling. "I felt something amazingly strong when I met you, Elizabeth. Sexual attraction for sure, but even more. A connection, if you will."

The romantic Elizabeth wanted to wallow in his flattering explanation, but the practical Elizabeth had learned the hard way to discount pretty words. She thrust out her chin. "It's called being horny. And I was. I am. I'll admit it. But let's not dress it up with pretty words." She couldn't let her guard down. She was terrified of being vulnerable. And this beautiful man had the power to hurt her. She knew it in her bones.

One dark eyebrow angled heavenward. "Such cynicism. What are you scared of, Elizabeth?"

His quiet words held not a note of sarcasm or anger. If anything, he sounded genuinely concerned.

Tears burned the back of her throat, and it took her a moment to speak. She managed to look at him steadily. "I'm not a sweet, young thing. I know how men think. And I'm all in favor of sexual attraction, believe me. But it's fleeting at best, and it isn't fair or necessary to make it more than it is. If I decide to go to bed with you, it will be because I want to scratch an itch. That's all. You're a nice guy, but I don't need to be wooed. I'd prefer us to be honest with each other."

He leaned back on his hands, still staring at her with an intense, probing gaze that seemed to see past her hastily erected defenses. "Okay, then." He pursed his lips. "I'm not sure how to sort through all the crap you just dished out, but apparently I need to slow down and let you decide when to scratch your itch. Is that it?"

She trembled, feeling ashamed and totally out of her element. "Don't make fun of me," she said sullenly. How dared he call her on her inconsistency? His seductive lovemaking had totally destroyed her usually clear thought processes.

She stood up and wrapped her arms around her waist. "I'm going back." She stumbled away from him, tears sheening her eyes.

He caught up with her before she'd gone a half dozen steps. He grasped her shoulders and turned her around. "Slow down,

Elizabeth. You're getting all worked up over nothing." He folded her into his arms and held her close.

She could feel his heart beating against her breast. She smelled the scent of warm grass and aroused male. She wanted to burrow into him and ignore all the stuff she had said. God, this was much too hard. She should have known better. Maybe if she stayed right here in his arms, she could freeze time.

He rubbed her back in comforting circles. She felt him sigh. His breath brushed her ear. "I can go slower, if it will make you feel better. Instead of going back to my room and screwing our brains out, what if you call your cousins and see if they would like to go out to dinner with us? My treat. I'd like to meet them."

Enrique couldn't miss the way she froze in his embrace. She wriggled free of his arms and faced him, a breezy smile on her face. "Let's not. I'd rather go back to your room. If the offer is still open."

He was, for once in his life, speechless. Elizabeth didn't want to introduce him to her family. It shouldn't have hurt so much, but damn, it did. Was he that much of a liability?

He turned back to the spot where he had made her gasp and writhe in three separate but equally powerful orgasms, and he began packing away their lunch. He sensed Elizabeth behind him . . . hovering, but he couldn't look at her.

Clearly, she considered fucking a man she had just met the lesser of two evils. She was embarrassed by him . . . or by them. His injured pride demanded that he send her home with a curt *No, thanks.* But his prick was far more practical. He still ached from the near miss when they were interrupted, and he wanted nothing more than to have Elizabeth beneath him, crying out her release as he thrust into her warm, wet passage.

He had inserted two fingers in her vagina that last time just as his tongue pushed her over the edge. Feeling her inner muscles clamp down on him made him dizzy with hungry anticipation.

What would it feel like when he was actually inside her? How would he last more than a second or two when he was already so eager to possess her? He couldn't think straight.

He could have sworn they were no more than a mile or two from the house, but the return trip seemed endless. The afternoon sun was hot, and the earlier breeze had evaporated. Sweat dotted his forehead and dampened his chest and back. He was tired and frustrated and still he hadn't reached a decision about what to do with the endlessly complicated Elizabeth. He could boot her out, or he could make love to her all afternoon and evening.

He was kidding himself if he thought the choice was not already made.

When they were finally back in his room, Elizabeth spotted her pocketbook on a chair and grabbed it up. Her body language was transparent. She was intent on making a clean getaway.

He growled at her. "What do you think you're doing?"

She clutched the bag to her chest. "You never answered me. I thought you didn't want to."

He removed the purse from her hands and tossed it aside. "Don't be an idiot." Her eyes widened in shock just as he shoved his mouth down on hers. The taste of her lips brought his momentarily subdued libido roaring back to life.

She murmured a protest, but since her arms were twisted around his neck like a noose, he didn't pay it much mind. He finally broke the kiss with a gasp and dragged her toward the bathroom. Somehow, with her help, he managed to get both of them naked and into the shower. Once there, the sight of her wet, sleek curves dried his mouth and made him fall back against the tile wall. "You're a knockout, sweetheart."

She blushed, looking bashful and eager at the same time. He soaped up the washrag and began with her breasts. His little Elizabeth liked that, a lot. When he moved the bar of soap between her legs, she moaned and sank sharp teeth into his shoulder.

This time he stopped short of letting her come. He settled for kissing her and learning every inch of her lithe, lovely body with wet hands and a determined assault.

At some point, Elizabeth seized control. She sank to her knees and took him in her mouth. His legs threatened to buckle, and even though the water began to run cold, he didn't stop her.

But when the temperature turned icy, they both gasped and tumbled out of the glass enclosure, reaching for warm towels. He dried her reverently, loving the feeling her ivory skin and the way it turned pink and pretty when he rubbed her down. She had a bit of sunburn on her nose and cheeks and the tops of her shoulders, so he was gentle.

She tried to return the favor, but he couldn't bear it. Not when he was shaking all over with lust and the driving need to possess her.

He scooped her into his arms and carried her out to the enormous bed. With one hand, he tossed back the covers and lowered his precious cargo. He joined her and kissed her roughly. His control was hanging by a thread, and if he didn't have her soon, he'd go mad.

She stopped his intent assault on her breasts with a hand to his collarbone. "Enrique . . ." Her voice was small, almost timid.

He braced himself on his arms, the muscles trembling. Her eyes were dark and filled with something he couldn't identify. "What?" he asked hoarsely. Surely she couldn't deny him . . . not now.

She wet her lips. "I haven't done this in a very long time. So please be careful when you . . ."

He shook his head, trying to assimilate her words amid the roar of need in his brain. "How long?" The question was hoarse and blunt.

Her lips trembled, though her hands were touching his waist in placating caresses. "Almost twelve years."

He stared at her, his mind fuzzy. Shit. This changed things. He wasn't sure how, but he knew that it did. He bent his head and kissed her as tenderly as he could at the moment. "You're going to tell me why," he said firmly. "But not right now. Later."

"Later," she repeated slowly, her gaze fixed on his. She nodded, and he was satisfied.

He rolled on a condom and moved between her legs. "I'm going to fuck you, Elizabeth." He said the crude word deliberately, watching as color flared in her cheeks and her eyes glittered with shock and hunger.

She tilted her hips, and wrapped her arms around his neck. "Yes."

The first inch of penetration made him breathless. He stopped, suddenly afraid he might hurt her inadvertently. "Is this okay?"

She stroked his hair from his damp forehead. "It's more than okay."

He gained another two inches and stopped instantly when she winced. He was beyond aroused, and she was incredibly tight. "Elizabeth." He would stop if he had to, but it might kill him to leave her now.

She wiggled a bit and the new angle helped him slide closer to the ultimate prize. She was panting, her eyes half closed. And she was silent.

"Elizabeth?" He ground the word from between clenched teeth. "Look at me."

She did, and when their eyes met, he felt something deep inside him shudder and melt. He'd never experienced whatever was happening between them, and it might have scared him if he hadn't been so damn horny.

She tried to smile. "I'm okay."

He kissed her nose, her lips, her chin. "You sure?"

When she nodded, he pushed harder and she cried out. He didn't need to ask this time. She was flushed with arousal, her nipples tight and hard. Her vagina squeezed him so tightly, he was in imminent danger of finishing too soon. He gasped for breath and pulled out, only to slide in again in one smooth thrust, which took him up against the mouth of her womb.

When she groaned from deep in her chest, he reached between them and found her swollen clit. He teased it with three firm strokes, and Elizabeth climaxed instantly, forcing him into an explosion of his own that left him weak and spent in her arms.

When the pulse in his ears quit deafening him, he rolled to his side and pulled her up tight against his chest. "Don't move a muscle," he demanded hoarsely. "Give me five minutes and we'll try for round two."

Four

In one brief period between spectacular couplings, when Enrique was dozing to regain his strength, Elizabeth made a stunning realization. The sex she had once shared with jerkface wasn't as amazing as she thought. Perhaps it had even been borderline boring.

Clearly her relative inexperience going into that affair had clouded her judgment. She'd had two long-term boyfriends before that, but neither relationship had been what you would call passionate. More convenient than anything else. So when jerkface came along, it had been exciting and wonderful to be pursued . . . to be captured . . . to be culled from the herd of available women.

It felt damned good to have the other females in the office look at her and know that she was the chosen one. And on a good day, jerkface could be sexy and funny and charmingly Hugh Grant–ish. A more experienced woman might have seen through his polished act. But not Elizabeth, much to her shame.

She curled on her side and watched Enrique sleep. He was an amazingly generous lover. Every moment in his arms was a revelation. She had suppressed her sensuality for so long, it was a minor miracle that she was able to experience the full range of pleasure he had to offer.

Despite the way he coaxed her into multiple orgasms when they were outdoors, she had been no less hungry for him once he had her beneath him in the bed. Foreplay via the shared shower was nothing outrageous. Men and women did that all the time, she was sure.

But for her, the easy intimacy was eye-opening. This was what had been missing from her life. This was what her still-young, healthy body yearned for. This was what all the books and movies were talking about.

This was amazing sex. Hot, sweaty, creative, wonderful sex.

She wanted to wake him, but he looked exhausted. Jet lag, along with extravagant sex, was bound to take it out of a man. So she cuddled close and caressed his broad back with her hand, gently enough to soothe and not wake him.

She had almost dozed off herself when she felt his hand nudge between her legs and begin to explore. She caught her breath. "You seem a trifle single-minded."

He licked her belly and parted the swollen folds of her sex with his fingers. "I call it focused." His voice was muffled against her thigh.

She put a hand in his hair, gripping tightly when he brought her to near flash point with almost no effort at all. She panted, pulling harder to get his attention.

He reared up, scowling. "Ow. That hurts. And I don't think physical abuse is the correct response to a man stroking your—"

"Don't say it." She released his hair and watched him wince as he rubbed his scalp.

He glared at her with mock anger. "Did I do something wrong?"

Her lips quirked. "You're the freaking Michelangelo of my Sistine Chapel, but I think we might need to come up for air."

His eyes widened. "Now?"

Her unrealized orgasm mocked her every bit as much as he did, but she tried to ignore the throb between her legs. She scooted up toward the headboard. "In the first place, I want you inside me the next time I come."

He grabbed her ankle and pulled hard. "That can be arranged."

She screeched, tugging ineffectually on her leg. "Wait. I'm not finished talking."

He paused, but didn't release her. "Okay. I'm listening."

She waved a hand toward the windows. The drapes were open wide, and although there was no chance of anyone looking in at them, she had finally come to her senses enough to be just the tiniest bit uncomfortable. "It's not even dark outside. And we've been—"

"Making love?"

She frowned. That phrase didn't really apply here, did it? "I was going to say *fooling around*, but the point is, I'm not used to sexual activity in the daytime."

He grinned at her. His hair was tousled, and his eyes were slumberous with unappeased sexual hunger. He was a magnificent male animal in his prime. He played with her anklebone lazily, raising gooseflesh all over her body. "I have a modicum of experience in that arena, sweetheart, and I promise you, it's neither immoral nor particularly naughty. So tell me . . . what's this really all about?"

She tugged on her foot, and this time he released her. She drew her knees to her chest and backed up to the top of the bed, wrapping the sheet around her. She felt way too exposed, particularly with Enrique looking as if he'd like to devour her in two or three big bites.

She sighed. "I need to go home, Enrique. Today was fun, but

I can't just put my life on hold to have sex, naughty or otherwise, with a man like you."

That wiped some of the good humor from his face. "A man like me?" He was stretched out with his head propped on his hand, seemingly unconcerned with his nudity. His heavy penis lay quiescently against his thigh, and try as she might, it was impossible not to notice.

She cleared her throat. "You have to know how attractive you are. And the look you have: that bad boy/sun god/pirate thing. I'm sure you have girls falling at your feet. But I'm just a regular woman. With a job and people I have to look after. This was great today. But I can't be the woman you want. I'm sorry."

He didn't seem particularly impressed with her speech. If anything, he looked contemplative.

When his silence dragged on, she glared at him. "What? What are you thinking?"

He rubbed a hand over his chest, drawing her attention to his sleek pecs and taut abdomen. He stared at her until she felt her face flush. And then he shook his head. "I'm thinking that if all I wanted was some easy ass, I sure as hell would have set my sights on someone a lot less complicated than you, Elizabeth Killaney."

She gaped at him, shocked at the matter-of-fact way he spoke. "Complicated?" She picked on the one word that jumped out at her.

He rolled to his back, staring at the ceiling. "If you'll recall, I was the one who suggested that you introduce me to those important people you feel responsible for. You're the one who chose an afternoon of debauchery instead."

She crossed her arms over her chest, feeling guilty and embarrassed, and yet still surprisingly aroused. "I don't see the point in introducing you to my family. You're temporary. This is temporary." She waved a hand to indicate the rumpled bedcovers. "Let's not make it more than it is."

"Hell, no," he said, and now the sarcasm was evident. "We wouldn't want to do that."

She felt small and naive and socially clumsy. Despite their perfect lovemaking, they seemed out of sync in every other way. "Don't be mad," she whispered. "I had a lovely time today."

He rolled off the bed and onto his feet in one fluid motion. He shrugged into the heavy robe provided by the hotel and turned to glare at her. "Why don't you send me a thank-you note then?"

She wanted to stand up as well, but she couldn't figure out a way to ditch the sheet and preserve her modesty. "You're angry," she said sadly.

He paced to the window and back. "Hell, yes, I'm angry. Sex like we just had doesn't come along every day. It's special and rare and I thought it might be fun to try again. But I'm not going to badger you into it."

She nibbled a fingernail. "Special?" It had seemed so to her, but given her lack of opportunities for comparison, she hadn't assumed the same for him.

He raked both hands through his hair. "Of course it was special, Elizabeth. I thought the top of my head was going to explode. You're amazing."

She smiled hesitantly. Perhaps she was letting her sexual in-securities cloud her common sense. "It *was* pretty hot."

"Damn straight." He nudged the damask-covered ottoman away from the foot of the bed. Then he stared at her with a chal-lenging gleam in his eyes. "But we can do better."

She raised her eyebrows. "As a businesswoman, I understand and applaud your determination."

He held out his hand. "Come over here and let me prove it to you."

Enrique understood simple lust. But the need to take her over and over until she admitted how well matched they were was a new concept. He was hell-bent on seducing away every last one of her reservations. If it took him all night. Fortunately, Elizabeth was naturally competitive and also unwilling to back down from a challenge.

He watched as she slid off the bed and approached him. She had a death grip on the sheet, and her eyes were dark with arousal.

He tugged at a corner of the soft cotton. "Ditch the armor, Elizabeth. You don't need it."

She dropped it so quickly he was startled. Holy shit. Startled, but appreciative. He held out his hand. "I want you, Elizabeth." She seemed to be hung up on plain speaking, and he was happy to oblige.

Slowly she placed her small hand in his larger one. "So it seems." She dropped her gaze to his cock, which had returned to attention as soon as it realized where things were headed.

He lifted the back of her hand to his lips and kissed it. "I want you tummy first over the ottoman."

He felt her little jerk of shock. And yet the look on her face showed excitement and not apprehension.

She knelt slowly. Even seeing the back of her neck turned him on. Such vulnerability. Such feminine strength. Elizabeth tried to convince the world that she was hard as nails . . . capable, dependable, and down-to-earth. And all those things might be true. He was impressed by every one of her stellar qualities.

But what drew him irresistibly was the deep vein of vulnerability that perhaps no one else saw but him. She seemed totally unaware of her beauty and sexuality. She had promised to tell him the reason for her celibate existence, and he wanted to hear it. But not now.

He had other plans at the moment.

He untied the belt on his robe and dragged it free of the terry loops. Elizabeth was facing away from him, but she had not completely followed his instructions.

He put a hand on her smooth, warm shoulder. "Bend over, Elizabeth."

She didn't turn her head. Instead, she slowly moved on top of the stool. He took each of her arms and pulled them behind her. When she didn't protest, he secured her wrists with the robe's tie.

The height of the ottoman was just enough that Elizabeth's knees didn't quite touch the floor. But her ass was beautifully displayed.

His mouth watered and his dick went stone hard. He shrugged out of the robe and walked across the room to the thermostat, bumping it up a notch or two. No need for his Elizabeth to get chilled.

He approached her from behind, letting her anticipation build. Her face was turned to the right, her cheek resting on the cushion. He squatted beside her and brushed the hair from her face. "How do you feel?"

She managed a tremulous smile. "Naughty."

He traced her lips with a fingertip. "Well, I concede that while daytime sex is perfectly acceptable, *this* might definitely be construed as naughty."

She exhaled and wiggled her hips, trying to get comfortable. "So what now . . . spanking?" The question held nerves and breathless arousal in equal parts.

He chuckled and smoothed a hand from her nape down her spine to the sweet curve of her ass. "I don't think we know each other well enough for that. I only want to give you pleasure. So relax."

He'd pocketed a small bottle of lotion in the bathroom. Now he uncapped it and squeezed small dots of liquid down her spine. She shivered, but otherwise didn't respond. He took his thumbs and put them side by side, applying pressure and sliding slowly from the top vertebrae all the way down to her tailbone.

Elizabeth made a sound that was a cross between a purr

and a moan. Hearing it made him shake. He added more lotion and used his palms this time, starting with her shoulders and working his way downward in a carefully mapped-out sensual grid.

At her ass, he paused for more lubricant. And then he squeezed and plumped and stroked her firm, resilient flesh until they were both panting. He kissed her luscious buttocks, once on each cheek. "You have the most amazing ass, Elizabeth."

She shivered again as he lightly brushed his thumbs down her crack. "It could stand to lose a few pounds."

Her wry comment amused him even in the midst of his fascinated hunger. "Nonsense," he muttered, offering two more kisses in homage to such perfection. "Not even an ounce. If I were a sculptor, I'd create your ass in marble. Every curve is poetry."

She laughed breathlessly, her fingers pulling perhaps unconsciously at the knot at her back. "I can tell you're a native Californian. Only on the West Coast could a guy get away with saying stuff like that."

He double pinched her butt, enjoying the pink marks he created. "You doubt my sincerity?"

She licked her lips, her voice a tad hoarse. "I think you've watched one too many movies."

He sighed, kissing his way up her spine and resting his aching erection in the cradle of her ass. "I will never lie to you, Elizabeth. And movies might be fiction, but they exist to point out the truths of human existence: despair, hope, friendship, betrayal, lust, love."

She pushed back against him, silently cajoling. "You're talking about creating a world we *want* to exist. That doesn't mean the silver screen is real."

He sheathed himself in a condom, spread her legs, and prepared to enter her. "I know what's real, Elizabeth. Never fear." He positioned the head of his cock and pushed deep. The walls of her vagina clenched around him, and his vision fuzzed at the edges. She was so hot and tight, he had to work to get all the way in. She moved against him, coaxing, teasing. . . .

Every time he withdrew, she made an almost soundless whimper of need. Such stuff could go to a man's head. He picked up the pace, shoving harder, feeling his balls slap against her. He gripped her butt, loving the position of dominance. He would never hurt a woman, but the caveman in him got off on this elemental claiming.

He held back, the muscles in his neck clenched as he tried to make sure she was with him. He reached one hand beneath her to fondle her nipple. He pinched it and Elizabeth shuddered and cried out, every contraction of her sweet, hot passage milking him and finally sending him over the edge. He came so hard, he saw stars behind the darkness of his closed eyelids.

In the silence afterward, Elizabeth whispered a request. "Do you think I could get up now? I have to pee."

Elizabeth groaned inwardly when Enrique burst out laughing. God, she was so incredibly gauche. Maybe if she rented a few more movies herself, she might learn a thing or two about romance. Something a shade more alluring than uttering a bathroom request right after a man screwed her senseless.

He was still grinning when she returned from the using the very lovely facilities. She had paused long enough to do a quick bit of personal hygiene, and then to don the robe that matched his.

He had replaced the ottoman in its original location, and he now stood with his arms up over his head, stretching and yawning.

She hovered on the far side of the bed. "I should go." She couldn't look at all that magnificent male flesh and not want to jump him again.

He just shook his head and stalked her. "I'm ordering room service, and don't argue." He grabbed the ends of her sash and tugged her toward him.

She focused her gaze on his neck just below his Adam's apple. "Shouldn't you get dressed?"

He pressed up against her deliberately. "Is my nudity bothering you, Elizabeth?"

She sighed when he kissed her temple and the curve of her cheek. "I don't think I can eat dinner with your whoopee hanging out."

He roared with laughter. Her face turned red, and she clambered onto the bed, pretending to study the room service menu he'd tossed there. She was conscious of Enrique's gaze on her, but she kept her head bent. She wasn't kidding. He *had* to put on some clothes. It wasn't fair.

Finally, much to her relief, he picked up his discarded robe from the floor and put it on. Then he sprawled on the bed beside her and put his head in her lap. She stroked his hair absentmindedly, studying the choices.

He turned his head and kissed the inside of her knee, where the robe had slipped away. "Let's make it easy. How about a couple of chef's salads?"

She wrinkled her nose. "I was thinking more along the lines of steak and baked potatoes. I seem to have burned up a lot of calories today, and I'm starving."

He smiled at her upside down. "You're a refreshing woman, Elizabeth Killaney. Do you know how often I see females who order green salad with the dressing on the side?"

She pulled his hair. "Are you calling me fat?"

He moved so swiftly, she never had a chance to protest. He had her flat on her back with him on top in less than five seconds. "You're perfect." He rubbed his cock against the notch of her thighs and then slid down to lick her belly button.

She caught her breath and ran her hands through his thick hair. "Enrique . . ." His name came out in a long, ragged sigh.

Suddenly he sat up with an aggrieved exclamation and looked down at his penis, which had risen to the occasion once again. "Damn it, hand me the phone. If I don't feed you now, I'll never get around to it."

She giggled and listened as he placed their order for immediate delivery. Of course, with most room service, the word *immediate* was open to interpretation, so who knew how long it would be? But it was probably not enough time to chance another erotic encounter in the interim.

Enrique insisted on shaving while they waited, despite her assurances that it wasn't necessary.

He scowled. "Take a look in the mirror. Between the sunburn and the whisker rash, your skin is in bad shape. And I refuse to be further responsible for ruining something so lovely."

What girl could argue with that?

They ate out on the balcony, even though it was getting cool. Elizabeth realized she had given up on the idea of leaving. If he offered, she would stay the night. It was as simple as that. He made her happy, and even if that was a very brief state of affairs, even if she was being foolhardy and impulsive for once in her life, she was content to sit back and enjoy herself.

She quizzed him as they worked their way through their delicious meal. He admitted to being an only child. He spoke with affection of his parents, who lived in northern California. She licked a drip of butter from her chin and tried not to think about calories. "Tell me more about them," she said. "What do they look like?"

He nodded toward the room behind them. "My billfold is on the armoire. See for yourself. I think it's the third photo."

She put her plate on the small round table and scooted past him to walk though the sliding door. Having carte blanche to rifle through a guy's wallet was intriguing and unexpected. She picked up the expensive brown leather bifold and extracted the photo sleeve.

His parents were both tall. They were a very handsome couple. His mother had dark hair and dark eyes. But his father must have contributed the hazel eyes and chestnut hair to the gene pool. They stood with their arms around each other, and the simple physical intimacy between them shouted their love more clearly than words.

She replaced the pictures and looked at Enrique's driver's license as she wandered back out to the balcony. Her heart fell to her shoes, or it would have if she had been wearing any. A giant knot lodged in her throat. Her little sound of distress must have caught his attention, because he half turned in his seat.

"What is it?" he asked. "What's wrong?"

She felt breathless and a little sick. "You're twenty-nine years old?" It started out as a question and ended up with a shrieked accusation.

He got to his feet, frowning. And then puzzlement followed. "Yeah . . . well, twenty-nine and a half. I'll be thirty this fall."

She literally felt the blood drain from her face. Her hands and feet went numb and her limbs trembled. She backed up into the bedroom. She couldn't speak. The enormity of the disaster was overwhelming. *My God, he's younger than Jeannie.*

He followed her inside, pausing only to close the door for warmth and privacy. "What's wrong, Elizabeth?"

She waved the billfold in his face. "You're *twenty-nine* years old, damn it."

Now he was frowning. "So?"

She felt like her head was going to explode, like her hair was going to catch fire, like her entire body was being sucked down into a nauseating whirlpool of disbelief. She tossed the offending billfold onto the bed. "I'm thirty-nine, Enrique. *Thirty-nine.*"

A puzzled frown still marked his handsome face. "I don't follow."

She wanted to punch him in the nose. The depth of her disappointment and angry disbelief choked her. "You don't follow." She said it mockingly, hearing her shrewish tone and unable to stop herself. "I'm ten years older than you." Oh God, she'd said it aloud.

Finally, he seemed to comprehend the source of her meltdown. He tried to take her in his arms, but she jerked away. "Elizabeth," he said quietly, "don't be silly. This is nothing."

She tossed the billfold on the bed. "Demi Moore might be able to get away with it, but not someone like me. People make fun of older women who try to hook up with younger guys. It's embarrassing." *And I've already had one dreadful love affair where people pointed and gossiped and laughed behind my back.*

"It's not that big a deal. Does it really matter?" he said, his expression troubled.

She stared at him in silence. Her anger and her frustration funneled away, leaving her mortally tired and so damn sad. "It matters," she whispered. "It matters a hell of a lot."

She turned and looked blindly for her clothes. Not the ones this *teenager* had bought her. But her own slightly conservative but very suitable clothes. She knew she was exaggerating, but she was so humiliated.

She locked herself in the bathroom and dressed rapidly. She felt sick. This was so much worse than finding out jerkface was married.

And hearing her say that in her head stopped her cold. Why? Why was it worse? The face in the mirror paled even more as she faced the unpalatable truth. Her relationship with jerkface had been a blow to her self-confidence and self-esteem. But this . . .

She sank down on the vanity stool and buried her face in her hands. Oh God, this hurt beyond belief. Enrique had touched something deep inside her, and he made her feel things that were so precious and new. Enrique had represented possibilities.

They hardly knew each other, but in his kind, gentle, utterly masculine strength, she had felt a sense of homecoming . . . of belonging.

And it was all a lie, a sharp-edged twist of the irony knife.

She rose to her feet, reaching for a calm she didn't possess. She splashed water on her face and tidied her hair. When she looked in the mirror, the woman staring back at her was under control, at least outwardly.

She left the sanctuary of the bathroom and faced what had to be done.

Enrique was standing in almost the exact same spot where he had been before. His hair was standing on end, and his lips were pressed together in a grim line. His hands were shoved in the pockets of his robe.

She didn't even try to smile. She knew she couldn't. She picked up her pocketbook, even though it meant stepping uncomfortably close to the silent man whose eyes she couldn't quite meet. But her car keys were inside the purse, so she had no choice.

She finally made herself look at him. "Goodbye, Enrique."

He didn't reach for her. He didn't try to argue. He didn't even speak.

With one last glance at the lovely room and its strikingly handsome occupant, she opened the door and left.

Five

Enrique was so angry, his stomach was in a knot. And for a man who rarely lost his cool, it was shocking. He wanted to spank her and kiss her and yell at her, but instead, he stood there like an android without a power supply and watched her walk out of his life.

So he was younger. What was the big deal? Did she think people would disapprove? Hell, no one would even know unless Elizabeth and he chose to tell them. Ten years was not that big a deal. There was no visible difference in their ages. And Lord knew he'd always been an old soul.

In high school and college, he'd looked with faint disdain at the wild youths bent on destroying their lives and their futures with endless partying. Enrique liked sex and booze as much as the next guy, but he was practical and focused on his studies.

His parents had worked hard for their money, and he wasn't about to dishonor them by throwing away his opportunities. He'd been called mature for his age, but it was more than that.

He knew what he wanted out of life, and he was determined to get it.

He dressed rapidly, avoiding any glance at the bed. His body still felt the warm buzz of sexual completion and satisfaction, but he also wanted her again. He was pretty sure he would never stop wanting her.

He had to get out of this room. It was making him nuts. He'd always enjoyed driving to clear his head, and here in Asheville and the surrounding countryside, he could even call it work.

As he strode downstairs and out to his car, he lectured himself forcefully. He would *not* follow her home and pressure her. If Elizabeth felt anything for him at all, she had to come to terms with it in her own time . . . in her own way. If he pushed her, he might ruin any chance they had of ending up together.

He didn't pause to question how he knew they belonged together. He had the experience to assess what was real and what was movie magic. Elizabeth Killaney was as real as they came. Forthright, grounded, almost comically self-aware. She was one in a million, and she had dropped into his lap like an unexpected blessing.

He was damned if he would let her go.

Elizabeth cried until the tears dried up, and then she crawled into her lonely bed and prayed for morning to come. She didn't want to sleep. She didn't want to dream. She didn't want to remember.

But the memories came anyway, starting with the recollection of how foolish she had felt ten years ago. Knowing that all her fellow coworkers were laughing behind her back or at the very least commiserating because she hadn't been smart enough to sniff out a rat.

That was bad enough. But this . . . this thing with Enrique. Oh God, she would be mortified if people thought she was trying to snag a younger man. Particularly since he was a completely dazzling specimen of brains and brawn, and she was a no longer twentysomething, depressingly practical, average-in-every-way, unexceptional woman.

She wasn't wallowing in false modesty. She knew her strengths and her weaknesses. She was smart and loyal and attractive in an understated way. She had a head for business, and she had drive and determination. She was extremely protective of those she loved. She had a sense of humor.

All in all, she was a nice person. But she wasn't up to tangling with someone of Enrique's level of sophistication. Nor his level of sexual experience.

She'd chosen poorly a decade ago and had lived to regret it. At least this time the cat was already out of the bag. She knew the truth. Enrique was too young for her. Too handsome. Too everything.

And since she'd known him such a short time, it would be much easier to get over the affair than it had been with jerkface. Then she snorted. Affair? That was ridiculous. What they shared was an extended one-night stand that just happened to take place during the daylight hours.

She burrowed under the covers and closed her eyes. Instead of shutting it all out, she deliberately allowed herself to remember Enrique's lovemaking. Passion and sweetness. Hunger and slow, drugging pleasure. Finally, she drifted off to sleep with a small, sad smile on her face.

In the shop the next morning, she picked up a bottle of lotion identical to the one she had been using in her shower the last few days. She unscrewed the lid and sniffed it. The number ten fragrance was pleasant but not overpowering. The blend of ingredients was their best yet for moisturizing the skin.

She replaced the cap and put the bottle back on the shelf. She couldn't help thinking that something about the special brew had influenced Enrique's behavior.

Why else had he left her alone the evening before and then practically pounced on her when they ran into each other the next day? That second morning she had used the lotion again, never dreaming she would see him when she went to the Inn.

If she had known what was coming, she would have deliberately changed her shower routine just to see if it made a difference. But that didn't explain the fact that after she and Enrique showered together, she'd had no trace of the number ten lotion on her skin and yet he'd wanted her as fiercely as ever. So maybe the lotion idea was just a silly game of make-believe.

Diana called out to her from the office. Elizabeth squared her shoulders and put on her happy face. Her family depended on her. She wouldn't allow her world to be turned upside down by a broad chest and a sexy smile. She was sensible and responsible.

And heartbreak was only heartbreak if you allowed it. Her wild fling was over. So there.

Enrique had an informative chat with the manager of the gift shop in his hotel. He pumped her unashamedly for information about the Killaney cousins. What he found out was no surprise. Combined with the information Elizabeth had shared with him, the picture came into focus.

She was the driving force behind Lotions and Potions. The business venture with the three cousins was her idea. She was the one who had worked tirelessly to make sure it all came together.

The other two women played integral roles, of course. But Elizabeth's drive and passion propelled the train. She was one hell of a woman.

Elizabeth picked up the phone and then set it back in the cradle. Could she do this? *Should* she do this? She'd spent the last four days trying to decide if she had it in her to be spontaneous and sexually free. In truth, neither description fit what she knew about herself.

But she had never wanted a man as much as she wanted Enrique, and it seemed a criminal waste to throw away the opportunity to be with someone who was funny and smart and amazingly talented in bed. She remembered him saying something about two weeks. How much of that time had passed? The longer she waited, the less chance there was to spend precious days with him.

She picked up the phone a second time and dialed the number of the Inn. It was only eight thirty in the morning. She hoped Enrique had adjusted enough to the time change by now so she wouldn't be waking him. The operator put her through. He answered on the third ring, his voice deep and pleasant.

"Enrique?" Her voice cracked on the third syllable. She imagined him on the other end. What was his expression?

"Is it you, Elizabeth?"

"Yes."

He sighed. "It's about damn time. I fly out in six days. I'd almost given up."

"You could have called me."

"No," he said quietly. Firmly. "You would never have been happy if this was not your decision."

She twirled the phone cord around her finger. "You know me well for such short acquaintance."

He laughed roughly. "I'm only just beginning." After a pregnant pause, he spoke again. "Dare I hope that you've changed your mind about us?"

Her chin trembled. "Yes. Our age difference aside, there's no future for us, but I want to be with you until you leave." Even his voice was enough to make her weak with longing and excitement.

He cursed softly. "I wish you had told me this in person."

"I couldn't face you. I was afraid you were still mad. And I don't do confrontation well."

His voice lowered to a caress that made her legs weak. "I will never say no to you, Elizabeth."

She swallowed hard. "That's a sweeping statement. It gives me all sorts of ideas."

He chuckled. "Bring them on, sweetheart. Bring them on."

They met for lunch at a crowded restaurant. Elizabeth still felt awkward and unsure of herself, and there were a few things she wanted settled before they ended up in bed again. A public audience would keep them from doing anything rash. Or so she hoped.

He met her with a kiss on the cheek and a smile that made her insides go all squishy. She'd used the number ten shower gel that morning, just in case it really did have erotic properties. She needed all the help she could get.

They spoke of inconsequential topics until the waitress had taken their order and disappeared. Then Enrique leaned across the table, taking her hands in his. Elizabeth tugged them back.

His brows narrowed in a frown, but he didn't say anything.

She put her hands in her lap and smiled nervously. "Here's the thing, Enrique. I'd prefer that we keep our relationship under wraps."

Turbulent emotions flashed in his eyes. His spine straightened, and he picked up a fork and drummed it lightly on the table. "Would you care to explain that?"

She took a breath and nodded. "I'd be more comfortable if we didn't go public with our sexual relationship. I pretended to be sick today, but I've decided to tell Jeannie and Diana that I'm taking a week's vacation."

"Won't they ask where you're going?"

That part bothered her. "Yes. I think I'll have to tell a little white lie."

"And you're okay with that?" He didn't bother to disguise the disapproval in his voice.

She winced. "It's not ideal, but I can't exactly say that I'm planning on having a week of hot-and-heavy sex with a guy who's in town on a business trip. They would flip out . . . maybe have me committed. Or check to see if aliens have taken over my body."

"So the truth would be that bad?"

She nodded fervently. "Trust me. It would. They'd want to meet you, and they'd tease me and start making romantic plans. It would be awful."

The waitress brought their salads and drinks. During that little interchange, Enrique's expression never lightened. He did not look like a happy man.

Elizabeth took a bite of spinach drizzled with raspberry vin-aigrette. Then she chewed and swallowed. Still Enrique hadn't moved. She put down her fork. "What's wrong?"

His jaw was granite hard, and he almost looked sullen. "I've never been anyone's dirty secret. I don't think I like it. And I *wanted* to meet your cousins."

She sighed. "Try to look at it from my perspective. You'll be gone soon. Back to the land of sunshine and beaches. No one there will give a flip about what happened while you were in North Carolina. But I have to live here. And even though Diana and Jeannie and I are closer than many sisters, I don't want to have to explain you . . . us . . . this aberration on my part."

He took a sip of iced tea and stared down at his baked salmon. "And where do you propose that we conduct this clan-destine affair?"

She looked around to see if anyone was listening. He hadn't bothered to lower his voice. Fortunately, the nearby patrons were intent on their own conversations, and the noisy lunch crowd made an effective cover.

She smiled at him nervously, wishing the devil-may-care

beach bum would return. At the moment, Enrique looked like judge and jury. She shrugged. "I thought I would move in with you at the hotel. If that's okay." She added that last bit hastily. Perhaps he was the kind of man who didn't like women to sleep over.

He finally started eating, and she relaxed a fraction. But she needed some kind of affirmation. "So does that work for you?" After a long silence, she prodded. "Enrique, what do you think?"

He looked up at her, and finally the lazy gleam of sexual interest had returned to his eyes. "I made the mistake, Elizabeth, of saying that I would never tell you no, so I think my agreement is a foregone conclusion." He shook his head with a wry grin. "Eat your lunch. I actually have to work for a living this afternoon."

He took her with him. She'd wondered if they would go straight back to the hotel and have sex, but Enrique was perhaps even more responsible than Elizabeth Killaney. He had a list of things he still needed to accomplish before he left Asheville, and Elizabeth tried to squash her feeling of disappointment. Of course the man had work to do. Sex could come later.

They dropped her car at her house without going inside, and they headed out of town. Enrique had found an interesting spot for a location shoot, so he'd made an appointment with the couple who owned the property to discuss possibilities. Now, with Elizabeth in tow, he was off to see if he could close the deal.

Their destination was fifteen or twenty miles west of the city. They had long ago left the main road and were now meandering along a perfectly lovely two-lane highway. Elizabeth knew the general area, but she couldn't remember ever actually driving along this road.

Enrique finally pulled over by a split-rail fence that marked the boundary of a broad, grassy rectangular field. In the distance, the mountains peeked up over the trees at the edge of the forest.

An old barn close to the road looked like a strong wind would knock it over.

Enrique put the car in park and opened his window. The sweet smell of honeysuckle scented the light breeze. He turned to smile at her. "What do you think?"

She gazed out at the recently mown expanse. It appeared that the owner was allowing it to lie fallow for a season or two. She imagined that some years it would be planted with corn or another crop.

She shrugged. "It's a field."

He leaned over the center console and kissed her cheek. "Use your imagination, Elizabeth. Pretend you have a camera and look again."

She would rather see where that kiss could lead, but he had already moved back to his own side of the car. She gazed out at the serene, bucolic setting. Minus a power pole or two, it could exist almost anywhere in time.

She cocked her head, trying to imagine the passive scene through a camera lens. "Why are you so interested in an empty field?"

He put the car in gear and eased out onto the road. "The movie has a jousting scene. I think this would be pretty close to perfect."

The house where they were headed was only an eighth of a mile farther. They pulled into the gravel driveway and got out. The white frame structure, built sometime in the twenties probably, was like a hundred others in the area. Its occupants, Bethel and Amos, had been married for sixty-one years.

Over cookies and lemonade, the old couple expressed an understandable wariness. Elizabeth felt sorry for them. The news was full of scams perpetrated on older citizens. And despite Enrique's genuine charm and reassurances, they were naturally skittish.

Elizabeth didn't know if she was doing the right thing or not, but she decided to butt in. She reached in her purse and took out a business card, handing it to Bethel with a smile. "I own a shop in town. And this man is a friend of mine. I can promise you that all he's talked about is true. If the producer and director approve this location, you will be paid very well for your time and inconvenience. But the choice is yours. If you want to pass, I'm sure Enrique will understand." She felt him stiffen beside her, but she ignored him. "A lot of movies have been filmed near here, and your farm is lovely. It's a generous amount of money for very little effort. So talk about it with your children if you like. But he *will* have to know something soon."

Bethel looked at Amos. They could probably communicate without even speaking after such a long marriage. Finally, Bethel looked back at her guests. "I think we'd be foolish to pass this up, Miss Killaney." She turned to the silent Enrique. "Young man, you've got yourself a deal."

Back outside, Elizabeth leaned against the car and tossed her purse through the open window into the backseat. "Whew. That was close. I was afraid they were going to kick you out."

Enrique stood, tall and handsome, in the bright afternoon sunlight. He folded his arms across his chest. "At first I wanted to smack you, and then I wanted to kiss your feet."

She grinned smugly. "You can thank me later."

His raised eyebrow and suggestive leer made her laugh. He took her arm. "C'mon. They said we can walk the property. Who knows? I might find another jewel."

Her khaki capri pants, scoop-neck top, and cork-soled espadrilles had been appropriate for lunch. She paused a moment to worry about their suitability for farm attire and then thought, *What the heck?* She could always buy new clothes.

Enrique led her along a path from the house into the woods. Clearly no one had spent much time there in recent days, because he was forced to hold aside briar bushes so they could pass by. Eventually the trail came to a small sunlit pond. One corner was covered with algae, but the other side boasted pretty lily pads. A frog plopped into the water with a croak and a splash as they approached.

Enrique took Elizabeth's picture and then they walked on. A few hundred yards later, they exited the woods and were standing in the field. Enrique squinted his eyes and estimated the dimensions.

Elizabeth studied the scene again and decided she might be able to imagine it filled with horses and lords and ladies. It must be a lot of fun to create that magic from nothing more than a fallow field and someone's fertile imagination.

Enrique took her hand. "Let's take a look inside the barn. With a bit of exterior carpentry and some cloth hangings, it could be transformed into a 'stand' for the audience viewing the joust. Or considering the derelict condition it's in, it might be torn down completely . . . with Bethel and Amos's permission, of course. Which they would probably give, because it looks like they haven't kept livestock in years."

Inside the rickety structure, dust motes danced on rays of sunshine that peeked in through missing boards. The smell of old hay and manure permeated the air, but not in a bad way. The place seemed a bit sad, as though its original purpose had been lost and now it was just waiting to die.

Elizabeth shook off her fanciful thoughts. Enrique was the moviemaker. She was too practical to invent entire new worlds.

He turned suddenly and slid his arms around her waist. "I've always wanted to have sex in an old barn."

She searched his face, sure that he was kidding her. "You're lying."

He cupped her butt and pulled her closer. Well, maybe he was partly telling the truth. His erection was full-fledged already.

He took her mouth in an urgent kiss. "I've wanted to do this ever since you called this morning."

She hooked a leg around his thigh. "What took you so long?"

They had each been tiptoeing around the unspoken white-hot need to meld their bodies. He scooped handfuls of her hair into his fists and pulled her closer. "I haven't been able to sleep," he groaned. "I've missed you."

The husky words made her melt, and she tried not to think about the possibility that he'd said them to a hundred other women. She pressed even closer, dying for the feel of his hot, muscular body against hers. "You have a very lovely hotel room back in town." Her words were breathless, barely audible.

He bit the side of her neck. "Too far."

She glanced around wildly. The place was more dirty than romantic.

He read her concern, his face tight with hunger. "You can be on top."

At that moment and in her condition, it seemed a fair concession. They undressed each other rapidly and he pulled her down on top of him. She grinned when he took a condom from the pocket of his discarded pants. "I love a man who thinks ahead."

She helped him put it on, and then he held her with his hands on her waist and her legs sprawled on either side of his narrow hips. His fingers were dark against her pale skin. She saw him swallow, and his face changed. The urgent, lustful need transmuted somehow to reflect unmistakable tenderness. "Thank you for giving us another chance," he said softly, his beautiful eyes searching hers. The diffused sunlight picked out flecks of amber in his irises.

She licked her lips. "I didn't have a choice," she whispered with complete honesty. "I've never met anyone like you before. You make me happy."

He joined their bodies with one mighty thrust and groaned. "I hope that's not all I make you." And then neither of them was inclined to talk for the next few minutes as they moved together urgently, first slow and sweet and then harder and faster.

She felt him stretch her, felt the power and heat of him deep inside. She braced her hands on his shoulders, looking down at him, the striking face that had become so dear and so familiar so damn quickly. She squeezed his cock with her inner muscles and smiled when he groaned and shivered. She closed her eyes and tilted back her head, feeling him grow even larger.

She was awash with emotions that frightened her. Only in the movies did such magic happen so quickly. He knew her body. He read the nuances of her sexual need and answered each unspoken cry. The perfect intimacy of the moment made her want to weep.

But there was no place for sadness. Not now.

He pressed harder, making her gasp. She braced her hands on his shoulders, and then almost lost her balance when his strong arms clasped around her waist and pulled her down onto his chest. They kissed wildly, his tongue thrusting in her mouth while his cock thrust deep inside her.

The dual assault made her crazy. She felt her climax coming and tried to hold back, but pleasure broke over her in a crystalline wave of shimmering joy.

She gasped and shuddered and seconds later experienced the powerful force of his orgasm as it rocked through them both.

They lay there spent and panting for long, silent moments. Far in the distance, the mournful moo of a cow echoed down the valley. Elizabeth felt like a character in a Western novel, all sweaty and rumpled in the arms of the sexy sheriff. She could feel the rapid thump of his heartbeat. She sneezed and grimaced when Enrique laughed at her.

He played lazily with her breasts. "I should have thought to ask if you were allergic to hay."

She nuzzled his collarbone, entirely content with her current position. "Wouldn't have mattered."

"Oh?" His big hands played with her butt.

She nodded, licking her way up his neck. "I seem to lose all common sense when you get within three feet of me."

He moved up her back, caressing, lightly tickling. "I adore your common sense, Elizabeth. But it's not what I love best about you."

Her heart stuttered and threatened to stop. *Love?* She swallowed and tried to speak lightly. "Don't keep me in suspense. I'm always ready to hear compliments."

He sat up suddenly, wrapping his arms around her to keep her in his lap. The new position, especially with his quickly recovering erection, gave rise to some very interesting possibilities.

He lifted her ass a couple of inches and realigned their bodies. He hadn't reached maximum hardness yet, but there was enough of him to make her gasp and then moan as he probed tender, overused muscles and sensitive inner flesh.

He groaned and held her so tightly her ribs threatened to crack. "I love how you fuck me."

She smiled against his neck, even as her body accepted him eagerly. No one had ever complimented her on such a skill, and she discovered that she liked it far more than being recognized for her business acumen.

She rubbed her breasts against his chest, shivering at the sensation of his hard, warm body caressing her nipples. She never wanted to leave this barn. Perhaps she could buy it and erect a monument with a plaque that read: *Here on this spot, in the year 2008, Elizabeth Killaney decided to become a sexually adventuresome woman.*

Enrique tightened his grasp and his breath rasped in his throat. "Are you close, Lizzie, my girl?"

The endearment shocked and pleased her. "Close only counts in horseshoes and hand grenades," she muttered.

He choked out a laugh and shifted his angle of concentration just enough to stroke her clit firmly. She cried out as that one brief stimulus sent her racing for the top.

Enrique shuddered, his chest heaving. "If we're going with military metaphors, then hang on, 'cause I'm gonna blow."

Six

$\mathcal{E}$ventually, they had to stand up. Enrique's back was covered with debris, and he had a nasty scratch on his bum. Elizabeth kissed it to make it better, a non-Red-Cross-approved treatment that nearly initiated round three.

She enjoyed using her hands to brush all the dirt and dust and straw from his impressive shoulders, back, and waist. Enrique stood docile until her hands rubbed over his ass and then he growled at her. "Enough. It's getting late, and I don't want Bethel and Amos calling in the National Guard to find us."

She gave him one last caress and waited as he stepped into his pants, socks, and shoes. A man *dressing* shouldn't qualify as an art form, but Enrique made it sexy as hell.

He was entirely comfortable with his nudity. She, on the other hand, once the sexual euphoria had partially worn off, was happy to cover up her body. It wasn't ugly, and she really didn't have any issues with her physical self-image, but no sense taking chances that Enrique might notice a stray bit of cellulite, or her bony knees and elbows.

When they were both fully clothed, he cocked his head, shoved his hands in his pockets, and gave her a long, curious look.

She shifted nervously under his intense regard. "What's the matter?"

He reached down and picked up his key ring, which had fallen into a small mound of moldy hay. "It's time, Elizabeth."

She frowned, genuinely confused. "For what?"

"For you to tell me why it's been so long since you had sex."

He watched as the color drained from her face. He was pretty sure she assumed he had forgotten her quiet confession in his room at the hotel.

Forgotten? Hell, no. If anything, he had obsessed over her whispered request for gentleness, wondering why the heck a woman who possessed so much natural sensuality would turn her back on sex. He was damn glad she had told him, though. The first time he had entered, she was so tight it felt like screwing a virgin. Not that he ever had. But a man could imagine these things.

And the way Elizabeth's body had gripped his like a warm, wet glove had threatened to make his eyeballs cross. He'd been addicted to her from that first instant. Or really, from the first moment she had fallen into his arms on a public street in broad daylight.

His body had learned the feel of hers in an intimate way, and now, it never wanted to let go.

He waited her out, content to let the fraught silence grow until Elizabeth cracked.

But he had underestimated her ability to think on her feet,

even after mind-blowing sex. She met his gaze calmly despite her pallor. "You're right about Bethel and Amos. We need to go back and rescue the car."

He wanted to argue. He hated the invisible wall that protected her secrets from him. Perhaps it was irrational, but he wanted to know everything about her . . . even if he didn't care for the answers.

He glanced at his watch. "Shit," he muttered, feeling surprisingly irritated for a guy who had just gotten his rocks off in the arms of a sexual goddess . . . twice. "All right. We'll go. But this isn't over."

As they wandered back through the field, he held her hand again. It seemed to be a compulsion. If he were making his own movie, he'd be Robin Hood dragging Maid Marian back to the hideout for some serious alone time.

His band of merry men would just have to get lost.

Bethel did indeed peer out anxiously at them from between her muslin curtains as they returned, responding to Enrique's wave with a little flutter of her fingers. It was probably a good thing he and Elizabeth hadn't lingered any longer in the barn. Amos might have taken a notion to come looking for them and gotten an eyeful.

Elizabeth was quiet on the drive back into town. She sat with her hands clasped in her lap, gazing out the window. When they neared the turn onto the interstate loop that circled the city, he broke the oddly uncomfortable silence. "Am I taking you to the hotel now, or do you need to go by your house?"

He could tell from her face that she hadn't thought through all the logistics of their supposed affair.

She nibbled her lower lip. "If you'll drop me off, I can pack a bag and then drive out there."

Though it pained him to think it, it occurred to him that she didn't really even want him to go inside her house. And frankly, it hurt. He sighed. "Elizabeth . . . you don't need your car. Why don't you let me come in and wait while you get ready? Then we can go together."

Their low-key argument lasted up until the moment he parked at her curb. And then the decision was taken out of their hands. A gorgeous blonde was just coming out of Elizabeth's house. A neighbor, perhaps. She looked up when she heard the car and her nose wrinkled in confusion.

Elizabeth got out of the car slowly. It was clear that the jig was up, and he was curious to see how she would handle things.

The blond woman's expression was a cross between concern and suspicion. She crossed the small grassy yard, met them on the sidewalk, and frowned. "Elizabeth? What's going on? You said you weren't feeling well, so I brought you some soup after we closed the shop."

Enrique stood quietly as the blonde gave him a head-to-toe inspection and her frown deepened.

Elizabeth smiled weakly. "Um, I felt better. And a friend of mine called. He's visiting from out of town, so we went for a drive."

The blonde's frown darkened. She put her hands on her curvy hips. "Who is he?"

Enrique stepped forward and held out his hand. "Enrique Cantilano, ma'am. And I'm guessing you're one of the cousins."

Her grip was firm and the steely-eyed stare she leveled at him warned him in no uncertain terms that Elizabeth had a protector. He smothered a grin, and kept talking to cover the silence. "Elizabeth has told me a lot about her family. It's very nice to meet you . . ." He raised an eyebrow, waiting for her to fill in the blank.

Elizabeth had gone into some sort of zombie trance, leaving the blonde to handle the social niceties. The other woman finally smiled, but it didn't reach her eyes. "Jeannie. Jeannie Killaney. And how exactly does our Elizabeth know you?"

He produced his best charm-the-pants-off-of-them smile. "I've been scouting some movie locations here in Asheville. Elizabeth and I met quite by accident one afternoon and struck up an acquaintance. Isn't that right, Lizzie?"

Elizabeth had gone from red-faced to pale and back to red-faced again. She was wringing her hands, perhaps unconsciously. She nodded slowly. "Yes. That's about the extent of it."

She gave Jeannie a nervous grin. "We were just going out to eat. I wanted to change clothes first."

Jeannie leaned toward her cousin and brushed her cheek. "Why do you have straw in your hair?"

Now Elizabeth was the color of ripe tomatoes. Enrique took pity on her. "I've had her tramping through the woods. Not all movie work is glamorous, I'm afraid. But I suppose we'd better be going. We have reservations."

Elizabeth shot him a grateful glance, but Jeannie was having none of it. "Nonsense," she said firmly. "Diana is cooking tonight, remember? So she can show off her culinary skills for Damian? She was really disappointed that you were sick."

Jeannie turned to look at Enrique. "I'm sure she would want me to invite you as well, Mr. Cantilano."

He smiled, ignoring Elizabeth's indignant squeak. "I would love to come. And please, call me Enrique."

Diana's kitchen and apartment were small, but she had set a pretty table in the living room with spring flowers for a centerpiece. Her fiancé—a big, brawny guy who clearly adored the woman in his life—seemed happy to see another male face at the table, nevertheless.

Jeannie was the only one without a date, but no one appeared concerned with the odd number. As a dinner party, it was extremely casual. Enrique fielded questions about his job and even his family and his background. It was clear from the outset that although Elizabeth was the eldest of the three cousins, the two younger women felt the need to be protective of her. Enrique thought it was very sweet.

And Elizabeth never seemed to realize that her kinfolk were effectively vetting her suitor.

Damian was already part of the inner circle. That much was clear. And plans were under way for his and Diana's wedding.

Enrique loved watching Elizabeth in the center of this tight-knit family group. And was it his imagination, or did her face actually grow wistful in the midst of all the wedding talk? Given what he knew of her down-to-earth take on life, he would not have pegged her as a romantic, but now he wondered.

Over dessert, Jeannie poked a bit for more details about Enrique's plans. She had thawed from her original frosty attitude, but Enrique sensed that he was still very much on probation.

Jeannie sat back in her chair and took a sip of her wine. "So, Enrique . . . Elizabeth tells me you have to head back home in about a week."

He nodded slowly, sensing one of those moments that make or break a man. "Yes, but I'm actually considering making my home in Asheville."

Elizabeth's choked gasp was audible. He pounded her on her back while she drained half of her water glass and tried to breathe. Her eyes were round and shocked. "You can't be serious."

Her less-than-glowing reception of his statement was hell on his ego, but he responded calmly. "You all may not realize it, even though you've lived here for a while, but outside of California, of course, North Carolina has more production complexes and sound stages than any state in the nation."

That sparked an animated conversation, which led to him sharing anecdotes about famous people he had met in the business, and that led to even more questions about his job. Although he was not averse to bonding with the Killaney clan at large, he was anxious to be alone with Elizabeth and to gauge her true reaction to his intentionally shocking statement. She'd barely said a dozen words to him in the interim.

In another half hour, he made a move to leave. Thankfully,

Elizabeth followed his lead, and soon they were in his car heading down the road. He remembered that after Jeannie showed up on Elizabeth's doorstep, they had all three left immediately to go over to Diana's house. Since Elizabeth had never actually gone inside and packed anything, he assumed she still needed clothes and an overnight bag.

He drummed his fingers on the steering wheel as they stopped at a red light. "Where to now?" he asked lightly. His silent passenger was making him nervous.

She fiddled with her seat belt and sighed. "It's been a long day. Why don't you take me home? I'll call you tomorrow and we can talk."

He bit his tongue to keep from yelling at her. Without another word, he stepped on the gas and sent the car hurtling down the road.

Elizabeth felt like the time she had accidentally taken a double dose of cough medicine and was so hyped up she stayed awake all night. Her thoughts and emotions were all over the map. Everything she had intended *not* to happen had come true. Enrique, her amazing secret lover, was out of the bag or out of the closet or whatever stupid metaphor you wanted to employ.

He'd met Diana and Jeannie and charmed them. Well, not without a fight. Her two cousins had been definitely cool in the beginning. But Enrique, given half a chance, could win over the most hardened of skeptics. His warmth and genuine decency shone through.

And then he'd gone and ruined everything. Why in the heck would he say something so stupid? Moving to North Carolina? Leaving California? Why on earth would he even mention such an unlikely possibility?

And though her heart had made an involuntary leap when it heard the news, her head urged caution. This changed the whole dynamic of what was happening between them.

She clenched her hands in her lap. "You missed my turn," she said quietly.

Enrique shot her a sideways glance. "I'm not taking you home."

Gooseflesh broke out all over her body at the sound of his voice. She'd never heard him use that particular tone. He was pissed.

She shivered in reaction to his unspoken aggression. She'd already told him she didn't do confrontation well, but it seemed that was where they were headed, come hell or high water.

He drove to a city park near the center of town and stopped the car. Although it was dark outside, the area was well lit, and even at nine at night, it wasn't deserted. A few joggers circled the paths, and the occasional high school couple could be spotted making out.

She tried to swallow her nerves, but she was shaking inside. "Why are we here?"

He reached over and unfastened her seat belt. "We need to talk. And since we seem to have difficulty staying focused, I thought we should pick a spot with no beds and no barns." He opened his door. "Get out of the car, Elizabeth."

He headed for the nearest bench, but she tugged on his arm. "I want to walk," she said. At least that way she wouldn't have to feel his far-too-perceptive gaze on her face while she talked. And she had a pretty good idea that he expected her to be the one to do most of the talking.

So they began a circuit of the park . . . not touching . . . not looking at each other. His hands were jammed in his pockets. Her arms were wrapped around her waist. A body-language expert would have had a field day with their solitary personal space.

Enrique didn't waste any time. His jaw was granite hard, his sensual lips a terse slash in his sober face. "I want to know why you haven't had sex since Clinton was in the White House."

Elizabeth wished she could say it was none of his business.

But to put it so bluntly would be hurtful and rude, and she would be lying. She winced inwardly. The memories were no less painful with the passage of time. She sighed. "I was in a relationship with a new guy where I worked. We'd been at it pretty hot and heavy when I found out that he was married. His out-of-town wife had finally sold their house and was moving with their young child to be with her husband."

Enrique stopped dead in the path. "Bastard."

The vehemence in his single growled word made her feel marginally better. She kept walking, forcing him to follow. "Yeah. He was. Nobody else knew about the secret family, either, but when his wife and kid showed up at the office one day, the shit hit the fan. I was an idiot, and the whole world was witness to my stupidity. It never occurred to me to ask if he was married. And everyone knew we were an item. I couldn't hide. It was humiliating and embarrassing and, quite frankly, the lowest point in my life."

"What did you do?" His words were quiet . . . curious . . . nonjudgmental.

She shrugged. "I thought about staying and toughing it out. It was a fantastic job and I loved it. But I was afraid if I was still in the picture, someone might say something to his wife, and the poor woman didn't deserve that." She swallowed hard, still remembering how awful it was to simply walk away. "So I left. Went home. Tried to reinvent my life."

"Is that when you came up with the idea for Lotions and Potions?"

"Yes. But I worked in my family's business for several years to save up some capital. Long hours, lots of overtime. When I finally decided to go for it, I worked my ass off, even with Diana and Jeannie giving a hundred percent. But I needed something to make me forget. I sure as heck didn't have time for men. And then later, when things finally settled down . . ." She trailed off, unable to articulate her feelings about jumping back into the dating pool.

"You were skittish."

She nodded without speaking, a lump the size of Kansas in her throat. Some of their fellow nocturnal enthusiasts had departed, leaving the place mostly deserted. She and Enrique were on the back side of the park at the moment, and because of a couple of burned-out streetlights, the shadows were deep and protective.

Her throat hurt from her determination not to get all emotional. It was a long time ago. It was over.

Enrique put an arm around her, and they kept walking. He had his hand on her shoulder, and the warm grip of his fingers made her feel safe.

When he reached in his pocket and handed her a handkerchief, she looked up at him. "I'm not crying," she insisted.

His smile was faint. "But you want to, Lizzie, don't you?"

He kept his eyes straight ahead after that, and she dabbed at the tears that escaped despite her best intentions. God, he made her feel so . . . She couldn't even come up with a word. It was like that moment when you were little and returning home from a trip and one of your parents carried you half asleep from the car to your bed and tucked you in. Warmth. Security. Unconditional love.

Love. No, not after a week. But maybe something on the way to love.

He squeezed her arm. "You didn't do anything wrong, Elizabeth. Con men and liars succeed because they are good at what they do. No one else suspected . . . did they?"

She sniffed and crumpled his handkerchief in her hand. "No. But that was almost as bad. They were all looking at me with pity and that *Thank God, it wasn't me* expression. I felt like such a fool. I'd always been Elizabeth, the smart, levelheaded one. The practical, never-frivolous girl who had a head for business and didn't take crap from anyone. Then suddenly I was the office joke."

"So you gave up on men."

She stumbled on a loose pebble, and his arm tightened. He pulled her closer to his side and swung them around until her back was against a tree and his body was pressed against hers. Now he stared down at her, his eyes impossible to read in the gloom. "Ask me again if I'm married."

Her mouth gaped, then snapped shut. "Are you married, Enrique?"

He kissed her forehead. "No, Elizabeth. I am not."

A tiny giggle escaped her. Then a ragged sigh.

And finally, he smiled. "But do you believe me?"

She nodded slowly. "Yes, I do."

He put a hand to her face, his fingers warm against her night-cooled skin. "I'll wait for you to believe it in your heart. Trust takes longer."

She wanted to nuzzle her face in his palm like a kitten seeking affection, but his roughly uttered pledge reminded her of his earlier bombshell. She stiffened her spine, though with him so close, it had little effect. She searched for the right words, but there was no way to dress this up.

She turned her face and kissed his fingers. "It isn't practical to move all the way across the country for someone you just met."

Even in the darkness she caught the flash of his white teeth as he grinned. Now he played with her collarbone, stroking it and teasing the little hollow above it. He had his other hand propped on the tree trunk above her head. The close intimacy made her giddy.

He brushed his lips across her cheekbone. "You're right. It isn't. And at the risk of damaging your fragile psyche, lovely Lizzie, I am honor bound to tell you that my moving plans were in the works long before I met you. This . . . us . . . is simply icing on the cake."

She was embarrassed even with the gentle humor in his voice. Perhaps she had allowed her ego to run away with her. She pursed her lips. "Well, I'm glad to hear it."

He chuckled and this time kissed her mouth full-on. "I'm not in love with you, Elizabeth."

She inhaled a sharp little breath and then melted into him. "I'm not in love with you, either." His erection, thick and full, probed insistently at her belly, making her knees weak and her panties wet.

He moved both his hands to her breasts, stroking and fondling them until she thought she would come on the spot. His breath came out in choppy pants. He licked the shell of her ear. "But I reserve the right to fall in love with you at any point in the near future. When you think an appropriate length of time has passed."

He rubbed his thumbs over her nipples, and when she cried out, the sound seemed to shock some sense into him. He dropped his face to her shoulder, his body shaking. She kissed his neck and then the curve of his ear, all the way down to that damn pirate earring.

She ran her tongue around it, circled it with her teeth, and tugged gently.

Enrique went rigid and the word he uttered was coarse but right on the mark. He moved his hips against hers urgently, effectively. She was ready to strip naked when he groaned from deep in his chest and shoved himself backward.

He glared at her. "Why the hell do you have this effect on me?"

She batted her eyelashes. "It's the older woman/younger man thing. I unconsciously seduce you with my mature lovemaking techniques."

"Like celibacy?"

His wry question surprised a bubble of laughter from her throat. "You're still too young for me."

He slammed the heel of his hand to his forehead. "Good Lord, woman. Give it up. We both know you're using the age thing as an excuse. No one is going to think twice about the two of us as a couple."

"So we're a couple now?"

He grabbed her wrist and started dragging her toward the car. "Don't push me, Lizzie. I'm feeing neither practical nor level-headed at the moment. And the idea of fucking you in a public city park is growing on me."

She allowed him to stuff her in the car, and managed not to laugh when he had trouble getting the key in the ignition. He broke every speed limit and made it to her house in 7.5 minutes.

On her doorstep, she paused, feeling the unmistakable significance of the moment. She was inviting Enrique into her house, her life, her bed.

He pinched her ass. "Anytime now, woman."

She hesitated, shivering in the evening chill. "I think I forgot to make my bed this morning."

He took the key from her trembling hand and opened the door, curling an arm around her waist and ushering her inside. "Then I'll take you on the kitchen table."

Just hearing him say it in that gravelly, rough voice made her gasp. "Promise?"

He blinked in surprise. "I was kidding . . . I think."

She waited impatiently for him to lock the door, and then she grabbed handfuls of his shirt and pulled him close. "I wasn't."

His eyes darkened and his cheeks flushed. "Okay, then." He looked beyond her with an unfocused gaze. "I don't see it."

She bit his chin. "See what?"

"The table." His hands were inside her pants now.

She reevaluated her priorities. "The coffee table's closer."

He stripped her so fast, she got dizzy.

When she tried to help him, he refused, tossing pants and shirts and socks in urgent motions. He shoved his hands in her hair, his wild eyes meeting hers. "Top or bottom?"

She wanted to giggle, but when his mouth came down over hers in a ravenous kiss, the urge passed. "Bottom," she murmured, not caring where or how, as long as it was fast and soon.

He eased her down onto her back, shoving aside a stack of magazines in the process. The polished wood was cold on her bare flesh, but she was burning up. Enrique's cock was firm and ready, and when he moved between her thighs and then nudged her legs even farther apart, she moaned.

He joined their bodies with a forceful thrust. The feel of his hot length pulsing deep inside her made her wrap her legs around his waist in an effort to draw him even tighter. "Enrique," she murmured.

He didn't respond. He was too busy screwing her senseless. The sheer rightness of it made her smile even as her body crested the first peak. She held him tightly as he groaned and went rigid seconds later.

She brushed the damp hair from his forehead, feeling the not unpleasant weight of his torso pinning her to the table. "That was fun," she said lazily, daring to contemplate a future totally outside her neat life plan.

He rolled to the floor, taking her with him. She shrieked and laughed when he managed to keep their bodies joined. He flexed his hips. "No, it wasn't."

She stared at him, shocked by his unchivalrous comment. "I beg your pardon."

He kissed her tenderly. "It wasn't fun, my lovely Elizabeth. It was magic."

I Dream of Jeannie

One

$\mathcal{J}$eannie kept a close eye on the man standing in the far corner of the store. He seemed harmless enough, but you could never be too careful. At Lotions and Potions, they did have the occasional shoplifter, though that was a rare occurrence . . . and it was usually a teenager.

This man was definitely not a shoplifter. He was dressed conservatively, and though he wouldn't be Diana's or Elizabeth's type, he was definitely on Jeannie's hottie scale up near the top. His simple white button-down shirt was tucked into plain khaki slacks with a brown leather belt. The clothes fit him well and showed off broad shoulders, a flat stomach, and a nice ass.

He picked up a bar of soap and examined it with great interest. She supposed she could go over and offer to help him, but most customers liked to browse undisturbed. So instead, she continued to study him.

His blond hair wasn't a buzz cut, but it was short. And the

severe style showed off his angular face. In repose, his features were almost austere.

The sleeves of his shirt were rolled up to his elbows, and his forearms were tanned and lightly covered with hair. She felt a funny sensation in her stomach and sucked in a sharp breath. Wow. Sexual attraction. She'd almost forgotten what it felt like.

She hadn't been on a date in far too long, and it was a darned shame and a miscarriage of romantic justice. She wasn't any less deserving of love and sex than the next woman. She had needs. Wants. Desires. Plenty of them. She was a seething cauldron of hunger at times. Like when the moon was full and the scent of gardenias filled the air and soft music played on the stereo.

And it didn't help that her two cousins practically radiated sexual satisfaction every day now. She had to grit her teeth and smile and try to pretend that she wasn't the least bit envious of the fact that they were getting laid. Frequently.

But was Jeannie? No. Men were usually intimidated by her looks or her brains or both. She'd learned a long time ago not to complain to other women. No one wanted to hear the beauty queen bitch about how tough it was to be pretty. Not that she'd ever actually been in a pageant.

She thought they were lame, and scholarship or no scholarship, they were simply another chance for men to objectify women. But she kept her opinions to herself. If cute girls wanted to exploit their looks, it was no skin off her nose. But she had brains in addition to her coveted cup size, and she'd much prefer to get ahead in life using her smarts and not her body.

She wasn't vain. She couldn't claim credit for the symmetry of her features and the curves of her body. They were an accident of birth, and if they occasionally got her out of a traffic ticket or guaranteed her fast service at a bar, it was nothing she did on purpose.

Men were another story, though. She'd developed breasts in the eighth grade, and ever since, her sexuality had been a curse.

Guys looked at her and saw a party girl. The fact that their image of her was totally false meant nothing. It wasn't until they went out with her a couple of times and realized she wasn't some simpering playdate ready to spread her legs on cue that they decided the chase was too much effort.

Nice guys didn't even bother. And that pissed her off. A lot. Where was it written that a decent, average-looking guy couldn't hook up with a pretty blonde? She was willing to bet that there had been a thousand guys whose company she might have enjoyed that had simply never gotten up the courage to ask her out.

In her twenties she had downplayed her sex-kitten looks deliberately, hoping to come across less as Marilyn Monroe and more like the girl next door. But it didn't work, so she'd finally said to heck with it and had reverted to wearing the clothes she liked.

When Elizabeth called five years ago with the offer to join her and Diana and make Lotions and Potions a reality, Jeannie had been one semester and a half dissertation away from finishing her doctorate in chemistry. But it had been a fight every step of the way.

Not that the academics were beyond her. Her damned IQ was disgustingly high. But at that point, she was already fed up with trying to live down her big-boobed blonde image and trying to prove that she had brains. So she walked away . . . and that was that. Not finishing something she started left a bad taste in her mouth, but Elizabeth's proposition was too exciting to pass up.

And frankly, Jeannie was heartsick. Even with a degree, would she ever be allowed to fit in at the doctoral level in *any* academic community? She had a sinking feeling that her looks would always be judged first and any credentials she possessed would be secondary.

Becoming part of this new business venture with her two

cousins had been and still was the most professionally rewarding thing she had ever done. And if there were days when she
thought wistfully of her almost-but-not-quite doctorate, she tried
not to let it bring her down. Though the chances were slim, she
might go back one day.

The mysterious man in the shop had worked his way closer
to the front, and now he was giving her the occasional sideways
glance. She frowned slightly. He looked familiar somehow. Was
he a regular customer? She didn't think so. But she had a fairly
good memory for faces, and something about his was ringing a
bell.

Finally, he got close enough that she decided to greet him.
She stepped out from behind the counter. "May I help you?"

He looked straight at her for the first time, and she shivered
inwardly. His eyes were a dark gray-blue . . . intense, piercing.
And a small scar high on his right cheekbone gave character to a
face that was classically handsome. Straight nose, firm jaw, aris-
tocratic forehead.

She was the tiniest bit rattled, but she didn't let on. She gave
him an encouraging grin. "Do you need help finding anything?"

Nathan felt the impact of her smile in the pit of his stomach and
then quickly lower. She was stunning. He'd had only a passing
glimpse of her the one and only other time he had been in the
store. But even that quick sighting had made a deep impression.

Now the full effect threatened to rock him back on his heels.
This woman was the kind of female whose beauty launched
ships, sent soldiers off into battle, inspired sonnets.

He cleared his throat. Spouted his carefully prepared pretense for being there. "I'm allergic to bee stings, and a friend told
me that one of your products serves as a natural repellent. I'd like
to buy some."

Immediately her smile dimmed, replaced by a sincere look
of concern. "That is so dangerous. But yes . . . we do have some-

thing. I'm assuming you keep a sting kit handy." Her arm brushed his as she passed him, and his heart jerked in his chest.

He followed her like a puppy, trying not to notice that the back view of her was every bit as luscious as the front. Long, slender legs, a rounded ass that flared from a narrow waist. She was a walking wet dream. A centerfold in the flesh. He hurt just looking at her.

She turned suddenly and he nearly rocketed into her. She smiled faintly. "Sorry. This is what your friend was probably talking about. It actually serves as a very effective repellent across the board."

He took the pink tube from her warm, slender fingers and stared at it blindly. They were standing so close he could feel the heat of her body . . . could smell the faint fragrance of lilacs on her skin.

He swallowed hard, trying to remember why he had come here. "I'll take it," he said, hearing the annoying squeak in his voice and wincing inwardly. Was he destined to make a fool of himself in front of this incredible woman? Probably so.

He followed her to the cash register and paid for the cream. When she handed him his change, a receipt, and the small floral paper bag, he took it automatically, managing not to gasp when their hands touched.

Her gaze was on his face, and she was probably wondering if he was mentally challenged. He was botching this errand badly. And that wasn't acceptable. He had to know the truth at all costs, or else his sanity would be in question.

He twisted the top of the bag in his hands. "You're Jeannie— is that right?"

Her smile warmed him through and through, and she seemed pleased that he knew her name. "Yes," she said softly. "Jeannie Killaney. And you are . . . ?"

Even the lift in her pretty eyebrow was sexy. He spread his legs a bit and stiffened his knees. He hadn't been this nervous since his first lecture as a grad assistant. He managed to look straight at her without blushing. "Nathan Hardison. I'm fairly new in town."

She put her hands in the pockets of her skirt, making the neckline of her dress shift just a tad. If that subtle movement had been geological, entire continents would have collided.

She cocked her head. "Well, welcome, Mr. Nathan Hardison. I hope you like it here."

With her as a resident? Damn straight. He crumpled the bag between his sweaty palms and blurted out his request. "I need to speak with you. In private. Could we possibly step outside for a moment? Take a walk, maybe? I'm not a stalker," he said hastily. "I swear. I'm not trying to pick you up or ask for a date. I won't keep you long."

Her eyes narrowed, and now she assessed him from head to toe. He felt woefully unprepared for the silent inspection, and it was a good bet that he didn't measure up. But she shocked him.

She wrapped her arms around herself, causing her bountiful cleavage to deepen. Now her smile was mocking. "It's okay if it *is* a date," she said softly. "I wouldn't mind."

While his brain analyzed that shocking statement, his tongue ran away with him, making ill-advised conversation without a filter. "It's not," he insisted. "Not at all. Just conversation. We could grab a drink. In the park. In public."

Her good humor fled. "Fine," she said dryly. "I get the point. It's not a date. And if it's so all-fired important, then yeah . . . I'll take a walk with you."

He glanced at his watch. "Now?" He had the craziest impression that he had hurt her feelings, and he felt lower than dirt. No one should do anything but admire this lovely woman from afar and give her anything and everything her heart desired.

He watched as she had a brief low-voiced conversation with another saleslady, and then she turned back to him. "Okay. Let's do this."

Immediately his cock and balls voted a fervent yes. He ground his teeth, clenched his jaw, and bit out a heartfelt curse beneath his breath. Nathan Hardison was in trouble, no doubt about it.

They had their first argument at the beverage kiosk. She wanted to pay for her own drink. He said no.

She glared at him. "This is not a date," she reminded him with silky tones.

He handed the guy a twenty. "Then call it a business meeting," he muttered.

They walked the two blocks to the park in silence. Once there, he looked around for a deserted bench. Sadly, there were none. It was a beautiful day, and they weren't the only ones who had decided to enjoy the perfect weather.

Jeannie left him standing on the sidewalk and wandered over to a flat, comfy spot beneath the shade of an oak tree. He hastened after her, watching mesmerized as she sank to the ground and modestly tucked her smooth, flowing skirt around her knees.

He joined her, frowning. "Won't you get grass stains on your dress?"

She took a long sip of her lemonade and somehow managed to leave a glistening drop of it on her lower lip. He wanted badly to lick it away.

She shrugged. "It will wash out. Life's short. Don't you know that, Mr. Nathan Hardison?"

He knew she was taunting him, and he despaired of ever getting the upper hand. She made his skin itch and his scalp tighten. He wasn't used to being around a woman who was so . . . well, everything. He stumbled as he squatted beside her and then nearly spilled his root beer down her bosom.

Only her quick action saved them both. She took the drink from his hand and tugged his arm. "Oh, good grief. Sit down before you hurt someone, Nathan."

Hearing her say his name made him weak. And that was somewhat of a miracle, since as recently as six months ago he'd been on the brink of becoming an engaged man.

He closed his eyes briefly, feeling the residual frustration, anger, and shame. What an idiot he had been. He deserved everything they said about him. And more.

Jeannie finished her drink and leaned back on her hands, studying the branches overhead. "So tell me, Mr. Hardison, what brings you to Asheville?"

He managed to swallow a mouthful without choking. "I'll be taking a position at WCU this fall. But for the spring and summer I'm doing some consulting work for the North Carolina Arboretum."

She sat up and tucked her arms around her knees, her long-lashed eyes lighting up. "How interesting. What's your background?"

He mutilated the empty plastic cup in his hands and stared at it. Looking straight at Jeannie made him forget how to string words together. "I did my doctoral work in biology and ecology at the University of Virginia. Then I taught for a few years in southern Ohio."

"Were you tenured?"

It was a commonplace question. No reason to think she was fishing. He shifted uneasily, embarrassment like a tight wad in his stomach. "No. Close, but not quite. It wasn't a good match, so I moved on."

He had figured out already that she was sharp. He could see the questions in her eyes, so he bumped the conversation along. He had no desire to rehash the last year of his life. He dredged up a smile. "How about you?"

Little pieces of sun rays had sneaked though the leafy canopy overhead and were dappling her with shards of warm light. He'd never seen skin so soft and smooth and perfect. Her eyes were the most amazing shade of rich chocolate brown. And her lips were painted a soft rosy pink.

If he were an artist, he would paint her exactly as she looked right now: relaxed, smiling, ready for an afternoon of lovemaking. *Whoa. Bad idea.*

Not the sex . . . but definitely the trip down imagination lane. He didn't need a boner. Not now. Not when they had barely met.

He realized she had been talking for several minutes, and he jerked his attention back to the present and listened carefully as she continued.

". . . so Elizabeth gets credit for the original idea, but we all developed the business and got it started. We've been here five years."

He nodded, wondering what her bra looked like. Was it one of those lacy, naughty ones, or did she need something more utilitarian to support her ample breasts?

Thinking about her naked body was getting him nowhere. Or at least nowhere it was smart to go. He cleared his throat. "It's a great store."

She brushed an ant from her sleeve and gave him an exasperated shake of her head. "I don't mean to be rude, Nathan, but we've been here forty-five minutes and you've yet to tell me what's so important that we needed a private conversation. And I really need to get back."

He gaped at her and then stared at his watch. He could have sworn they had been there no more than ten minutes. Had she bewitched him? "Well, I . . . uh . . ."

She rose gracefully to her feet. "Why don't you come by my house this evening? I'll fix dinner and you can tell me this big important secret."

He stood up as well and raked his hands through his hair. "You don't have to do that," he said, feeling guilty and excited all at the same time.

The twist of her mouth was wry. "Don't worry," she said. "It's not a date, I promise."

. . .

Jeannie chopped tomatoes with a ruthless, measured precision. The beginnings of her homemade spaghetti sauce bubbled on the stove, and the steamy kitchen smelled of garlic and spices.

She was mad at herself and mad at Nathan Hardison. If he had simply blurted out whatever it was he had to say, she wouldn't have given in to the temptation of inviting him to dinner. It was a rash, ill thought-out impulse. The man might have a girlfriend.

His ring finger was bare, so he was probably single, but he could conceivably have a perfectly lovely sweetheart tucked away somewhere who would not at all appreciate having Jeannie cook for her man.

Jeannie tossed the tomatoes in the pot and started in on the onions. Well, that was just too damn bad. He didn't have to say yes. But in truth, she wasn't sure she had given him the option of saying no. While she jotted her street address and phone number on a scrap of napkin that had been wrapped around her drink cup, Nathan stood quietly, looking ill at ease and oddly expressionless.

Perhaps he was afraid of her. Men didn't like assertive women. She'd learned that lesson the hard way. But she wasn't kidding about having to get back to work, and he seemed in no hurry to talk about whatever it was that bothered him. So she cut to the chase.

Maybe she should have invited his mystery girlfriend. So he would feel safe. Ha. Not in this lifetime. She was deeply attracted to Nathan Hardison, and she was determined to find out if the feeling was mutual. If she sat back and waited for him to ask her out, chances were it would probably never happen.

She had left work an hour early, but even so, it was a flat-out rush to get everything ready. She scooped up the tiny pile of diced onion and added it to the mixture. Then she opened the oven and removed the perfectly browned pecan pie she had prepared earlier. It smelled even better than the main course. She set the table in her roomy kitchen. No sense in using the dining room. It had been pretty clearly established by both sides that this was *not* a date.

Even so, she used her favorite Kate Spade china with the red stripe, and she pressed real cloth napkins. No reason for Nathan Hardison to think she didn't know how to entertain. She opened two bottles of wine since she didn't know his preference, and she filled crystal goblets with ice water. Then she stood back and surveyed her table.

Flowers. She'd forgotten the flowers. She dashed out the back door and cut a cheery bouquet of red and yellow tulips. When those were arranged in a nice vase, she checked her watch, hissed in dismay, and ducked into her bedroom to change into a simple ivory linen sheath.

She was already wearing her favorite diamond-stud earrings, so she left it at that, ran a brush through her hair, and spritzed a quick dash of perfume at her throat and wrists. Her pulse was racketing away, and she was breathless for no good reason.

This was so stupid. She lectured herself as she put the finishing touches on her dinner. She didn't even know the man. And he had been insultingly clear about the no-date thing. But she couldn't help it. He excited her. And she wanted that wonderfully fizzy feeling to last for as long as possible.

The spinach salad and crusty bread were no trouble at all. Everything was ready and waiting ten minutes before he rang her doorbell. She would only need four or five minutes to cook the pasta later. She smoothed her damp palms down her hips, fluffed her hair, and went to let him in.

Nathan's collar was tight, and he wondered despairingly if putting on a tie had been the correct way to go. But he was having dinner with a beautiful woman, and it seemed the least he could do.

When Jeannie Killaney left him standing in the city park, his composure in shreds and his brain mush, it was a good five minutes before he'd been able to gather himself together and walk back to his car.

Something about the woman dazzled him, made him a stuttering, sweaty-palmed embarrassment to his gender. But good Lord, he had just cause. She was sexy with a capital *S*. Her easy smile, her husky voice, and the way her hair bounced around her shoulders like it had a mind of its own. She was so damn . . . alive.

That was the best explanation he could come up with. And her natural sensuality made a man's thoughts go straight to rumpled sheets, sweaty bodies, and long hours of screwing. He shivered despite the warm spring evening.

He didn't even know himself. As a rule, he was extremely comfortable in almost any social situation. He was accustomed to lecturing in front of a hundred or more undergrads. He'd presented papers at conferences. He wasn't a shy, klutzy moron. So it was disconcerting to realize that Jeannie Killaney had the power to reduce him to the equivalent of a stammering thirteen-year-old boy.

Why had she invited him to dinner? True, he had been slow to spit out what he wanted to talk about. But that didn't mean she had to be so nice about it. There was no reason at all for her to open her personal life to him . . . unless she wanted to know him better.

Wow. Was that egotistical or what? She probably could have any guy on the planet, married or not. No red-blooded male would be able to say no to her. Unless he was already deeply involved with another woman. And even then, he might be tempted.

Jeannie Killaney was a woman in a million. Of course, on closer acquaintance she might turn out to be a disappointment. There was no guarantee she was fun to be with. After all, you couldn't have sex twenty-four/seven. There were more mundane things like shared interests: conversation, recreation, procreation.

Whoops . . . scratch that last one. He couldn't think about Jeannie pregnant, or his johnson would never behave.

He looked at his surroundings for a few minutes, hoping to capture some kind of composure. He liked her Colonial two-story brick with the blue shutters. It was neat and welcoming. Her yard was pretty as well, though he could certainly help her with a bit of landscaping. Perhaps some forsythia in that corner.

Damn. He was doing it again. Mentally weaving himself into her life. Stupid, stupid, stupid. He leaned his forehead against her front door and banged it gently on the polished wood. His recent track record with women said he didn't know shit about how to see through the crap to the real female beneath.

So he needed to tread with caution.

He straightened his spine and reached out to press the doorbell.

Two

*J*eannie breathed a sigh of relief when she opened the door and saw him there. Number one, because she had been afraid he might not show. And number two, because he had the same effect on her libido as he had this morning.

She wanted to drag him straight up the stairs to her quiet, dimly lit bedroom and have her way with him. She held out her hand just for the hell of it, wanting to touch him again.

He squeezed her fingers and released them rapidly. Did he feel the same shock of heat lightning that made her nipples perk and her throat go dry?

She backed into the house, allowing him to close the door. She felt jittery and excited, and this might all be for nothing.

She blurted out her foremost thought with an appalling lack of manners. "Do you have a girlfriend?"

He blinked, caught off guard in his inspection of her home. "Um, no."

Jeannie smiled brightly. "Good. I wouldn't want her to get

the wrong idea. Not that this is a date. I know it's not . . . but still . . ."

He didn't say a word in response to her rambling, overly chirpy monologue.

She motioned to the living room. "Have a seat. Pour yourself a glass of wine. I need to check on one thing in the oven, and I'll be right back."

She bolted down the hall and into the kitchen, leaning against the refrigerator in order to catch her breath. God, she was being a total airhead. No wonder people made dumb-blonde jokes.

She went to the sink and ran cold water over the backs of her wrists. She dried them with a dishtowel and took several long, slow breaths. If she wanted to get to know Nathan Hardison, she needed to calm down.

And there was still his curious errand to ponder. It was a measure of how much she responded to his quiet masculinity that she kept forgetting about his secretive mission. His reason for seeking her out.

She smoothed her hair with her hands and went to join him. She found him standing, studying her bookshelves, glass of wine in hand.

He turned when she entered and cocked an eyebrow. "Interesting collection you have here. And I'm guessing I'm not the only one in the room with an academic background. Organic chemistry maybe?"

She sat down on the sofa and crossed her legs, gratified when his gaze went to her knees and then quickly back to her face. She spread one arm along the back of the seat. "Very good, Sherlock. Any other dark secrets about me you've ferreted out?"

He remained standing, which for some reason made her feel small and feminine and deliciously vulnerable. He smiled, and it brought a wicked charm to his face. "I gather you're a Stephen King fan."

She chuckled. "That's not so hard to guess."

"And you have a fondness for English history."

"Guilty."

"And you enjoy the Romantic poets."

She felt her cheeks flush. "On occasion." She patted the cushion beside her. "Why don't you sit down? Dinner will be another fifteen minutes." A lie, but a girl needed to pace herself.

He joined her, and she caught the smell of woodsy aftershave. He had an easy strength about him that she liked. Men who continually tried to prove how macho they were always seemed silly and pretentious to her. But she sensed that Nathan was a rock. A steady presence you could rely on in a crisis or a storm.

He set his empty glass on the table beside him and sighed. "I suppose you're wondering why I sought you out."

"I was hoping it was my charm and personality," she said, batting her eyes theatrically.

He grinned. "I'll plead the fifth on that one."

"Party pooper." She pretended to pout, enjoying the gentle flirtation.

His hands lay palm down on his thighs, drawing her attention inexorably to his muscular legs, as well as to his sexy arms. Some women might go for the nice ass and the pecs . . . but even though Nathan had nothing to be ashamed of in those areas, she had always been seduced by the look of a man's hands.

Nathan's fingers were nice . . . long and tanned and perfect for cupping a woman's—

He unwittingly interrupted her flight of fancy. "Something strange has been happening to me, and I have to know if you have any clues as to why."

She jerked her gaze away from the area below his waist and tried to be a good hostess. "Strange?" His jaw was smooth. He must have shaved right before coming over.

"Jeannie. Are you listening to me?"

She stood up abruptly, needing some space between her and

temptation. She nodded. "I'm hanging on your every word. Go for it."

He dropped his head, staring at the design in her ruby-and-indigo Oriental rug. His voice was low and rough with some unnamed emotion. "I've been dreaming about you. Every night for the last three weeks."

Her hand clenched around the slender wine goblet. "Come again?"

He lifted his eyes to hers, and in his gaze, she saw reluctant embarrassment and genuine bafflement. "I don't understand it. I've only laid eyes on you one time before today. And yet at night in my head, we—"

She put a hand on the floor-to-ceiling bookcase to steady herself. "We what?" she asked urgently.

His face flushed a dull red, and she reeled inwardly. Good Lord, first Diana's and Elizabeth's whirlwind romances and now this. It couldn't be true . . . could it? Was that mixture they concocted really magic?

Then she stopped her mental train wreck and snapped back into the Jeannie who believed in science and not foolish fancy.

"Never mind," she said quickly. "Forget I asked." She sat down on the piano bench and faced him. "I think I know why you've been having those dreams," she said simply, keeping her voice even.

Hope and relief marked his face and he sat up straight. "You do?" She could see how badly he wanted to hear her explanation.

She nodded slowly. "You must be as attracted to me as I am to you."

Nathan wanted to slap the side of his head to stop the ringing in his ears. Surely she hadn't said what he thought she said. Although it made sense . . . at least the part about him being attracted. He was. Definitely. And it only took one brief sighting several weeks ago to imprint her image on his subconscious.

And then he processed the remainder of her sentence. His eyes widened and he swallowed hard. "You're attracted to me?" Even as he said the words out loud, they sounded like some weird foreign language. In his world, the gorgeous starlets did not hook up with the geeky professors.

He jerked to his feet and removed his weak, susceptible male self to the other side of the room. She watched him with a small smile that made the hair on the back of his neck stand up.

"Yes," she said softly. "I am definitely attracted to you. Is there a problem with that?"

He ran his finger beneath his collar, wishing like hell that he hadn't worn the constricting necktie. "No," he muttered. "No problem.

She joined him, coming so near he felt perilously close to grabbing her and devouring those full, pouty lips. Just when he thought she was going to lean forward and kiss him, she brushed his forearm with her fingers and turned away. "Come into my kitchen . . ."

The old spider-and-fly verse came to mind, but he followed her blindly, drawn in her wake by a powerful beam of lust that held him captive but willing.

If he hadn't already fallen under her spell, dinner would have done the trick. A brilliant, gorgeous woman who liked to cook. He must have stumbled into another dimension, and he sure as hell didn't want to go back to the real world anytime soon . . . not when this one was fulfilling every one of his fantasies.

Over spaghetti and meat sauce, they sparred verbally, flirted shamelessly, and felt each other out in the literary sense. Their politics were the same, though their views on a few issues differed.

She dazzled him. No woman he knew had such a grasp of currents events or such an appreciation for the nuances of global policies that were of concern to a scientist.

They went from topic to topic seamlessly, and under it all ran a slow, heated current of sexual interest. He studied her face and couldn't find a single flaw. Her only imperfection was that she rooted for the wrong baseball team.

She was an Orioles fan. He backed the Reds.

It might have been hours or days that they sat at her table. If he weren't an educated man, he would have sworn that some kind of magic drifted in the air.

When the two candles between them sputtered and went out, he glanced at his watch. "Damn, it's midnight."

She looked at him from beneath her lashes. "Do you turn into a pumpkin or something?"

He grinned. "I was hoping more for the handsome-prince role."

She widened her eyes and sat back in her chair. "Too bad this isn't a date," she drawled.

His penis flexed and twitched and pleaded for action. "Why exactly is that?"

She shrugged. "If this was our first date, you might kiss me good night . . . or even—"

He leaned forward urgently. "Even what?" He interrupted her without compunction.

Her slim fingers played with a table knife, drawing patterns in the cloth. She met his hot, eager gaze head-on, her deep brown eyes warm and full of mischief. "Ask to sleep over."

He gulped. "And what would you say to such an impertinent request?"

It was her turn to grin. "I'd tell you I don't sleep with a guy on the first date."

He grabbed her wrist, feeling the narrow bones, the soft skin. "But this isn't a date." He rubbed over her pulse with his thumb.

She stared down at their hands, his large and a bit rough, hers satin smooth. "That's true," she murmured. She looked up and caught him staring at her breasts. Then she licked her lips in an unconscious motion that cut him off at the knees.

He tightened his grasp. "I would give my right arm to share your bed tonight, but I don't want to be someone you regret in the morning." Even as he said it, he cursed his own stupid sense of honor. Women didn't expect to be treated like princesses anymore.

Hell, you'd think he'd never had a one-night stand. He was making more out of this than it warranted, for sure.

She smiled wistfully, and he could see in her face that they weren't going to be sharing a bed. Not that he was surprised. Despite the nuclear proportions of the heat flaring between them, he sensed that Jeannie Killaney was a careful, analytical woman.

She cocked her head, standing up so he was forced to release her. "Why did you come in the store the first time?" she asked quietly.

The unexpected question puzzled him. He leaned back in his chair and watched her move dishes and tidy the counter. "My sister was in town helping me fix up my new place. She saw your shop and wanted to go in. Then she ended up buying me some shaving cream for my birthday."

Her head snapped around and her gaze sharpened. "Which fragrance? Was it the one with eucalyptus?"

He detected something odd in her voice and her question, but he couldn't pin it down. He nodded slowly. "Yeah, eucalyptus."

"And do you like it?"

He shrugged. "It's okay. I've been using it every day. I'm just as happy with the cheap stuff from the grocery, but I will admit that your version leaves my skin feeling good." He choked out a laugh. "This is why men don't buy or discuss beauty products. We feel ridiculous."

He rose to his feet and carried their dessert plates to where she stood.

After she put them in the dishwasher, she lifted a hand to his cheek. "It's nice to know our products are appreciated," she murmured, "even if it's reluctantly."

Before he could react, she took her hand away, and he was disappointed. He ran a single finger down her cheek. "Do you use your own concoctions?"

Her mouth opened on a little O of surprise. Perhaps she was shocked that he had taken some initiative. She shouldn't have been. He wanted badly to touch her all over.

She stood perfectly still, almost as if she were holding her breath. And she didn't say a word until he finally broke the tenuous connection and folded his arms across his chest. "Well, do you?" he said.

She nodded. "Of course." Her pupils were dilated and her chest rose and fell as though her breathing was ragged. She looked around the kitchen blankly. "Would you like another cup of coffee before you go . . . or a nightcap?" Her voice was soft and low. The prosaic question sounded like an invitation to bed.

He quit second-guessing himself and pulled her into his embrace. "What I'd like," he said quietly, "is a good night kiss."

Jeannie felt his arms tighten around her. There was nothing tentative or shy about the way he held her. Her breasts flattened against his chest, and their legs tangled. He bent his head and covered her lips gently, his kiss firm and sure. She tasted her pie on his tongue, and it was amazingly erotic. He tightened his grip. The bottom of her stomach fell out, just like that moment a roller coaster crests the top. She shivered.

It wasn't the kiss of two people who had met for the first time only that morning. It was a yearning, breathless kiss, all groans and trembling and jerky heartbeats.

She wasn't sure who pulled away first. Probably not her. She would have happily gone on kissing him until her lips and legs went numb.

He cleared his throat, looking as shocked and scattered as she felt. He ran a hand through his hair. "Well . . . okay then."

She straightened his tie as best she could. It looked like he had been attacked. "Drive safely." She barely heard her inane words. His chest was hard and warm beneath her fingers. She wanted to stroke him and grab him by the tie and drag him up the stairs.

They were standing in her front hallway. Nathan allowed her restless hands to touch him for several more moments, and then he put his hands in his pockets and jingled his keys. It was difficult to keep her hands above his waist.

Finally he captured both of her wrists in his big hands. "Stop, Jeannie." The words were gruff, but not unkind.

She looked up at him. His eyes were dark, and a red flush covered his cheekbones. His lips were a sensual slash above his firm jaw.

He sighed and dropped his forehead to hers. "How do you feel about painting?"

She blinked, confused by his question and turned on by the way his firm grip held her captive. "I can sketch a little bit, if that's what you mean."

He chuckled. "I meant walls. Mine. I made the mistake of letting my baby sister go hog wild with her decorating skills, and she insists that my guest room needs two coats of maritime blue before she can finish."

She tugged halfheartedly at her wrists, but he didn't release her. For some reason, that made her hot. She was one messed-up female. "So you're asking me to do physical labor?" It wasn't her fault that the word *physical* came out sounding so sexy.

She felt him shudder. "Yeah. This Saturday. Then I could take you out to the arboretum and show you the bonsai exhibit."

She tilted back her head and their lips met by accident. Or at least, that was her theory. His mouth moved over hers urgently, hungrily. Then he released her and stepped back with a muttered curse. "Enough, Jeannie."

She managed to look innocent. "Sorry. Guess you'd better go."

He glared at her. "You're not helping matters."

She glanced deliberately at the front of his slacks, where an eager erection tented the cloth. "I suppose not."

He reached behind him to open the door, as if he needed an escape route. "So you agree?"

She raised her eyebrows. "Hard work and tiny trees? How could a girl refuse?"

He laughed. "Go ahead. Make fun of me. I'm a science geek. I'll be the first to admit it." Then his face softened. "But I have a feeling it takes one to know one." He pulled a card from his pocket and wrote something on it. "Here's my e-mail. Let me know if you're free. I'll swing by and pick you up around nine."

Nathan kicked himself all the way home. Was he totally out of his mind? Any normal guy would have invited her out for dinner and a movie. But not Nathan. No, sir. He'd press-ganged her into working for him, and then dangled a nature outing in front of her.

It would be a miracle if she even took the time to write him a Dear John letter in cyberspace.

But even though his dick was aching, he felt better than he had in a long time. Jeannie Killaney was an amazing woman, and for some inexplicable reason, she seemed to like him. And maybe . . . if the gods were kind . . . he might actually convince her to wind up in his bed.

Jeannnie floated through the next several days, and she was not at all a *floaty* kind of person. She wanted to regale Elizabeth and Diana with tales of her newfound hottie, but at the same time, she wanted to keep Nathan a secret, her own, private, can't-wait-to-see-what-happens-next secret.

By the time she knocked on his front door on Saturday

morning, she was fully aware that she was bound to be disappointed. And as insurance, she had insisted on driving herself rather than allowing him to pick her up. The other day had been an aberration. That kind of connection was very likely a mirage in her sexual desert.

She had replayed their nondate again and again in her mind, and clearly, abstinence and a bad case of horniness were to blame for her intense response to a man she barely knew. Animal attraction was not to be trusted.

She had been around the block a few times, and she was not easily impressed. But something about Nathan made her feel like a teenage girl, all sighs and fluttery anticipation. It was disconcerting, but she was prepared to enjoy the experience for as long as it lasted.

He opened the door, and her stomach fell to her shoes. He was naked from the waist up. He had a folded navy bandanna tied around his head, and a torn, ancient pair of faded jeans hung from his hips.

His bare chest was tanned and sculpted with sleek muscles that made a woman's hands tingle with the need to touch them. Even his feet were bare, and she knew she was in deep trouble when looking at his naked toes made her weak in the knees. Good Lord, she had to get a grip.

She smiled breezily, projecting her usual confidence, even though at the moment it was a lie. "Jeannie Killaney reporting for duty. Point me toward the bedroom." She gulped when his face went blank and his cheeks flushed. He got all dark-eyed, aroused, predatory male on her, and swear to God, she hadn't meant to sound so provocative. But apparently her subconscious had other ideas.

She brushed past him and took a look at his apartment. It was clear he hadn't lived there long, but she could see signs of his designer sister's handiwork. There were a couple of pretty salmon-and-forest pillows on his leather sofa, and the walls had been done in a deep ivory with one small section painted tangerine.

It looked warm and masculine at the same time. She dropped her purse on the coffee table. "Well, when do we start?"

The look on his face said he was ready to start you-know-what at any moment. She decided to ignore the sexual vibe in the room and forge ahead. "I like your place." The tiny kitchen off to the right was compact but cheerful, and she assumed the hall led to the two bedrooms and presumably a bathroom.

He shoved his hands in his back pockets. "Thanks." He stared at her stretchy black ankle-length pants and formfitting pink knit top. "You *did* know we were painting?"

She shrugged. "Of course. These clothes are old as dirt." She had never been afraid of hard work in her life, but she also saw no point in dressing like a dockhand. A woman could be stylish in any situation if she put a bit of thought into it.

She kicked off her own shoes and took a rubber band from her pocket. With a quick twist, she put her hair up in a ponytail and then donned the Orioles baseball cap she had brought along. "Let's do this. Those bonsai trees won't wait forever."

Nathan dipped a roller in rich blue paint and tried not to stare at the dip in the rear of Jeannie's skintight pants. When she squatted to work near the baseboard, her top went up and her bottoms went down, and Nathan was privy to the most luscious strip of skin at the small of her back.

He wanted to lick his way up her spine and bend her over for a quick, hard tumble. His hand shook and he smeared paint on the white doorframe. Shit. Whose dumb-ass idea was this? Being cooped up in a ten-by-ten room all day with the woman who made his body ache was a sure recipe for frustration. The fumes must have addled his brain. Because he was actually contemplating how amenable she might be to the idea of the two of them in bed. All night. Not sleeping.

Jeannie muttered when a blob of paint landed on her narrow, elegant foot. He was at her side in moments, brandishing a damp cloth. "Let me," he said gruffly. "I'd hate to see that pretty pedicure messed up."

She sat back on her butt abruptly when he took her foot in his hand. He might as well have been stroking her bare breast. That was how hot it made him to rub the paint from her foot. Her skin and bones seemed unbearably fragile in his grasp, and her trim ankle led to her calf, which led to her thigh, which led to her—

Jeannie wiggled her leg. "That's enough, Nathan. The paint is gone." Her voice sounded breathless.

He stared at her bright pink toenails and tried to think rationally. "Right. Okay." He released her reluctantly and sat on his heels.

Jeannie had leaned back on her elbows while he cleaned her up, and her lovely breasts were thrust upward, just begging for attention. Her eyelashes were at half-mast, and he couldn't see her expression. But he did see the small spot of blue paint that sat innocently on the curve of her cleavage.

Without conscious thought, he moved over her on his knees, his thighs straddling hers. Her eyes flew open and she made a gargled kind of squeak. "Nathan?"

He was mesmerized by that little dot of cerulean on a sea of creamy white. With the one last unstained portion of his wet rag, he dabbed at her chest. Her bosom heaved and he thought he heard her moan.

He rubbed slowly, his fingertips grazing the cleft where her plump, beautiful tits pressed together. God, he wanted to peel away her top and scoop those incredible curves into his hands and—

"Nathan." She might have said his name more than once. He wasn't sure.

He tossed the rag aside and looked down to meet her gaze.

What he saw in her eyes made every centimeter of his body tighten in fierce, desperate hunger. He slid his hands into her hair and cupped her head, lifting her into his embrace. The ball cap fell to the floor. Her hands came up to his shoulders, and at first he couldn't tell if she was pushing him away or hanging on.

Maybe she couldn't either, because when he found her mouth with his and took it in a gentle kiss, she whimpered and groaned almost as if it pained her to feel his need.

They kissed slowly, but there was nothing tentative about it. They were ravenous, seeking, far past where they should have been on such short acquaintance. It was as though he had come out of a deep, debilitating fog and found his way home. It felt so damned right.

Who knew what might have happened next? But it remained a mystery, because he cursed like a sailor when the cell phone in his pocket rang with shrill insistence.

Jeannie had the gall to laugh as he scowled at the number on the screen and flipped open the phone. "What?" He barked at his sister and then had to apologize.

He scowled when Jeannie scooted out from between his legs and escaped from the room. He dragged his attention back to his caller. "This had better be important."

Three

Jeannie stood in Nathan's small bathroom and stared in the mirror. What in the devil was going on? There was no way in hell that she and her cousins had concocted some sort of potent aphrodisiac. It was illogical. It wasn't believable. It wasn't scientific.

Yet what other explanation could there be? Nathan and she were like oppositely charged magnets. Get them close to each other and suddenly they were lip-locked. Geez . . . he must think she was the easiest woman on the planet. Kiss her once and she was ready to do the horizontal hokeypokey. And she didn't even know his middle name or his favorite color or his shoe size.

She did know his preference in underwear, though. Those damn jeans fell so low on his lean hips that she'd been faced all morning with a tantalizing view of the waistband of a pair of white boxers. White. Plain. Utilitarian. Nothing at all sexy about them.

But tell that to her recalcitrant female parts. They were all dancing the mambo and preparing to break a long, frustrating man fast. Unless Jeannie could find a way to slow things down.

Perhaps she should just come right out and confess that the shaving cream he had been using might be responsible for his inexplicable dreams and the incendiary lust between the two of them.

Yeah, right. And then she could watch his eyes glaze over while he called for the men in white coats to take her away. The man was a scientist. So was she. They both lived and died by the scientific method.

It was far too soon to chance a *Gee, you're never gonna believe this* explanation. Better to let things progress on their own.

She washed her hands and face and put the ball cap back on her head. It was sprinkled with pinpoints of blue, and a long stripe of color ran from her earlobe down the side of her neck. She remembered scratching an itch, which probably accounted for that one.

Unfortunately, in addition to the spot Nathan had cleaned from her breast, another very obvious smudge decorated her shirt right above the left nipple. She tried to remove the paint with a damp tissue, but that only made a big wet spot right in the middle of her boob.

Finally she gave up and headed back out to face the music. She found Nathan securing masking tape around the window frame. She watched him for a moment, enjoying the play of muscles in his back as he stretched to reach the edge near the ceiling.

He grunted in frustration when he realized he couldn't quite do it. He grabbed the ladder and dragged it into place. It wobbled wildly when he stepped up on it, and Jeannie ran forward.

"I'll hold it steady," she said. "Where did you get this piece of junk, anyway?"

He looked down at her. "I got it out of the Dumpster," he said sheepishly. "It didn't look so bad until I got it inside. And besides, I have a perfectly good ladder in storage back in Ohio. I just haven't had a chance to move the last of my stuff yet."

Her eyes were on a level with his ass as he worked, and she stood patiently, enjoying the view. She managed not to cop a feel, and it didn't hurt that her hands were occupied holding the sides of the ladder.

She grinned, knowing he couldn't see her. And then her inherent nosiness reared its head. "So you never did tell me why you left Ohio."

He tensed. It was hard to miss, as close as she was to him. She heard him sigh, and then he finally answered her. "It's a long story."

She handed him a second roll of tape when his ran out. "I'm not going anywhere."

He finished taping and jumped down after warning her to get out of the way. Then he picked up his pan and roller and went right back to where he had been working earlier. He ignored her completely, his eyes on the wall. But eventually the story unfolded.

"I was there for seven years, three as an adjunct and four more as assistant professor. I *was* on tenure track, but I had mixed feelings about it, even before the incident that forced me to leave."

She decided not to interrupt with annoying questions. Men hated that. So she waited semipatiently, and he finally kept talking.

"One of our female PE professors went on maternity leave at the beginning of the last fall semester. They hired several people to fill in on a part-time basis, and then found someone locally to take over the aerobics classes for about eight weeks. The new woman was very attractive and had a great personality. The students loved her."

Jeannie hated her on the spot.

He bent to get more paint and kept going. "I wasn't dating anyone at the time, and she was very cute. A couple of my good friends had married recently, and I was feeling like the odd man out. I was lonely, too, I guess. So we started dating."

"How did it go?" Try as she might, she couldn't bite back her question.

Again, she saw him tense. "Pretty well, at first. I tend to be too serious sometimes, and she was so bubbly and fun that I thought it was a good match. But it was a small town, and pretty soon, everyone was teasing us about wedding bells. All I wanted to do was go out with someone on a casual basis and not feel like a fifth wheel when I was socializing with my friends."

Did you have sex with the bubbly woman? Jeannie would have given just about anything to hear the answer to that, but even she wasn't that brazen. She dragged her attention back to his story.

He was attacking the wall now with broad, forceful slaps of the roller. "Someone saw me in the jewelry store buying a gift for my sister's birthday. Before you knew it, the rumor was all over town that I was going to propose."

"And you didn't want to?" Well, heck. A question popped out anyway.

He sighed, loud enough for her to hear. "I thought about it once or twice. I wasn't getting any younger, and she seemed like a nice, sweet girl. Someone I could imagine growing old with. But then she went out of town for a week, and when she came back, everything went to hell almost overnight."

"What happened?" Jeannie had ceased painting, just so she could concentrate on Nathan's story. She could imagine him lecturing in front of a classroom of young people. He had a pleasant voice and an easy way of speaking that sure as heck kept her attention.

He finished the wall he was working on and started edging paint around the window with a small paintbrush. He stopped suddenly, and she was shocked at the flash of bleak humor that darted across his face.

He looked straight at her and grimaced. "She told everyone who would listen that she had been abducted by aliens, and they had taken her to their spaceship and performed experiments on her body."

Jeannie burst out laughing and then realized uneasily that Nathan's face was sober. She bit her lip. "I'm sorry. I thought you were kidding."

"I wish to God I was. Needless to say, the story spread like wildfire. The radio station picked it up first. Then local TV and, finally, one of the lesser-known tabloids. I was horrified and quite honestly deeply concerned that she needed immediate psychiatric help. But she loved all the interviews and the attention, craved it in fact, and even when we were alone, I couldn't make her crack. She swore it was the truth."

Jeannie touched his arm. "How awful, Nathan."

He scowled at the wall. "You can't imagine. I knew it was over between us. The woman was a nutcase. But I felt responsible somehow, and no one else seemed to care that her story was a cry for help. And then it got worse."

"What do you mean?"

"The head of my department called me into his office and told me that my close association with such an obviously deluded young woman reflected poorly on me as a professor and on the department and the school. He threatened me none too subtly about the possibility of my never getting tenure, and I got so pissed that I walked out."

She winced theatrically. "I'm guessing that didn't go over well."

"Not hardly. But I had to deal with the circus that my life had become. I managed to contact her parents, who came and packed her up lock, stock and barrel and took her home to Florida. She'd been missing for nine months, and they hadn't been able to trace her to Ohio. When it was all over, I went back to the department head and told him I was resigning effective the first of the year."

Even though progress on Jeannie's wall had slowed considerably, they were virtually finished by this time. Her stomach growled loudly, and finally, Nathan's expression lightened.

"C'mon," he said, wiping his hands on yet another rag. "Let's eat some lunch."

He insisted on fixing her a peanut butter sandwich, and she didn't have the heart to tell him she hated the stuff. But she chewed and swallowed anyway, her soft heart feeling for what he had been forced to endure. Embarrassment. Sadness. Starting over.

She took a sip of her milk, the only beverage he had in his fridge, and couldn't resist hearing the end of his tale. "That took guts . . . quitting, I mean. I know how sticky it can be to get tenure."

He passed her a bag of chips. "It wasn't as reckless as it sounds. I had known for some time that I wasn't a good fit there. Luckily for me, I had a small legacy from my grandmother to tide me over. So at least I knew I wasn't going to starve. It gave me the luxury of looking around for a position that really excited me."

"And you think WCU is it?"

He grinned, and this time it reached his beautiful blue-gray eyes. "Oh, yeah. North Carolina is definitely growing on me."

They washed all the brushes and rollers together, side by side at his kitchen sink. As the streams of blue water disappeared down the drain, Jeannie realized that she could never tell him the silly tale about a moonlit night and a weird mixture and a trio of sudden, unlikely romances. That information would go with her to the grave.

He'd been with one woman who made up unbelievable stories. . . . Jeannie wasn't about to risk seeing the look on his face if she shared her suspicions that his shaving cream might be infused with a mysterious aphrodisiac. He would probably run for the hills, and she liked him far too much to see that happen. Maybe it was the kind of anecdote they could laugh about one day in the future, the distant future . . . when their children were grown and she and Nathan were in their rockers on the front porch.

For now she had other things on her mind. She glanced down at her shirt and pants, ruefully aware that she was pretty much covered in dried paint. "We'd better postpone that trip to the arboretum," she said. "Neither of us is fit to go out in public."

Nathan dried his hands on a dish towel and leaned against the kitchen counter. "We could go tonight. After dark. Then it wouldn't matter."

She frowned. "But they lock the gates at closing, and I'm not into climbing fences or getting arrested."

He chuckled. "Where's your sense of adventure?" Then he held up his hands. "Just kidding. I have a key. One of the perks of being on staff at the moment."

She thought about wandering in the moonlight with Nathan as her guide. The idea had a certain appeal. "It's a deal. I guess I'll go home now and get some stuff done in the meantime."

Nathan took her arm and pulled her into the V of his legs. "Not so fast. I have a question."

He studied her face to gauge her reaction. She was warm and pliant in his arms and seemed entirely happy to be there. He liked the way her body curved into his so naturally . . . as though her subconscious was ready for something that her lips might not be willing to admit yet.

He tugged off her ball cap and loosened her ponytail until her hair once again fell soft and bouncy at her shoulders. He sifted his fingers through it.

She watched him with a small, secretive smile on her face. He would give a lot to know what she was thinking. He tucked a strand of golden hair behind her ear. "So here's my question."

She put a hand on his chest, not stroking, just touching his skin. Then she nuzzled her nose against his collarbone. "Spit it out, Nathan."

He sucked in a sharp breath when he could swear her lips

grazed his nipple. He swallowed hard, his thought process fuzzy. "How many dates does it take for you to be comfortable going to bed with a man?"

She hooked her thumbs in the belt loops at the back of his jeans. "No hard-and-fast rule."

He cupped her ass. There should have been a panty line under those figure-molding pants, but all he felt was warm, resilient flesh. "Does today count as a date?"

She shook her head. "Definitely not."

He frowned. "And why is that?"

Her hair tickled his skin as she rubbed up against him like a cat. "I didn't shave my legs."

That surprised him enough to make him laugh. "I'm not sure I follow."

She tilted her head back, her eyes brimming with mischief and humor. "If a woman doesn't shave her legs, that means she's not planning on even the possibility of sex. And if the possibility of sex doesn't exist, even hypothetically, then it's not a date."

"I see." He fell silent, trying to sift through the female logic. He understood the parameters of scientific logic, but this was another thing entirely. He kissed the top of her head, but softly, so she wouldn't notice. "Did you know that guys don't really give a shit about that shaved-leg business?"

She wiggled free of his arms and faced him. "Well, they should." She was indignant, and it made him smile.

He tried not to notice that her nipples were poking through the thin fabric of her shirt. "But what if a man seduces you against your will and you haven't shaved your legs. What then?"

Her eyes narrowed. "I am a mature, experienced, modern woman. I decide when and where I plan to have sex."

He snagged her wrists and pulled her back into his arms. "Is that so?" he muttered softly. And then he set about helping her make a decision.

Jeannie was in way over her head. Nathan's effect on her libido was insidious and impossible to ignore. He made her hot and weak and excited all at the same time. He had given up on gentlemanly, tender kisses and gone straight to shuck-your-panties carnal.

She gasped when he slid his hands inside the back of her pants and squeezed her butt. Then he turned her sideways and used one hand to do the same thing in the front. His middle finger found her clitoris and gave it a teasing stroke. She was wet already, and he had to feel the slickness beneath his fingers.

His lips brushed her ear. "You can say no anytime, Jeannie."

Say no . . . was he crazy? Her body was already racing toward an orgasm. She groaned and shuddered when his fingers met and played between her legs. Sweet God in heaven. That was her only coherent thought before her body arched and shivered in release.

He scooped her into his arms and strode toward his bedroom. She barely had time to register what was happening before he deposited her gently on the large bed and joined her.

He took her face in his hands, his eyes dark and serious. "Stop me now if you don't want this, sweetheart, because I'm going down for the count."

His hands slid beneath her shirt and squeezed her breasts. This time they both groaned . . . in unison. When she remained mute, he stripped away her top and unfastened her bra with disarming reverence. She'd never been a fan of her overgenerous breasts, but seeing the look on Nathan's face made her rethink her previous assessment.

He used his thumbs on her nipples and then bent his head. At the first tug of his teeth on her sensitive flesh, she shattered in a sharp, unexpected climax.

It was broad daylight. Her legs were unshaven, and she didn't even care.

Nathan was like a hurricane-force wind coming at her from

every direction, slow and soft for brief moments and then all passion and fury and incredible power.

He loved her breasts thoroughly before finally removing her pants and underwear. He paused a moment to tease her with the string of her thong panties. He drew it up tight, deep in the folds of her sex, and dragged it back and forth over the sensitive little nub of flesh that swelled and wept with her response.

The naughty game made her thighs clench and her hands grasp the comforter convulsively. Suddenly he snapped the fragile fabric with a deliberate motion and tossed the ruined scrap of silk aside. Before she could catch her breath, his face was buried between her open thighs, driving her up once again.

Only after her third orgasm did he remove his jeans and boxers. His penis was thick and throbbing with eager heat. After donning a condom with clumsy haste, he positioned his cock against her swollen sex and pressed firmly. Every one of her already overstimulated nerve endings reacted immediately. Ripples of honeyed arousal tightened her lower abdomen and built yet another wave.

She wanted to touch his body, to taste him, to feel his warm skin and firm muscles. But Nathan had an agenda, and he was carrying her along willy-nilly to some place she was desperate to reach.

He paused when only a couple of inches of his length were inside her. "Jeannie?" His voice was a harsh rasp. Sweat slicked his chest and dampened his forehead. His eyes were dark, almost navy, and the desperation in them matched her own excitement.

She put her hands on either side of his neck, her fingernails deliberately marking his skin. "Do it," she urged. "Take me like you want to."

He shuddered hard. All over. And then he started to move. The first moment he filled her completely was unlike anything she had ever known. This was more than sex. It was a claiming. An unapologetic dominance that her body welcomed.

But beneath the power and the control was a steadfast gentleness that she felt keenly. He was never lost to his own greed. He was never selfish.

The feel of him stretching her wider, deeper made her twist restlessly. She was so close, so damn close. But three orgasms made her body need more . . . like an addict searching for the next fix. Stronger. More powerful.

She wrapped her legs around his waist, her body jerking each time he rammed to the hilt. He grunted with the force of his assault. He was in her and over her and around her, capturing her without apology. Making her feel delicate and coveted and completely in his command.

For a strong woman, the ability to surrender totally and willingly was incredibly erotic. She whispered words in his ear, cajoling, urging, encouraging. Her hands played over his back, stroking damp skin, raking her fingernails down his spine, hanging on for dear life.

He came with a cry and a roar, grinding the head of his penis against the mouth of her womb and making their bodies seem as one. In the aftermath, the room was silent except for their labored breathing and the quiet tick of the alarm clock on the bedside table.

Nathan was pretty sure he blacked out for a moment. It had been several months since he'd had sex, but even so, the strength and power of his climax shocked him. He'd been like an animal with her. God, what was she thinking? What was *he* thinking?

He rolled on his side, taking her with him, and he freed one of his arms long enough to grasp a corner of the comforter and pull it over their still-joined bodies. He didn't ever want to leave her.

If he'd been able to let go of her, he would have studied her lush body, trying to memorize it against the day when he had to see her walk away. She was the warm, living embodiment of a

Greek goddess: long, shapely legs, curvy hips, a narrow waist, and beautiful breasts made to pillow a man's head.

He'd never met a more physically perfect woman. But all that aside, her natural sensuality brought him to his knees. He couldn't imagine what he had done to deserve this time with her, but he was determined to cherish her for as long as she allowed it.

He wondered if she was asleep. Her head was on his shoulder, and her breathing was deep and regular. He thought about what it would be like to wake up with her every morning. Again last night, he had dreamed about her. But the dreams were a pale reflection of reality.

Nothing his subconscious mind conjured up came close to matching the sheer physical pleasure and the heart-wrenching intimacy of what had just happened in his heretofore lonely bachelor bed.

He wanted to tie her up and keep her his prisoner. Make love to her until they both keeled over from exhaustion. And then he wanted to start all over again.

He had no illusions. He knew this wasn't anything permanent. Jeannie Killaney could do far better than a science nerd. But while she was in his life, right here and now, he would treat her like a princess.

Their lovemaking had surprised him on many levels. Entering her the first time had been a tight fit, and despite her arousal, he had seen her flinch briefly, almost as if it had been a long time since she'd had sex.

Not likely. A woman with her looks and charm would be constantly pursued. She was the woman all other females envied. She had the face, the body, and the personality. The whole package. And even as she aged, her allure for the opposite sex would still be powerful.

He sighed and tightened his arms around her. Her skin was soft and warm, and she smelled of jasmine and fresh paint. He grinned. She was a lousy painter, but she sure as hell had brightened his day.

He eased her onto her back and stared at her face. Her thick lashes were long and several shades darker than her hair. But now that he had certain irrefutable evidence, he knew that her pretty shade of blond hair with just a hint of strawberry highlights was not from a bottle.

He touched her face lightly with his fingertips, careful not to wake her. He traced her straight nose, her high cheekbones, the stubborn line of her chin. He let his fingers wander lower, gently stroking the curve of each breast. Her flat stomach caught his attention next, her sexy navel, the almost imperceptible curve of her soft belly, the moist tangle of baby-fine curls between her legs.

His heartbeat gained speed, pounding in heavy, jerky thuds. God, he never knew what it was like to experience such intense sexual desire. But it was more than that. He wanted Jeannie for his own. He wanted the right to slay her dragons, to protect her if necessary.

He removed his hand abruptly, realizing with sick certainty that he surely wasn't the first man to feel those things. She inspired love, devotion, and—though it shamed him to even think it—lust. But he wanted to believe that the lust was simply a base part of a more admirable whole. He saw her as more than an object of sexual fantasy, despite his disturbing dreams.

He had made some stupid mistakes, including one that had been horrifically public, and he had been embarrassed to admit it to Jeannie. But every wrong step he'd made in his life up until this point was valuable experience in recognizing a woman of worth when he found her. Since the first day he'd stepped through the doors of Lotions and Potions and was knocked up side of the head by a powerful attraction, he'd wasted no opportunity to ask people he met in Asheville about Jeannie and her cousins.

And every one of those people had nothing but glowing

comments, especially about Jeannie. You might expect people to be jealous of her seemingly perfect life, but unless they were hiding it well, no one resented her overabundance of gifts, both physical and mental.

And every minute he spent in her company convinced him more and more that they were right. Jeannie Killaney was a bright, decent, funny, sexy woman. And his response to her was not surprising. The only surprising aspect of the whole situation was that she seemed to have a thing for an ordinary, passably good-looking, brains-over-brawn everyman.

He caressed her cheek. This time his gentle caress roused her. She blinked sleepily and stretched her arms over her head in a big, cute yawn.

Her eyes widened when he stroked her leg from her knee to more dangerous real estate. "Nathan?"

"Hmmm?" He was busy playing with her belly button.

"Can we do it again?"

Four

It was late when they finally drove out to the arboretum, very late. Nathan couldn't remember the last time he'd spent eight hours of a Saturday afternoon and evening in bed having uninhibited, mind-blowing sex. Oh wait, yes, he could . . . never.

Jeannie kept him laughing and talking and panting and fucking until he knew without a doubt that he was seriously, completely addicted to her. End of story. Only her cajoling pleas had finally coaxed him out of bed to fulfill his promise about the excursion.

The moon was past full, but there was still enough light to see clearly. He used his key to open the gated entrance out at the road. Jeannie slid over into the driver's seat, moved the car several feet inside the fence, and then waited for him to relock the gate and rejoin her.

They drove down the mile-long driveway and parked near the building. No need to try to go inside. There was an alarm system, and he didn't want to alert anyone to their presence.

As promised, he took her first to see the exhibit of bonsai trees. They were arranged on stone shelves in an outdoor setting that had been structured to resemble a traditional Japanese garden. He used his flashlight to illuminate shadowy areas, and waited patiently as Jeannie carefully read each small placard.

Afterward, they wandered the various areas: the holly garden, the heritage garden, the plants of promise. She demanded explanations and details that the usual visitor would never think to ask. It challenged him, and he had to keep on his toes, scientifically speaking, to satisfy all her questions.

When they stopped for a bit to enjoy the scents and sounds of the almost-summer night, they sat on a bench down near the creek and held hands in silence. The gurgle of the shallow water tumbling and splashing over rocks was a muted symphony.

After a long while, he spoke quietly. "Why aren't you working as a scientist, Jeannie?"

She shifted on the bench and withdrew her hand. It made him feel oddly bereft. Her words when they came were pensive and low. "I was almost finished with my doctorate when Elizabeth asked me if I wanted to join her and Diana in starting the shop."

"Couldn't they have waited?"

"Not really. Not then. There was so much to do during the start-up phase that it took all of us. In the early days, we re-packaged and sold products from other vendors, but we always wanted to develop our own line of lotions and creams and—"

"Potions?"

She laughed. "You got it. That was my area of expertise, so it made sense to get things rolling as quickly as possible."

"But you've never thought about going back?"

She didn't answer him at first, and he wondered if he had offended her. There was nothing wrong with the work she was doing at the shop, but it seemed a waste of her brain and her training, even if she *was* doing product development to some degree.

He sighed. "I'm sorry. Forget I asked. It's none of my business."

Her hand slid back into his, their fingers twining. "No. It's okay. I was really disenchanted with the whole academic process by the time Elizabeth first called me. I had struggled from the beginning to get people to take me seriously. And not just the men. The female faculty members were equally as or even more insulting and judgmental than their peers."

He frowned in the darkness, wanting to jerk a knot in someone's head. "I don't understand."

Now her voice was laced with weary sarcasm. "Big tits and big brains are mutually exclusive, Nathan. Or so I've been told."

He squeezed her hand. "I never realized," he said, feeling troubled by the vulnerability in her wry explanation. "Was it so blatant then?"

"Definitely. And I had begun to wonder if even finishing the degree would make a difference. So when Elizabeth called, I used it as an excuse to bail. What if I completed the doctorate and then couldn't get a job?"

"But sexual discrimination policies are being enforced more stringently . . . aren't they?"

She stood up, pacing restlessly. "In theory. But I'm always going to have the battle of people taking me seriously."

It was true. He knew she wasn't exaggerating. And yet it seemed so unfair. He stood up and moved behind her, wrapping his arms around her waist. "Will you ever go back and finish?"

She leaned into his embrace, her hands settling over his. "I don't know. Maybe. Sometime."

He wanted to make her feel better, but some things in life simply sucked. And this was one of them.

He tugged her hand. "Come on. I want to show you one last thing before we go."

Jeannie had flat-out refused to wear her paint-spattered top, so he had offered one of his plain cotton button-downs. She had rolled up the sleeves, and the hem hung a couple of inches below her ass, but it covered far too much of her delectable figure for his liking.

Even without visual provocation, he had sex on his mind continually. A double swing in one of the gardens was a perfect spot for a couple to read a book or while away a lazy afternoon. In the dark, it offered a whole new set of exciting possibilities.

He pulled her to a halt in front of it, and kissed her. "Could I interest you in a ride?"

She was quick on the uptake. "On the swing, or on you?" She nibbled his chin and licked the stubble of his late-day beard. They had showered together—oh boy, had they showered. And the memories were etched in his brain. But shaving would have wasted far too much of their precious time.

He tugged her with him, sitting in the middle of the swing and perching her on his lap with her back to his chest. "How about *on* me, on the swing? Call it a twofer."

She giggled, the sound young and happy. "I love a man who believes in giving full service."

"Just you wait," he promised brusquely. He wrapped his arms tightly around her waist and pushed off with his feet. The wooden structure wasn't meant to go very high, but the light breeze they stirred up tumbled her hair into his eyes. He buried his face in the back of her neck, wishing he could stop the sun from rising tomorrow morning.

After a few minutes, she crawled around on his lap, threatening permanent harm to his boys. She took his face in her hands. "Please tell me you didn't really mean *just* swinging."

He cupped her ass, loving the feel of her soft feminine parts mashing up against his dick. "Are you propositioning me, Miss Killaney?"

She slid her tongue in his mouth, and that was all the answer he needed. His mama didn't raise no dummies. He stood up and steadied her as she stumbled to her feet. With shaking hands, he stripped off the overconcealing shirt she wore. Jeannie hadn't bothered with a bra, and he knew for a fact that her ass was bare beneath those damn pants, because he'd been the one to trash her undies.

Jeannie was busy unzipping his jeans and shoving them to his knees. When they were both nude, he backed onto the swing and didn't even notice when a rough splinter poked his ass. At the last second, he had the presence of mind to retrieve a condom from his pants.

And then he forget how to think . . . how to speak . . . how to breathe, when Jeannie took his rock-hard erection in her hand, toyed with it for a few, throat-drying seconds, and then lowered herself onto it with a ragged sigh.

Feeling her hot, tight sheath take him in, even with the damn condom, made little yellow spots dance in front of his eyes. He figured he was about a quart low on bodily fluids, and he spared a passing thought to wonder how many times a man could ejaculate in a twelve-hour period.

He was willing to try for the record, God help him. Even if it killed him.

She put her hands on his shoulders. The temperature had begun dropping after dark, and Jeannie's skin was cool, her nipples hard against his chest. Though it was damn difficult to concentrate on anything other than his cock, he managed to use his feet to set the swing in motion. With a bit of effort, he synced his thrusts to the downswing.

Jeannie had closed her eyes after the first few seconds. Her fingernails dug into his shoulders, and he knew there would be marks on his skin come morning. The idea of being branded by her tightened his dick even more.

He pumped deliberately, loving her almost-silent gasps, relishing the squeeze of her inner muscles. All around them, the earth was moist and teeming with life. Deer wandered unseen in the nearby woods. Lightning bugs flashed in the darkness, and a barred owl hooted overhead. Something about the smell of the breeze and the sounds of the night made him feel free and wild and defiant.

Perhaps he never had to let her go. Perhaps it was possible to win her . . . to make her his in every way. She bit the side of his throat and his back arched in a vain effort to fuse them eternally. He fought to delay his climax. More. He wanted more.

Jeannie sobbed and moaned, her helpless sounds of pleasure inflaming him. Heat. Need. Passion. It was in him and around him and wafting over the trees on soundless puffs of scented wind.

He cried out at the last, as did she, and the echo of their release filled the night with raw joy.

The drive back to Nathan's apartment was mostly silent. Jeannie was wiped out, physically and emotionally. It scared her to feel so happy with a man she had no connection with, other than amazing sex.

True, they had a lot in common in terms of their academic backgrounds. But she was pretty sure that Nathan saw her as a sexy woman first and a brainy woman second. She was very glad he desired her. It would be stupid to be upset that he wanted to make love to her.

But did he really see more than the surface? She had waited all her life for a man who wanted the whole package—a man who would encourage her to be more than just a pretty face. A man who valued her skills and abilities.

It was asking a lot of his gender. But then again, the stakes were high. When and if she ever got married, she planned on it being permanent. She didn't want to make a mistake.

Even Nathan himself admitted that he'd judged that poor crazy woman on her looks and bubbly personality. Only later had he seen her for who she was. It was human nature to assess the outer package in the beginning. First impressions were important. But how did people ever actually know other people . . . really know them? And how could you decide if a man and a woman were really suited?

The intense sexual attraction between her and Nathan was rare and exciting, but that would fade in time to a more realistic level. Would there be anything left when it was gone?

When they got back to his place, he wanted to follow her home. She shook her head firmly. "Completely unnecessary. I've been driving myself home at night for a lot of years. I don't need an escort. But I appreciate the thought."

He put his hands on her shoulders. "Can I see you tomorrow?"

His husky request was temptation personified. She touched his cheek. "I'm not blowing you off, I swear. But I have a family thing tomorrow, and we're doing midyear inventory at the shop this week. I won't have a moment to breathe. But next Saturday is free."

He scowled. "A whole week? Damn, woman. You know how to hurt a guy."

She kissed his chin. "I'll make it worth your wait, I promise."

His face lightened. "That sounds intriguing."

He walked her out to the car. It was almost midnight, and the parking lot was quiet. She opened her door and turned to face him. "I had a nice time today," she said primly, not sure about how to thank a guy properly for amazing, wall-banging sex.

He chuckled and hugged her. Already his embrace felt familiar and comforting, even with the momentarily quiet undercurrent of sexual awareness.

He kissed her gently, his tongue teasing her lips and then stroking into her mouth. "I'll work on earning a better adjective next time. Something more than *nice*."

Her arms went up around his neck. "You are a very sexy man. I'm not sure the vocabulary exists for what happened today."

"You got that right." He tucked her into the car and held the door. "Drive safely."

She nodded, wishing she had said to hell with it and invited him to come home with her. "Good night, Nathan. I'll be in touch."

He crouched to give her one last kiss. "Goodbye, Jeannie. Sweet dreams."

Then he closed her door and stood alone in the dark as she drove away.

Jeannie had lunch with her cousins on Monday. It was rare for them to have the opportunity to eat together when the shop was open, so they often got together at the beginning of the week.

Diana and Elizabeth were full of wedding chatter. Jeannie listened patiently, enjoying their excitement and enthusiasm. But she was restless with the need to share news of her own. Over dessert, she finally got the chance.

She felt self-conscious, which was odd, because the three of them shared everything . . . or at least mostly everything. There were certain sexual details that needed to remain a mystery.

She finished off her iced tea and leaned forward, lowering her voice. "Do you guys remember the night we made that weird batch back in April?"

Both Diana and Elizabeth stared at her in surprise. Jeannie had been the one to insist that nothing *magic* had happened that evening.

Elizabeth frowned. "Of course, we do. Diana and I still wonder if some kind of chemical reaction produced an aphrodisiac effect. Not that we're complaining. We found the men of our dreams. So what's up? Don't tell me that your scientific brain might actually concede the truth of the matter?"

Jeannie bit her lower lip. "I met someone."

Diana's shriek of excitement drew attention from other tables, and Jeannie felt her cheeks turn red. "Keep it down, for heaven's sake. I still think it's unlikely that our potion did anything. It's coincidence, that's all." Perhaps she wanted to be convinced.

Elizabeth pressed for details. "So spill it, Jeannie. Who is he? How did you meet? Is he cute? What's his ranking . . . ? Is he a solid ten?"

Diana's avid gaze sharpened. "Did he use one of the number ten products?"

Jeannie's cheeks burned with embarrassment. "His sister bought him shaving cream. He came into the store and said he had been dreaming about me for three weeks."

The other two women fell back in their chairs, their eyes round with awe. Elizabeth's words were soft. "So it's true. My gosh, I can't believe it."

Jeannie waved a hand. "Let's not get carried away. All of this could be a happy accident of timing."

Diana snorted. "Yeah, right."

Jeannie tried to be the voice reason. "We know that phero- mones exist and can be blamed for sexual attraction. Maybe some- thing we used in the number ten batch falls into that category."

Diana stared at her two cousins. "Or maybe we did cre- ate a bit of magic that night. Some things in the world can't be explained. It's possible that our mixture really is a love potion. Three new men in barely six weeks. This is so cool."

Elizabeth was ready to move on to more immediate con- cerns. "So tell us about the guy. Do we approve? Is he worthy?"

Jeannie smiled. "Worthy of what? You're so goofy. He's a sci- entist. Moved here from Ohio. Right now he's working at the arboretum, but in the fall, he'll be teaching biology and ecology at WCU."

Diana lifted an eyebrow. "Is he a stud?"

Jeannie tried not to blush again. "He's quite attractive," she said, with massive understatement. "Not as exotic as Enrique or as overtly macho as Damian, but he's really hot in this restrained, volcanic-sexuality kind of way."

Diana fanned herself dramatically. "Wow. I can't wait to meet him."

Elizabeth summoned the waiter for their checks. "Why don't you invite him for dinner, Jeannie? I'll cook one night this week. He can meet us and bond with the guys. Damian and Enrique can check him out."

Jeannie shook her head. "Oh, no. Way too early. I don't want to scare him off. Besides, I told him I was going to be really busy and that I couldn't see him again until next Saturday."

Diana shook her head. "Only you could keep a man dangling for a week. He must be smitten if he agreed to that."

Jeannie wrinkled her nose. "He didn't exactly agree, but I didn't give him much of a choice. I thought we needed to slow things down a little bit . . . get a handle on our feelings."

Elizabeth was signing a credit card clip, but her head snapped up, her face shocked. "My God, you've already had sex with him."

Diana shrieked again, and Jeannie wanted to disappear under the table. "Will you be quiet?" she hissed. "I don't need everyone in Asheville to hear about my sex life, if you don't mind."

Elizabeth pounced on that. "So there *was* sex," she crowed. "Hallelujah. Most of the men you meet are afraid to scale the ivory tower."

Diana giggled when Jeannie spit out a mouthful of water. Jeannie glared. "You make it sound like I'm some unattainable prize."

"Well, aren't you?" the other two asked in unison and then howled with laughter when Jeannie's disgruntled expression set them off.

Elizabeth cocked her head. "C'mon. Give us the juicy details. PG rated, of course."

Jeannie clasped her hands in her lap, uncomfortably aware that recounting the weekend's events might make her sound impulsive and reckless. She was neither. But you couldn't tell it by the way she had acted.

She sighed. "He came over for dinner Friday night. It was very nice. We connected . . . had lots of common interests. Saturday I went over to help him paint a room in his apartment. That night he took me to the arboretum for a stroll in the gardens."

Diana narrowed her eyes. "You've left out a lot of hours."

Elizabeth nodded her agreement. "And I know for a fact that the arboretum is not open that late."

Jeannie's blush got cranked up all over again. "He had a key to the gate, and we walked in the moonlight."

"That explains the arboretum," Elizabeth agreed, "but what about all the hours in between? How long can it take to paint a tiny room?"

Jeannie was stumped. Her two cousins pinned her with their knowing gazes, and they could detect a lie from her a mile away. "We had sex that afternoon," she said baldly. "Is that what you wanted to know?"

They were all three whispering now, not wanting other tables to overhear something so intimate. Diana's face was filled with naughty mischief. She leaned forward, resting her arms on the table, and lowered her voice even further. "How many orgasms did you have?"

"Diana!" It was Jeannie's turn to screech.

Elizabeth patted her shoulder. "You might as well come clean. We're not leaving until you do."

Jeannie stared from one to the other. They were excited for her. Happy for her. She loved them like sisters. "I think it was only five," she muttered, closing her eyes so she wouldn't have to see their reactions. But that was a mistake, because when she did, every detail of Saturday's abandoned, multi-orgasmic love-making appeared in perfect detail on her mental screen. Her skin warmed, and she realized what a dope she was. A week? How stupid. She wanted to see Nathan Hardison now. Today.

Elizabeth snapped her fingers. "Earth to Jeannie. Wow, honey. When you take the plunge, you don't waste any time. Are you sure we can't meet him? He must be a fantastic guy. I've never seen you this addled."

Jeannie wrinkled her nose. "Trust me on this. When the moment is right, you both will be the first to know. But for now, I think we'd better get back to work."

About that time an attractive older woman at a nearby table rose to her feet and approached them. She flashed a friendly smile and handed them each a business card. "I hope you don't mind me interrupting, but I couldn't help overhearing part of your conversation."

While Jeannie died inwardly of mortification, Elizabeth shot her a don't-worry glance and responded with her usual poise. She was cordial but cautious. "No problem." She glanced at the small rectangle of thin card stock. "You work for the paper?"

The woman nodded eagerly, pulling up a chair without waiting for permission. "We're doing a June bridal insert that comes out next Saturday. One of our interviews fell through and I'd like to include your story."

"Our story?" Jeannie had a bad feeling about this. She might not be Britney or Anna Nicole, but whoever said there's no such thing as bad publicity was an idiot. Words, even printed words, could hurt.

The well-dressed woman beamed. "I heard you talking about your love potion. What a fascinating piece. Readers will devour it. Please say the three of you will sit down with me and let me write this up."

Jeannie wanted to blurt out an immediate, unequivocal *hell, no*, but then her cousins and the reporter would want to know why. And she sure as heck couldn't expose Nathan's private affairs.

Elizabeth, ever the business woman, was intrigued. You could see it on her face. But she pointed out the obvious. "We were mostly just joking about the new men in our lives. It's possible that pheromones in our latest product do have some power on the libido. It certainly seems to have a positive effect on *our* guys. But clearly there's no such thing as a love potion."

The reporter laughed. "Who knows? But it makes for a great tale. Especially during wedding season. And think of the publicity for your business. Please tell me you'll do it."

Diana grinned. "I'm game."

Elizabeth nodded. "Count me in."

All three women looked at Jeannie. She was trapped. And the knot in her stomach knew it. But really, what were the chances Nathan would read a bridal insert? Slim to none. The gods couldn't be so cruel.

With a weak smile, which was the best she had to offer, she gave in to the inevitable. "Fine. This is all pretty silly if you ask me, but as long as you quote us correctly and let us see a proof of the article before it runs, I have no objection."

The reporter's smile dimmed, but she nodded reluctantly. "I suppose we can do that. But trust me, your love potion is going to sell papers like hotcakes."

Five

It was the week from hell. Jeannie wasn't sure if her state of mind was influencing things, or if the world really was going to heck in a handbasket.

The annoying reporter insisted on meeting them later that afternoon in order to finish the story and meet her deadline. Diana and Elizabeth were happy to spin her a creative account of the spooky April night, the full moon, the bubbling pot, and then every detail of their subsequent romances.

Jeannie sat mute, desperately wanting them to shut up, but ruefully aware that they thought the whole thing was a lark. Fun and silly and entertaining.

Which it probably was for everyone but the woman whose love interest had already been burned by one crazy-ass lunatic. At one point the reporter looked coyly at Jeannie. "So how about you? A woman with your looks must have guys beating down the door. Maybe you don't need a magic potion. Or has it worked for you, also?"

Everything went quiet as they waited for her to reply. She wet her lips. Blurting out the truth wasn't an option. *A strange man started dreaming about me every night after he used the number ten shaving cream. We had unbelievably erotic sex on our second date, and I think I may be falling in love with him.*

She crossed her legs and clasped her hands in her lap. "I'm still waiting for Mr. Right to come along and sweep me off my feet."

The woman jotted that down, her face reflecting vague disappointment. Then she turned back to her two more cooperative subjects and pressed for any last details. By the time the interview was over, Jeannie wanted to crawl back in her bottle and put a stopper in the lid so no one could bother her.

And that was just the beginning. The inventory software crashed on Tuesday. Two of their employees came down with a virus on Wednesday. And on Thursday, one of the heavy but fragile shelving units collapsed, sending little shards of glass all over the store and destroying more than thirty-five jars of expensive body scrub.

By the time Jeannie got home that evening, she was ready to chuck it all and go flip burgers at the nearest fast food place. No responsibility. Free french fries. It sounded pretty damn wonderful at the moment.

She and Nathan had e-mailed back and forth at odd times during the week. And he had called her each evening. But their conversations were brief and stilted.

At night in bed, she felt his absence, though he'd never been upstairs in her house. She lay in the darkness and remembered the feel of his big hands on her breasts, between her legs, cupping her ass.

He was funny and tender and inventive in bed, and she knew without a doubt she'd never find a lover who pleased her more.

The whole thing about the dreams and the shaving cream still bothered her. There couldn't possibly be a connection.

Surely, after he'd seen her in the store that first morning, he'd felt a strong sexual attraction and thus had been imagining them together in his subconscious. That could logically account for the nightly dreams.

And she didn't need any stupid potion to fall for him. She was halfway there already.

Friday morning she was scrambling to get out the door on time when the phone rang. She decided to ignore it until she glanced at the caller ID.

She snatched up the receiver. "Nathan? Hey, there. I'm on my way to work." She was also smiling for no particular reason.

His voice sounded like he had just climbed out of bed, and that made her knees weak. "I can't wait," he said abruptly. "It's killing me."

A frown knit her forehead. "Wait for what?"

He groaned. "I can't wait until tomorrow afternoon to see you. Please let me come over tonight."

She twined the phone cord around her finger. She knew just how he felt. Hearing his voice made her insides go all squishy with yearning. "I won't get home until almost eight. We're open later in the evening starting this weekend. You know . . . summer hours."

He sighed, and even over the phone line, it made her shiver. "I'll pick up Chinese," he whispered cajolingly. "You have to eat something. And I'll leave whenever you tell me."

Yeah, right. Like she was going to let him walk away once she had him in her house. "Okay," she said softly. "That sounds nice."

He grunted. "There's that damn word again. You sure as hell test a man's mettle."

She grinned, feeling better already. "Nothing good in life comes easy. Haven't you heard that?"

"I don't want easy," he said with a chuckle. "I want you."

Perhaps the gremlins of fate were through screwing with her, or maybe everyone was in a better frame of mind because it was Friday, but the day actually went pretty smoothly. Jeannie couldn't resist telling Diana and Elizabeth about her early-morning call, and that set the two of them off . . . making plans, placing bets.

Jeannie just shook her head and let them go until they told her to leave early.

She shook her head. "No way. I'm not shirking my duty just because some hot guy wants to bring me takeout."

Elizabeth put her hands on her hips. "Scram," she said with mock fierceness. "You're working tomorrow until two. Diana and I can handle things here right now. Go home, take a bath, put on some naughty lingerie. But you have to promise to introduce us soon."

Their love and affection made Jeannie blink back tears. She really was very lucky. She might not be teaching in some fancy university, but her life was rich and full.

She made it home by six and ran around the house like a madwoman, tidying this and that, hitting the high spots with a dust rag, and then reserving an entire half hour to soak in a tub of oil-scented water. The fragrance was one of their own products, a heavy, lush, eastern-inspired combination of sandalwood, musk, and patchouli.

She shaved her legs, rubbed herself down with the matching body lotion, and picked out her favorite set of mint green panties and bra. The lace was sheer and provocative, and her nipples thrust against the delicate fabric as she thought of Nathan removing the sexy undies.

She set out candles in her bedroom, more than the two she usually kept on the mantel. Her bedroom had an old sealed-up fireplace with gas logs. This time of year, she liked to keep fresh flowers in front of the grate.

By seven thirty, everything looked suitably romantic. She slipped into comfortable jeans that made her butt look slim and then donned a thin cashmere, V-necked sweater in cotton candy pink.

A bit of long-lasting lip color, the kind that wouldn't come off in an intimate moment, and she was ready.

She flung open the door before Nathan could knock, and she dragged him inside. "I'm starving," she said, bubbling over with happiness. Her memory hadn't let her down. He was every bit as adorable as she remembered. "I've been waiting for this all day."

Nathan took a deep breath. *Down boy. She's talking about the Chinese food.* He set the bags on the small table in her foyer and gathered her close for a kiss. The first touch of her lips had him hard and shaking.

He'd spent six days trying to understand how she could have such an effect on him. Now he remembered. It was like touching fire and not getting burned. Feeling hot and dodging sparks and knowing that the cold outside their embrace was being kept at bay. She was made for him. Every inch of her soft, cuddly body fit up against his like some perfect, divine plan.

He released her reluctantly and was unable to say exactly how long they'd kissed. Jeannie looked flustered and mussed, and one look in the nearby mirror told him he was much the same.

She took him by the hand and led him into the kitchen. He watched as she went up on tiptoe and removed a couple of wine goblets from the cabinet. She poured them each a glass of chardonnay and joined him at the table.

He could tell she was feeling shy, and it charmed him. Her vulnerability made him want to cherish her. He took a long sip of his wine and prayed for the control to love her slowly tonight. To give her what she deserved.

They talked lazily over sweet-and-sour pork and egg rolls . . . one hunger appeased while another built. He had picked up a couple of pieces of coconut pie at a local bakery, and she ate it happily without a single comment about calories or diets or watching her weight. He liked that about her. She was comfortable with her body, and why not? It was spectacular.

Cleaning up the simple meal took a matter of minutes. Nathan shoved his hands in his pockets, trying to be a gentleman. "I brought a couple of videos to watch," he said lightly, "if you're interested."

She tucked a drying cloth over the handle of the stove and turned to face him. The way that soft, fuzzy sweater hugged her breasts ought to be a crime.

She came toward him, a half smile tilting the corners of her mouth. "I'd rather take you upstairs and make love to you."

Nathan wondered if he had stumbled into some freaky third dimension where all his fantasies were granted. He followed her up to the second floor and into her bedroom with his knees knocking and his dick as hard as marble. Just watching the gentle sway of her butt in front of and above him was enough to make him come in his pants. Almost.

Her bed was unabashedly romantic, and he realized that while he had been busy admiring her physical attributes and her impressive mind, he had missed a whole other side of her. The sweet, dreamy, feminine Jeannie. The woman who had decorated this room.

He stood just inside the door while she lit candles and opened a couple of windows to let in the sweet early-summer breeze. She turned finally and held out a hand. "Don't be shy," she teased. "I won't bite."

He caught his toe on the edge of her pretty pastel patterned rug and caught himself with an awkward stumble. She watched him with a gentle smile, and he knew she forgave him for his lack of savoir faire.

After all, a man couldn't expect to be at his most debonair

when blinded by such beauty. He took her hand and squeezed it tightly. It was as if a tingling thread connected them palm to palm.

He slid his free hand into her hair and cupped her head. "I've been telling myself all week that this couldn't possibly be as wonderful as I remember."

She turned her face and kissed his fingers. "I know. I did the same thing."

He slid his hands down her arms to her wrists. "I have these fantasies in my head," he muttered, driven to offer the truth.

Her eyes widened in pleased curiosity. "Tell me," she whispered. She swayed toward him, and he tightened his grip. The yearning between them was palpable.

"I'd rather show you."

She nodded slowly, standing obediently still, although she could have slipped away at any moment. Dusk was fading rapidly, and the shadows in the room deepened. Dancing flickers of light and dark decorated the walls and ceiling, mimicking the candle flames.

He undressed her carefully, every movement an homage to her loveliness. At the first sight of her rib cage, her breasts, her delicate collarbone, he sighed.

When he had her bare but for her bra and panties, he stopped. She looked like a forest sprite, a sexy woodland fairy clothed in palest green, ready to grant his wishes. His hands trembled, mapping the glowing curves and planes of her flesh.

She reached for the buckle of his belt, but he gently batted her hands away. "I want to play Old West outlaw and innocent schoolteacher," he muttered.

Her lips parted, her eyes widened, and her hands came up to cover her breasts. Almost as if she were already feeling the part. She pouted a bit. "But can't I at least help you get undressed?

He put his hand on his hips, adopting a swagger and a sneer. "I'm gonna take you fast and hard. Won't be time for that."

Her pale skin flushed from her breasts all the way up her throat to her face. "Oh, my." She backed toward the bed. "I don't care for smelly criminals," she said with a haughty sniff.

He advanced slowly. "You're my bounty, little lass . . . won fair and square in a poker game. What you want doesn't matter in the least."

The backs of her legs hit the mattress, and she sat down abruptly. He loomed over her, forcing her to lie back.

She put her hands over her head. "Please don't tie me up," she said with a theatrical tremble in her voice.

He gave her his best evil smile. "Wouldn't think of it," he purred, flipping her quickly and dragging her hips to the edge of the mattress. He stroked the small of her back with one hand and freed his aching cock with the other. He released her for a split second to roll on a condom, but she made no move to escape.

He reached between her legs and touched her lightly. She made a choking sound, and her hands grabbed the folds of her ivory satin comforter and clenched hard, as though preparing to hold on.

He positioned his penis, fitting it between the moist folds of her sex. He was in danger of exploding the moment he entered her, and he closed his eyes to shut out the sight of her body. He tried reciting the periodic table in his head: *Hydrogen. Helium. Lithium.*

Jeannie wriggled her butt and he lost track. Shit. He'd have to make it up to her the second time around. He eased into her, his hands clenched on her superlative ass. "Here you go, lass," he muttered. "Some real man's flesh for yer pleasure."

She arched her spine and pushed back against him. "Arrogant barbarian."

He pinched her bottom. "Cooperate, little hellion, and I might go easy on you."

She peeked at him over her shoulder, her brown eyes sparkling with humor. "Lying already. You promised fast and hard."

Even in the midst of the hunger gripping him, he managed a laugh. "You asked for it," he said, thrusting forward and burying his length tightly inside her.

Something about this angle made him crazy. It was the sexy curve where her narrow waist flared out to her rounded hips. Or the vulnerable nape of her neck. Or the way her breasts filled his hands when he reached beneath her to cup them.

He broke his vow. No fast and hard. Not when he could savor the moment. With a valiant effort, he maintained control. Slowly, ever so slowly, he slid all the way out and then back in.

He rested his forehead on her back. "I've been hiding out in the mountains for a long time, lass. You'll be required to service me regularly for a while."

Her voice was muffled in the bedclothes. "Promises, promises."

He smacked her butt lightly for her impertinence. "A man has needs, hungers, aches."

He slid free of her and turned her on her back. Her hair was a wild tangle around her face. Her beautiful eyes had the glow of warm brandy. Slowly, provocatively, she fingered her own nipples. "Perhaps I have a few hungers and aches and needs of my own, Mr. Outlaw. Mayhaps I like your impressive . . . . *sword*."

When she stared at his cock, it twitched and grew. He moved her on the bed so he could join her. He was still fully clothed, and she was completely, magnificently naked. He was on his knees, his hands on her thighs.

She reached out and stroked his erection. "Have you robbed any banks lately?"

"Too many to count," he growled. "And I could use a pretty accomplice if you're interested." He filled her with one heavy thrust.

She went wild beneath him, dragging his head down for a ravenous kiss and wrapping her legs around his waist. He fucked her hard, grunting and panting and sweating. In some vague corner of his mind, he was aware of ordinary sounds outside. A dog barking. A distant siren. He smelled the scents from the candles, tasted the dryness in his mouth from trying in vain to drag in much-needed air.

He lifted her head off the mattress, covering her mouth in a hungry kiss, gasping and shivering when her tongue dueled with his. Her body was hot and soft, limber and firm. He wanted to fuck her forever.

But six days of abstinence after last Saturday's sexual excess had made him weak. He draped her legs over his arms, slammed even deeper, and groaned as he felt her orgasm roll over her and drag him with it.

Jeannie played with his damp spiky hair and tried to catch her breath. Being screwed by a man who had not even bothered to undress made her feel like a sexual goddess. Infinitely desired. Completely and totally wanted. It was fun.

She nibbled his ear. His large body was deadweight on her, but she welcomed it. She felt whole and satisfied and deliciously lazy. But she was freezing in the aftermath. She bit the side of his neck gently. "Can we get under the covers, Mr. Outlaw?"

He grumbled something inaudible and crawled off the bed. While he was in the bathroom disposing of the condom, she wriggled beneath the soft sheets and light blankets and burrowed into a warm spot.

She was drowsy and replete when he came back. He stood beside the bed and looked down at her with a quizzical smile on his face. "Any room in there for me?"

She had the cover pulled to just below her nose. "No shoes in my bed," she said, her voice muffled.

He took the comforter and the bedclothes and stripped them away with one firm sweep of his arm. "Then we'll have to do it on the floor."

She squealed when he tugged on her leg and tumbled her

from the bed, catching her up in his arms to keep her from falling. She lay against him shivering and laughing, and he realized her skin was covered with gooseflesh.

"Shall I close the windows?" he asked softly, pressing little kisses on her nose and forehead. Across the room, he saw Jeannie and himself in the mirror over her vanity table, and it made him shudder. She was a lovely woman anytime, but nude she took his breath away.

She clung to his neck with one arm. "Leave them open," she whispered. "You'll warm me up . . . won't you?"

He eased her to her knees. "I'll make you a deal. Bring this outlaw's pistol back into shooting position, and I'll cover you up again."

He had left his trousers unzipped, but his penis was tucked back inside his boxers. Jeannie had him out and up in record time. Her lips on his cock were making him seriously crazy. He didn't last thirty seconds.

He dragged her to her feet, dumped her in the bed, shucked his clothes, and only barely remembered the condom. She slid off the other side of the mattress, shocking the shit out of him.

Her grin was taunting. "I'd rather die in the desert than submit to a dirty outlaw."

"We have a desert now? What happened to the mountains?" He approached her carefully.

She backed toward the window as though she meant to jump. He was pretty sure she wouldn't go out the second-story window in her birthday suit, but the tiny sliver of uncertainty urged him on in the game.

He glared at her. "Get back over here."

She folded her arms beneath her breasts, making them move in mysterious and wonderful ways. He dragged his attention back to her face. "Now, woman."

His captive seemed unimpressed with his order. She lifted her chin and glared back in silent defiance.

He cocked his head and lowered his voice to a cajoling whisper. "Return to me, lovely lass, and I'll taste that sweet treasure between your thighs. I'll lick and stroke and suck until you beg me to stop."

Her arms fell to her sides, and she blinked and swayed.

He held out a hand. "I'll make you soar, my angel. I'll toss you off the mountaintop and catch you and then start all over again."

She approached him slowly as though drawn by an invisible force, eyes wide, lips and cheeks rosy with arousal. When their fingers met and clung, she put a hand to his head, stroking his cheek. "Is that a wicked threat, Mr. Mean-and-Nasty Outlaw?"

He flipped back the covers and helped her get settled. Then he leaned over her on one elbow. "No, my lady. It's a promise."

Jeannie spread her thighs obediently at the touch of his hands and whimpered when his head bent and she felt the first pass of his tongue. His hair tickled the soft skin between her legs.

She was wet and swollen and almost unbearably tender. He seemed to know without her saying a word, because he licked her delicately, barely grazing her clit.

Her climax built so rapidly, it shocked her. In minutes she was moaning and writhing, held immobile by his mouth and his strong hands.

At the end, he suckled carefully on her clitoris. Sparks exploded behind her eyelids. He didn't let her escape. Even as her orgasm ripped through her and sent her spiraling over and over and over, he continued his gentle assault until she lay spent and drained in his embrace.

Her breath rattled in her throat and the smell of sex permeated the air. She tried to formulate thoughts, but her brain was short-circuited. All she could think about was keeping him in her bed always.

Finally, as her breathing and her heart rate slowed to more

normal levels, she slid down in the bed and curled against him with a sigh. "I never knew outlaws and professors were so multitalented."

He tightened his arms around her. "Wait until I show you how I plunder and pillage. . . ."

Six

Jeannie yawned and cuddled even closer. "Sounds like a lot of effort. Maybe we can save that for another day." She moved a leg between his, wanting to feel his warmth and strength all around her.

He stroked her hair. "I should go and let you get some rest."

She murmured a protest. "Not yet. Tell me how your week went. Better than mine, I hope."

She felt him shrug. "It was good. Challenging. I entertained some visiting grad students . . . looked over some plans for future expansion of the arboretum. Missed you." He rubbed her back with long, firm strokes.

She was too tired for any more fooling around, but even so, her body hummed. She sighed. "My week sucked, but you're making it all better."

She felt him smile against her cheek. "I'm glad."

She mustered enough energy to turn on the lamp beside the bed and then leaned on an elbow to look at Nathan. The fierce intelligence in his eyes was momentarily muted by a gleam of lazy, sensual satisfaction.

And surprisingly, with his big nude body sprawled in her soft, feminine bed, he looked far more like an outlaw than a professor at the moment. He lifted a shoulder. "What? You're making me nervous."

She laughed softly. "Right." Though she quaked with self-consciousness, she slipped out of bed and walked with studied nonchalance to the bathroom. She freshened up and looked in the mirror. *Yikes!* She took a brush from the counter and ran it through her hair.

She couldn't seem to squelch the smile on her face. Last Saturday wasn't a fluke. She and Nathan were amazing together.

When she returned to the bedroom, he had propped his shoulders against the headboard and the sheet was pulled to his waist. His cocky smile made her toes curl into the soft rug.

He folded his arms across his chest. "So if you're too tired for round three and you're not sending me home . . . what now?"

She climbed in beside him, brushing a quick kiss on his lips. "Well, we could talk. You know . . . since we jumped right past the getting-to-know-you phase."

He curled an arm around her and tucked her close. "Women—what is it with you and talking?"

She laughed. "It beats caveman grunts, don't you think? And besides . . . I have nothing to hide, do you?" Even as the teasing words left her mouth, she winced inwardly. Oh God, that damn article. She shoved the uneasy thought aside. Nothing was going to ruin tonight.

He played with her hair, lightly stroking the shell of her ear. A quiver of sexual awareness heated her skin, made her melt inside. It wouldn't be long before she pounced on him if she wasn't careful.

She swallowed and tucked her knees up to her chest. "You first. What did you want to be when you were in grade school?"

He laughed. "That's easy. I wanted to be Luke Skywalker and fight the Imperial Stormtroopers."

"Do all little boys have violent streaks?"

"All the ones I knew. I think it's in our DNA . . . you know . . . the need to conquer."

She put a hand on his knee under the covers. "Is that what you're doing with me? Conquering?"

His hand stilled on her hair. "I wouldn't say that."

"Okay. What *would* you call it?"

He turned their bodies so they were facing each other. His expression was almost troubled. "I think it might be falling in love."

She froze. The idea had been sliding around in her brain, but hearing him say it out loud was shocking. She wet her lips with her tongue. "Sex isn't love. It's animal attraction."

A rueful smile ticked up the corner of his mouth. "Don't try to lecture a biologist on animal attraction. I know what I'm talking about." He traced her lips with a gentle finger. "I know it's probably premature. We barely know each other. But I'm giving you fair warning. I've got it bad."

She took a deep breath. "Me, too."

They might have made love again, but the phone rang, and it was Elizabeth. While Jeannie talked to her cousin, Nathan got dressed. He'd laid his heart on the line, and while Jeannie's response had been all he could ask for, he needed to back off and give her some breathing room.

He fetched her robe from the bathroom and helped her slip it on while she continued her conversation. Then he went down to the kitchen and reheated some decaf Jeannie had brewed earlier.

She was completely dressed when she appeared ten minutes later. He was glad. If she'd been wearing nothing but the robe, he wasn't sure his resolve would have been strong enough to walk away.

She reached for the cup he handed her. "Thanks."

They stood in silence, sipping the hot beverages, their gazes meeting now and again.

He remembered one last important thing he wanted to say. "Jeannie?"

"Hmmm?" She set her cup aside, watching him warily.

"If you ever want me to, I'd be happy to read through your dissertation . . . the part that's finished. It might help to have an objective eye . . . someone outside your field. You know, to take a look . . . offer suggestions. I don't mean to be presumptuous, but when I was doing mine, I had a half dozen friends who read it over and over. It really helped, and I hope you'll let me do that when the time is right."

There was a funny look on her face. Shit. Had he stepped in it? Perhaps she was one of those people who guarded their work fiercely. He'd known a few. They simply didn't want other people reading what they had written until it was completely finished.

He put his empty cup on the counter. "Or not," he said, trying to smile. "It was just a thought."

He saw her swallow and he could have sworn that her eyes were watery. She leaned back against the fridge. "So you think I should finish it?"

Was that a loaded question? He had no choice but to be honest. "I really do. Even if you decide never to teach, it still gives you a great feeling of accomplishment to complete a milestone like that. And who knows . . . ? It might even be published."

A huge smile broke over her face and she launched herself into his arms. "You are the most amazing man, Nathan Hardison."

He staggered backward but caught his balance, not sure what had prompted such a response. He hugged her close, feeling his dick get hard when she rubbed up against him. "If you say so."

He glanced at the clock on the far wall. "I need to go, pretty girl. You have to be up early."

She released him reluctantly. "Are we still on for tomorrow after work?"

He kissed her swiftly to avoid temptation. "Of course. How about dinner . . . at a nice restaurant . . . so we can do more of that getting-to-know-you thing?"

She walked him to the door. "I can't wait."

She slept deeply and woke up before the alarm went off, humming and smiling as she showered and dressed. Nathan respected her work. He thought she should complete her dissertation. Even her cousins never said much about the aborted doctoral program. Not that they didn't care about her, but probably because they thought she was a big girl who could make her own decisions.

Witnessing Nathan's genuine interest and hearing his confidence in her ability to finish the job made her want to dance around the room. First, he said he was falling in love with her, and now this. Her heart was so full it threatened to burst from her chest and float up into the sky.

It was a busy Saturday. Elizabeth ran out and bought several papers from the nearest corner newsstand, but Jeannie didn't have time to stop and read it. Her cousins had approved the article. Wouldn't you know it? She had been a victim of Murphy's Law. The newspaper lady had come by with a proof on Wednesday during the one half hour Jeannie had been out of the shop running errands.

But Elizabeth and Diana said it was cute and funny and really clever. So perhaps Jeannie was worrying over nothing. She had already decided to show Nathan the article tonight and explain. She hated secrets. They made her break out in hives, and even though there was little chance he would see the article on his own, she wanted to be up front about the stupid formula.

They could laugh about it together.

He was due to pick her up at the shop at five. She'd brought a dress to change into, and she'd washed her hair that morning and painted her toenails and worn a sexy new pair of strappy sandals. It was going to be a great evening.

At two o'clock, the bell over the door tinkled loudly as a customer flung it open with unusual force. Jeannie looked up to see who it was, and her heart lodged in her windpipe. Her pretty shoes were going to be all for naught. It was Nathan, and he was pissed.

He stalked to where she stood and shoved the newspaper insert in her face. "What in the hell is this?"

His face was pale, his jaw clenched, and a thin white line around his tightly pressed lips gave testament to exactly how upset he was.

Without speaking she walked back into the office so they wouldn't create a scene. He followed, of course. She could feel the heat of his anger on the back of her neck.

She resisted the urge to wring her hands like a beleaguered heroine in a horror film. "I can explain," she whispered, her stomach churning with nausea.

"I trusted you," he muttered, and for a moment, she saw past the anger to his hurt and disappointment.

She held out her hands, pleading for his understanding. "It was a puff piece, Nathan. A lighthearted, funny joke. No one took it seriously."

"Bullshit," he said, shoving the paper into her hands. He dragged two items from his jacket pocket and slammed them down on the nearest desk. It was two tubes of their eucalyptus shaving cream, one brand-new and one three-quarters empty.

The glare in his cold blue eyes shriveled her inside. "The next time you need a sucker for one of your freaky test-tube trials, do me a favor and pick some other poor, fucked-up loser."

Then he stared at her with disillusionment and pain and disgust in his eyes. "Thank God, no one saw us together." And then he strode out of her life.

Jeannie sank into a chair, her legs too weak to hold her. Her chest hurt and she wanted to curl up into a ball and die. Surely the stupid article wasn't that bad.

She reached across Elizabeth's desk and picked up one of the thick inserts. There were orange blossoms and doves on the cover. She had to flip to page five to find the article. It was titled "Love Potion #10."

There was a nice photo of the front of their shop. And several well-written, charming paragraphs about how Diana and Elizabeth had captured the men of their dreams all because of a magical potion.

The whole thing was tongue-in-cheek. Anybody could see that. But perhaps the most damning paragraphs were near the end.

Elizabeth Killaney admitted that she and her cousin, Diana, saw a definite cause and effect when the men in their lives were exposed to the special "potion." Pheromones? Or did the Killaney gals do a bit of benign voodoo with this latest batch? Caveat emptor. Let the buyer beware!

Jeannie Killaney, the only unattached one of the trio of lovely ladies, is a chemist by trade. When asked about the unusual properties of their latest concoction, Ms. Killaney remained noncommittal. But the smile on her face told me that she's biding her time, waiting for Love Potion #10 to work its magic on some unsuspecting hero who will sweep her off her feet and never know what hit him.

She folded the paper carefully, laid her head on the desk, and cried.

Nathan was so hurt and distracted that he ran three red lights on the way back home. The screech of brakes at the last intersection, and the rude hand gesture from the understandably angered motorist, jerked him back to reality.

He eased off the accelerator and made the remainder of the trip at a more sedate speed.

In his apartment, he couldn't settle down. The other sections of the newspaper covering his coffee table mocked him. Sports. Business. Real estate.

Ordinarily he might never have opened the June brides insert, except for the fact that his sister was newly engaged. They'd been talking on the phone that morning, and she had asked him to flip through and give her the names of any photographers who had advertised.

She and her fiancé were thinking about getting married in Asheville. She had fallen in love with the area the first time she'd visited Nathan.

So he had flipped, and skimmed, and stopped in stunned disbelief when he saw the damn article about Lotions and Potions. It was more than mere advertising. The reporter had gone on and on about the mysterious April night and the boiling pot and the happily engaged Diana and Elizabeth. They sounded like a group of witches.

He, poor schmuck that he was, had walked into that stupid shop of his own free will, offered up his manhood and his dignity, and stood quietly by while Jeannie Killaney led him on a merry dance. In her eyes he was merely an experiment, a guinea pig.

His blood pressure shot up as he remembered the two of them in bed last night. He had to get out of here before he combusted.

He grabbed up his keys and headed for the arboretum. Surely something needed to be dug up or analyzed or studied. That was what he did, damn it. He was a scientist.

Jeannie didn't have the luxury of falling into a blue funk. Even though the shop wasn't open on Sunday and Monday, she had promised her cousins that she would accompany them on various little bridal excursions for Diana, to florists, dress fittings, and caterers.

It seemed that with almost everything available online now, even when the brides-to-be ran into a business that *was* closed, there was still plenty of work to be done at home with a computer and a pad and pen.

It was hard work being cheerful and supportive when your heart was breaking. And though a generous dose of sympathy and pampering would have been nice in the wake of her newly established and quickly demolished relationship, she didn't have the heart to tell Diana and Elizabeth what had happened. They would feel terrible about their part in the article, and really—they shouldn't.

The more she thought about it, the madder she got. And if healthy anger helped keep the sick feeling of distress at bay, the more the better.

The article truly wasn't that outrageous. She read it about a hundred times, and in the end, though she had to admit that from Nathan's perspective it was bad, no one else on the planet would really believe that the Killaney cousins seriously thought they had created a magic potion.

Still, it hurt that her connection with Nathan had been so new and so tenuous that it hadn't survived the first bump in the road. She wasn't some crazy, I-believe-in-aliens woman. She was educated and intelligent, and she didn't deserve to be lumped into the same category as miss fun-and-bubbly aerobics girl.

By the time Tuesday rolled around, she had been on a roller coaster of emotions. First she felt better, sure that Nathan would come to his senses. Then she felt worse when she admitted to herself that she'd found the perfect man, only to lose him again so quickly.

Work was her panacea. The article had generated a huge amount of extra customers, and all the female ones wanted to buy products in the number ten line. No matter how much the cousins stressed that it was just a joke, the women weren't dissuaded, particularly since Sunday's paper had run a little follow-up piece about hunky Damian and Enrique.

By Wednesday, Jeannie was back to anger. She was a catch, and if Nathan was stupid enough to pass her up, it was his loss. When the phone rang that evening, and she saw the number on the screen, she answered it with a snarl. "What do you want?"

Nathan ran a hand through his hair. He gripped the phone, white-knuckled. "Can we meet somewhere and talk?"

"What if someone sees us together?"

The ice in her voice froze a knot in his belly. He cleared his throat. "I shouldn't have said that. It was cruel."

"You think?"

The unmistakable sound of a dial tone filled his ear. He hung up with a pained sigh, wincing at the hostility in her voice.

Then he dialed the number again. He took it as a good sign that she answered. He hesitated, not wanting to make things worse, but he was still angry, even so. "Why did you do it, Jeannie, when you knew how I felt about that kind of exposure . . . ?"

After a long silence, she spoke, sounding as miserable as he felt. "It all happened by accident. The reporter overheard us joking around and being silly. She wanted to do an article. Diana and Elizabeth thought it would be good publicity."

"You could have stopped them."

"How? I'd never even told them about you. What was I going to say?"

That hurt. He absorbed the blow and spoke without pausing to evaluate his words. "I thought you three shared everything. Was what you and I had together so trivial that you couldn't even tell the two most important people in your life?"

He heard her little indrawn breath and knew his accusation had hit the mark. And he felt like shit for making her suffer. "I'm sorry, Jeannie. I shouldn't have said that either."

Her voice wavered, and he knew with sick certainty that she

was crying. "Well, hell, Nathan. Is there anything else you want to say and then apologize for? Any more sins to lay at my door?" There was a muffled sound and then she spoke again, her words barely audible. "Forget it. You're entitled to your feelings. But I've had enough of this conversation."

"Wait," he said urgently. "Don't hang up." But it was too late. She already had.

He stared at the phone, wondering when he had become such a prick. Was his injured pride really that important?

A few shots of Jack Daniel's and a good night's sleep went a long way toward putting him back on track. The next morning he decided some groveling was in order. It had taken him a while to see through his own self-important righteous indignation to the truth. He finally had to admit to himself that it was a cute story. And Jeannie could easily have told the tale of him using the shaving cream and dreaming about her. But she hadn't.

So where was the harm?

He'd let his temper and his unresolved feelings of embarrassment and regret about the incident in Ohio goad him into hurting the one woman he loved more than anything else in his life . . . far more than his job, his reputation, his good name.

As a teenager he'd had a stubborn temper, but he'd worked hard to learn how to control it. Obviously he still had a ways to go.

He thought about calling her back, but it was doubtful she'd be receptive. Some sins were too big to be forgiven overnight.

He needed to make a big gesture.

Jeannie stared at the phone, willing it to ring. Fat chance. The man she loved had actually called last night, and she had hung up on him. Twice. Not the action of a smart woman. On the other hand, her stomach still trembled every time she replayed his earlier words in her head. *Thank God, no one saw us together.*

He could have stuck a knife in her heart, and it wouldn't have been as painful. It was the ultimate rejection. And despite the fact that he had called, she wasn't ready to absolve him of all responsibility.

Diana came walking out of the office with a funny look on her face.

Elizabeth looked up from the cash register. "What's wrong?"

Diana shook her head. "I don't know. That was Randy in the bookstore down the street. He says we need to come out and see the billboard on top of the bus station."

Jeannie felt an odd flip in her stomach. No jumping to conclusions. Nathan was worried about public opinion. This had nothing to do with them.

The single customer in the shop at the moment paid and left, and the three cousins locked up, put out the *back in ten minutes* sign, and headed down the street.

Jeannie stared in shock at the enormous billboard, huge red letters on the white background: *I bought magic shaving cream at Lotions and Potions and now I'm in love with Jeannie Killaney*. It was signed *Nathan Hardison*.

Diana and Elizabeth burst out laughing. At that exact moment, the reporter from the paper appeared around the corner with a camera in her hand.

Jeannie stared at her blankly, and then her jaw dropped when Nathan stepped out of the bookstore, went down on one knee, and handed her a single red rose.

His dear, angular face was solemn, and he spared not a glance for the gathering crowd. "Jeannie Killaney, I was an idiot and I'm sorry. Will you be my girlfriend?"

She looked at the people milling around. She looked up at the billboard, which was big enough to stop traffic. She looked at her grinning, sniffling cousins. And then she held out her hand, a wry smile on her face and a rush of joy flooding her chest. "I suppose I have to now, or you'll sue me for false advertising."

And then she tugged him to his feet, wrapped her arms around his neck, and decided she would never let him go.

Later that night they lay in her bed, breathing heavily after a most magical round of hot, sweaty sex. Nathan's fingers still played lazily between her legs, and her breasts were crushed against his chest.

She nuzzled his chin. "I really am sorry about the article, Nathan. I can only imagine how it made you feel."

His arms tightened around her. "I overreacted. It wasn't nearly as bad as I made it seem. Forget about it. And I swear, I'll happily be a test subject for any new lotions or potions you want to rub all over my poor, naked body."

She giggled. "You wish." She sighed and licked his nearest nipple. "But as long as we're clearing the air, I suppose I should tell you something else."

He raised his head, alarm in his sleepy gaze. "What? Please don't tell me it involves cauldrons and bats."

Her lips quirked. "Smart-ass." She reached up and kissed him. "Nothing so sinister." Then she smiled at him with all the love and happiness in her heart. "I just wanted to let you know that I've been dreaming about you every night."

Epilogue

The three cousins leaned forward, one at a time, and signed their names on the lengthy legal document. Each of their faces was solemn, but excitement filled the air. Elizabeth was leaving that afternoon with Enrique for a trip to Ireland. To scout movie locations . . . and to track down some family ties.

Diana was six weeks pregnant. She and Damian had bought a house in Blue Oaks and were furnishing a nursery.

And Jeannie—well, Jeannie was enrolled for her final semester of doctoral work and, God willing, would be teaching with her sexy professor by this time next year.

The three of them waited for the lawyer to tuck copies of the sales document into envelopes and hand them over.

Elizabeth smiled faintly at her two cousins. "Regrets?"

Diana shrugged. "It was our business, but it was *just* a business."

Jeannie nodded. "She's right. We're selling bricks and mortar and inventory. Not our dreams."

Elizabeth hugged them both. "Thank you for these past six years. It meant the world for me to have you two as partners."

The three of them sniffled and kissed until the trio of handsome men in the back of the room intervened.

Damian spoke up first. "Okay, turn off the waterworks. It's not good for the baby." He put an arm around his wife and kissed away her tears.

Enrique scooped Elizabeth off her feet and twirled her in small circle. "No time for this, my lovely. We've got a plane to catch."

Nathan handed his love a soft cotton handkerchief and tried not to be pissed that the lawyer was ogling his beautiful Jeannie. "Let's get out of here and celebrate."

The three women nodded, smiling through their overflowing emotions.

A short while later, all six raised their glasses. Diana's was filled with sparkling water.

"To new horizons." Enrique kissed Elizabeth, making her blush.

"To lots of babies." Damian put a hand over his wife's tummy and beamed.

Nathan was the last. He curled an arm around Jeannie's neck and pulled her close for an extravagant, sloppy kiss. Then he smirked. "To Love Potion Number Ten."

Hannah and Morgan know what happens to
the sex lives of married couples, and they don't want to be
one more statistic. So they sign up for premarital sex therapy,
where they learn how to keep things sizzling,
even after walking down the aisle.

Turn the page for a sneak peek at

By Appointment Only

on sale in July 2008.

$\mathcal{E}$ven minus the requisite white wedding dress, the woman fleeing down the front steps of a large, imposing church in downtown Orlando had a definite "runaway bride" vibe thing going on. Morgan Webber was minding his own business as he strolled along the sidewalk when she literally slammed into his shoulder, threatening to send them both crashing to the pavement.

Only his bulk and her quick footwork saved them. She tossed out a muttered apology, evaded his grasp, and darted out into the street. He watched aghast, wincing at the cacophony of blaring horns and screeching brakes as she danced between the vehicles.

When she made it safely to the opposite curb, he actually glanced over his shoulder expecting to see a distraught groom in hot pursuit. But at the top of the steps, the sturdy oak doors, both decorated with large white ribbons, remained firmly closed.

Two things kept him from going on about his business. The first was simple curiosity. He sensed a drama in the making. But the second reason was even more compelling. The brief physical encounter smacked him square in the chest with a powerful sexual attraction.

His mystery lady was tall and slender and had masses of wavy brunette hair that bounced and tumbled on her shoulders. Even when she wasn't in a dead run, he suspected that her hair would seem alive with the current of energy she exuded.

While he watched, bemused, she unlocked a fuchsia Kia, rummaged in the glove compartment, and backed out of the car to do a reverse dash, once again ignoring the irate motorists who tried to keep from killing her.

As she retraced her route, he jogged up the church steps close on her heels, compelled by an urgency that was probably only a reflection of hers. But he ran anyway, unwilling to miss the next act in this unfolding mystery.

By the time he stepped into the cool, dimly lit church, his fleet-footed, graceful gazelle was kneeling beside a tiny, gray-headed, supine female, opening the woman's mouth and tucking a small pill beneath her tongue. A minister and a rail-thin octogenarian groom hovered helplessly nearby along with a bald, middle-aged fellow who was apparently the best man.

Morgan held his breath unconsciously until the old lady's eyes fluttered and opened. She looked up at her rescuer. "Stupid angina. Damn it, Hannah, my girl. What took you so long?"

In the flurry of nervous laughter that followed, Morgan allowed himself a closer inspection of the female who seemed to be in entire control of the situation.

"Hannah" grinned down at the small elderly bride. "Sorry, Miss Beverly. Next time let's leave those pills in your pocket."

Beverly snorted as she allowed herself to be lifted to her feet. "No next time about it. This is my last trip down the aisle."

Morgan lingered in the back of the church while the abruptly aborted wedding service continued. Shafts of sunlight filtered through massive stained-glass windows painting Hannah with a rainbow of soft colors. Her generous lips curved in a smile as she watched the older couple make their vows.

If she knew Morgan watched her, she made no sign. But surely she must sense his intense absorption. He felt almost dizzy from the force of his heart pounding in his chest. He told himself it was the leftover adrenaline from thinking she would be hit by a car at any second.

But the truth was, he'd been the one to be metaphorically knocked on his ass. And he was in imminent danger of appearing to be a stalker and a wedding crasher at that. So he slipped into a pew at the rear of the sanctuary and sat quietly until the ceremony reached its conclusion.

There was no recessional, merely lots of hugs and congratulations and then finally a deep, resonant silence when the bride and groom, minister, and best man disappeared through a hallway at the side of the chancel area.

Now only his Julia Roberts look-alike remained. She turned as if on cue and their eyes met. She was smiling, but it was a mocking smile. Whether it was directed at herself or at him, he couldn't tell. He rose to his feet and walked toward her. After a split second, she moved as well.

They met in the middle of the church. She cocked her head, her sultry lips and wide-lashed eyes—brown he saw now—making him sweat beneath his dress shirt. He'd had a meeting with the suits at the bank earlier, hence his unusual attire in the middle of a workday.

Though he topped six feet by a couple of inches, she was tall for a woman, and their lips were in touching distance. That odd thought shook him even more, and he swallowed against a dry throat.

Her ivory slip dress clung to her fit body and begged for a man's touch.

Finally she took pity on his mute state. "Do I know you?"

Her husky alto took what was left of the starch in his knees. He shook his head, trying to clear it. "No. But seeing a woman nearly run over . . . twice . . . tends to grab a man's attention."

She lifted a hand to his chin, shocking the crap out of him. Her long, slim fingers brushed his jaw in a brief caress that made note of the slight stubble she found. He'd been up at five a.m. to shave and dress, and it was now midafternoon.

When her hand fell away slowly, he forced himself not to grab for it. She lifted one perfectly shaped eyebrow. "Your name?"

He forced the words past the lump in his throat. "Morgan Webber."

She studied him like an exhibit in a museum, as if by analyzing his form she could come to some conclusions about his identity or his motives or even his moral character. Then her eyes lit with a combination of mischief and outrageous bravado. "Can I do anything for you?" she drawled, the words dripping with sexual overtones.

He studied her mouth with rapt fascination. "You could marry me," he said, only half joking.

She lifted an eyebrow. "I'm afraid I don't think much of that venerable institution."

He frowned. "And yet here you are."

She shrugged, the epitome of haughty sophistication. "I don't impose my views on others." Her naughty smile returned. "I'm assuming you have no desire to kiss the real bride, so perhaps I'll do as a substitute."

And then she wrapped her slim arms around his neck, found his mouth with hers, and proceeded, like some ancient sorceress, to steal his heart away.

He sucked in a startled breath and managed to get with the program in a split second. She tasted like whipped cream and coffee, and her body in his arms was all curves and slippery silk and sensuous woman.

Though his boner was perhaps a foregone conclusion, he

would have liked to disguise its importunate presence. But his stunning playmate was having none of that. She nudged her hips against his, making both of them groan. Her tongue whispered and fluttered on his.

He was breathing fast, too fast. His hands went to her hips, gripping her ass in an effort to get closer. He was pretty sure he was breaking at least nine of the Commandments and maybe a few he wasn't aware of.

But he couldn't stop kissing her. It was like a dream, a surreal but impossibly sweet image conjured up by the palette of muted, prism-spread hues that cloaked them like an intangible blessing.

He knotted his fist in her hair, testing its thickness, its softness. He'd waited his whole life for a woman like this.

He wondered if she knew how close she came to having him make love to her in front of God and a host of dead saints. But before their incendiary embrace reached its inevitable conclusion, the modest wedding party reappeared.

Hannah sighed and pulled back, her attention already lured away from him. She touched his face one more time, gently, as though fascinated by the feel of his skin. "You're a great kisser, Morgan Webber," she whispered.

And then his lovely, unexpected gift of a woman abandoned him without a backward glance.

He started after her and glanced down at his watch with a curse. He had a very important meeting in exactly forty-five minutes. One he couldn't miss.

Damn it. He took one more step toward Hannah and then stopped. He had people depending on him. This incident was far from over. But the conclusion would have to wait. Even if he didn't know her last name.